Bachelor Not for Sale
The Bachelor Series, 1

CHERYL BARTON

Published by:
Barton Book Publishing

Barton Book Publishing
P.O. Box 962
Reisterstown, Maryland 21136
www.crbarton.com

Ordering Information:
Quantity sales. Special discounts are available on quantity purchases by corporations, associations, and others. For details, contact the publisher at the address above.
Orders by U.S. trade bookstores and wholesalers. Please contact prez@crbarton.com

ISBN: 0615752748
ISBN-13:978-0615752747

Dedication

This book is dedicated to the memory of my brother, John Barton, III (December 26, 1962 – February 24, 2010), my inspiration to live each day like it's my last. I miss you so much and I think about you every day. I know you are smiling because I'm pressing forward and making my dreams become a reality.

Acknowledgments

I am so thankful for being blessed with the best parents, John & Barbara Barton. Without your love and support, I would not know that all things are possible. I can never thank you enough for always being in my corner and for being a great example of love that endures all. It's not a coincidence I'm releasing my first book about love in the same year that you are celebrating 50 years of love and marriage. I love your love!

To my daughter Chynae, my first reader and editor, I love you and hope that as you see me fulfill my dreams, you will know that your dreams are within your reach. Go get yours. I will be here to support you!

To my brother Brian Barton, Sr., thanks for being the best big brother and protector. In honor of my love for you, I have a character in my first book named Brian. Love you!

To my sisters from another mother, Rochelle Barfield and Melissa Bradshaw, I have the greatest love and respect for you both. There are many things that bind us together and our love for reading is just one.

To my brother from another mother, Dwayne Simpson, Sr., I love you to pieces. Continue to "Stand". No one sings it like you do.

To Ms. Mary Demory, the perfect mother figure, thank you for always being supportive.

To my Aunt Shirley and Uncle Jimmy. I am blessed to have the greatest family that always shows love and support. Thank you for always being there.

To the ladies who make up *Sisters About Making Moves*, a community service organization in Maryland, I love being a part of a group of ladies who are a positive inspiration to other women. Continue paying it forward.

1

Duron Knight's head was pounding, literally, to the same beat as his irritating door buzzer that someone was leaning on, too early for a Saturday morning. Peeping over at the clock on his nightstand, the hour was just after six in the morning, too early for visitors, unless it was a lady friend who meant to call him at midnight for a booty call, but waited until the morning to call on him.

He had gotten home and in bed only a few hours ago from a night of too much partying and far too much drinking with his best friends and business partners, Michael Bailey and Tyrone Davis. They had been out celebrating landing another major contract for the architecture firm, Pioneer Architecture & Design, the three of them owned together. It was a night to congratulate each other on all of their hard work. Now, all he wanted to do was sleep.

As he attempted to focus on sleep again, the pounding in his head and the irritating buzzer were not a good combination. Duron could recall little about the night before, but the ringing in his ears and the pounding in his head were a sure sign that he had drowned himself in more alcohol than he'd like to admit to and he was now paying the price.

The buzzing stopped and he thought his visitor had gone. After a quick attempt to find comfort to sleep, the annoying sound started right back up again with no sign of stopping, sending his aching head into a wild spin. Burying himself further down into his king-sized bed to try and smother any sound, Duron grabbed a pillow, pulling it over his head and tightly over his ears so that he could drown out the sound and ease his aching head. He listened as the sound stopped again and this time the silence was interrupted by the sound of the opening of his front door, the poking on the keypad of his security alarm system and the door shutting once again. Exhaling loudly, he knew of only one person brazen enough to show up early in the morning, unannounced without thinking twice. His level of exasperation kicked up a notch. He needed to rethink giving access to his home so freely, even to those he loved.

He waited for it and as soon as he heard the tell-tale sign of his visitor, he wished he had never given her a key and alarm code. Her impromptu drop-ins were oftentimes acceptable, but today wasn't one of those times.

He clearly heard the click, click, click sound of her high heels as she crossed the hardwood floor of his foyer, heading to toward stairs. There was only one person he knew of who would wear high-heeled shoes at six in the morning. No one wore heels this early to visit someone except his sister Loren and he knew she was the culprit. He loved her, but not early in the morning after the night he'd had, that he'd like to forget. Duron knew if she were in his house at the butt crack of dawn, she must want something and he had a feeling he wasn't going to like it. If there was a time that he wished he could will himself back to sleep, this was it.

"D?" Loren hollered, using his nickname. "Are you up yet?"

Loren listened and waited for a response. When none came, she walked slowly up the steps, loud enough to announce her arrival before she reached his room. Continuing to call out to him, she wanted to give him time to either tell her to go back downstairs, letting her know he was with his latest female conquest or tell her to go away, which meant he was alone and didn't want to be bothered. The second option was her favorite because to her, it meant to come up and disturb him, even at an early hour; at least that's what she liked to call her interpretation. She was sure Duron's opinion on that differed greatly from hers, but she didn't care. To her, he should be accustomed to her interruptions by now. There have been many over the years and each time he'd forgiven her because that's what big brothers did.

A few times she'd popped in on him at his condo, before he purchased his house and she had mixed up what she thought his response meant.

When she thought his response meant he was alone but didn't want to be bothered, she ended up temporarily losing her key and alarm code privileges and a little bit of her eyesight, seeing a little more of her big brother than she ever wanted to see.

Due to his very active sex life, a few times she'd caught him mid-hump with some chick or some woman was mid-ride, astride him going for broke screaming about him being the greatest. She loved her brother, but she was not a fan of his overactive libido and the women who found him irresistible.

In Atlanta, where they lived, there were plenty of women who couldn't wait to 'Ride the Knight'. When Loren first heard that term, she was out one night at a nightclub and overheard a woman talking about her brother. She thought the woman who made the comment was talking about the time of the evening, meaning 'night'. It wasn't until she eavesdropped a little more on the woman's conversation that she discovered she was actually talking about taking a wild ride on her brother, with the word not being 'night' as she originally thought, but 'Knight' referring to their last name.

Growing up with three older brothers, Loren was an eyewitness to many women her brothers went through, but Duron was by far the most charismatic when it came to attracting just about every woman he came in contact with. Being his sister, she didn't see the draw, but apparently every woman in Atlanta did and they were plentiful. Knowing her brother as well as she did, she had no doubt he obliged each one of them.

Loren continued her climb up the stairs while listening for any sign of early morning moaning or headboard banging and hearing none, she figured the coast was clear.

"D, you know it's me and I'm coming upstairs, so I hope your sleeping attire is sister-friendly and decent up there!" she hollered.

Hearing his sister's voice closer than it was before, Duron knew the inevitable was unavoidable. No matter how much he ignored her, she wasn't going to take his silence as a cue to go away. He grumbled knowing they were about to have an unwelcomed encounter.

"Go away Loren, it's too early in the morning for a brother/sister moment."

Though his head was buried in his pillow, he heard her laugh off his comment as she stood outside of his bedroom door.

Before entering his bedroom, Loren had placed her hand over her eyes and peeked through the slits of her fingers just in case she had to quickly cover them depending on what she saw. She put her hands down when she saw that he was alone, though barely noticeable under the covers and pillows on his gigantic bed.

"I can't believe you're still in bed this early in the morning. I assumed you would be up working out or heading into the office like you do most Saturdays, though I don't understand why."

Duron groused at her unwelcomed appearance in his room.

"When are you going to stop barging in my room? I could have been in here with someone and you've been on the other end of that kind of intrusion before. Ever heard of a phone to announce you're on your way? This is my home and I could use a little more privacy than what you give me by showing up all the time whenever you feel like it. You could have at least waited for me to tell you to come up," he said trying to sound annoyed.

Loren would not be deterred.

"Boy, please, you know I have seen you with many chicks in a few uncompromising positions and I have learned to listen for the signs and I didn't hear any, so I came on up. Why complain when clearly no one is here but you, which is surprising. That's so unlike you to be in your bed alone," Loren chuckled.

Duron tuned his sister out as she rambled on and didn't bother to make any attempt to move from her current spot in the middle of his room. After a few minutes of hearing her tell him more of how he should be used to her dropping by and preparing for it as soon as he hears her coming through his front door, he knew her leaving wasn't a possibility. With ease, as not to make his head pound any louder, he threw the heavy comforter off of himself and moved to get out of bed to wait for the ball to drop with the reason she was at his house being an annoying chatterbox even before the birds outside signaled they were awake.

"Late night big brother?" Loren asked.

"Something like that, so why are you here?" he said.

Finally getting up, he wasn't surprised to see Loren plop down on it looking at him like she had no plans to move anytime soon. That was also her way of letting him know she wasn't letting him get back in bed either. Ignoring her as she talked non-stop, he headed to the bathroom. As he reached the door, he stopped, having an idea of why she showed up. He had a thought that she must have seen the newspaper announcement and was worried about him.

Without turning around to face her, he said, "You saw it, didn't you? You saw the announcement in the paper and came by to see if I saw it too."

Duron's question was met with silence. He could tell she wasn't sure of how to respond, trying not to upset him.

"Yeah, D, I saw it last night. Mom called and told me about it and we called you a couple of times to check on you, but you didn't answer. I also called the condo and when you didn't answer or call me back, I decided to come by here this morning before my flight to Boston," Loren explained.

Duron remembered she was heading out of town on an early flight. Only because of that, would he excuse her early morning intrusion.

"Right, I forgot your friend is getting married tonight. What time is your flight?" he asked.

"It's at noon, and don't change the subject. So, are you good? I've been worried about you all evening."

He heard concern in her voice and unbeknownst to her and his family, there was no need for concern. There was nothing for anyone to worry about.

"I'm fine and you can call Mom and tell her the same thing because that's all ancient history for me. It's the past and I'd like for it to stay in the past."

He knew Loren was about to dig even more, so before she could, he turned and headed into the bathroom.

"D?" Loren said, wanting more confirmation that he was fine.

"Let me get a shower and I'll meet you in the kitchen," he said.

Duron shut the bathroom door and turned on the shower cutting off anymore conversation with Loren. She had him thinking about things he didn't want to think about – not today, not any day.

Removing the sweat pants he'd slept in, he slid the shower door open, hopped in and let the hot water pour over him as his thoughts went back to the wedding announcement one of his friends shared with him the night before. *ALLISON*. The one woman, as far as he was concerned, that gave all women a bad name.

As the water continued to pour down, Duron's thoughts drifted to memories of the love found and lost over a year ago.

Allison had been the love of his life. He thought back to a time when he lived and breathed her and thought she'd felt the same way. He was ready to make a critical life decision and propose to her when she pulled the rug from under their relationship and ripped his heart out of his chest. He remembered that day like it just happened.

He had planned the perfect evening for them that was to start with dinner at one of the finest restaurants in Atlanta. Then, they would head back to the penthouse suite he'd rented for the evening, for which he paid handsomely to have decorated with lots of flowers, champagne chilling on ice, special lighting and music for the perfect ambiance for a romantic evening made for celebrating. He'd hoped the evening would end with her saying yes to his marriage proposal and him spending the rest of the night making love to her, showing her in every possible way that she would never regret agreeing to become his wife.

He had been in love like never before and he was about to share with the love of his life the good news that all of his hard work in the business world was about to pay off. He'd had his struggles, but he was about to come into his own.

He and his friends, Michael Bailey and Tyrone Davis, earlier that day, had signed a multi-million-dollar contract for the design, development and construction of a major corporate office park in Chicago. Their company, Pioneer Architecture & Design, was an Atlanta-based firm, but with great connections and a great marketing and promotions team, they were able to land lucrative deals in other cities like Chicago and New York. The project was going to put them on the road to even greater success, which was a road that he and his two best friends had dreamed about since their days together as students at Howard University where they'd taken Engineering and Architecture classes together.

Duron had planned to tell her about his design for the office park he and his partners now owned that was currently home to their company and many others that leased office space from them.

A year ago, the office park was a mere dream for the three of them, but now it was one of the most popular business centers in downtown Atlanta. He thought she'd be excited about the plans for the condo level of the complex he now called his part-time home. He, Mike and Tyrone had been putting in a lot of time building their dream office building and he wanted to surprise her with it, hoping she would enjoy decorating it since they would be living there together as husband and wife.

Duron placed his hands on the tiled shower wall in front of him and dropped his head, allowing the hot water to ease some of the aching in his head as he recalled being nervous that day over a year ago, but very excited about the direction their lives were about to take.

When he arrived at the apartment Allison shared with her best friend he couldn't wait to see the look on her face when he gave her his good news.

Duron remembered the feeling of the five-carat diamond engagement ring he'd carried in his pocket. It was the first purchase he'd made after the business deal had been sealed. He couldn't wait to pick her up for a night to remember after telling her earlier in the week that he wanted to have a special dinner with her and to be sure she dressed up for the occasion.

He was surprised when he arrived and she'd opened the door, not dressed for the evening he told her to dress for, but casually dressed instead. He sensed something was odd when she didn't greet him with her usual kind of kiss; the kind that made his toes curl and had the little hairs on the back of his neck stand out as if he'd been shocked by electricity.

At twenty-six, Allison was smart and gorgeous and being with her, he felt like the luckiest man in the world. He had devoted a lot of time to making her feel like a queen, letting her know that he was and would always be her knight in shining armor. She was the first woman whose love made him easily give up other women and devote all of his time to her. Little did he know that what he thought was the beginning of an incredible new chapter in life for them, would come crashing down when she informed him that she loved him, but she needed more.

When he questioned her about not being dressed for the evening he'd prepared for them, she invited him in and nervously played with her hands without looking him in the face. He knew something was wrong when she wasted no time in telling him what was going on. That dreaded conversation was as clear to him now, as if it had just taken place.

"More? What do you mean you need more? More of what, Allison?"

"Just more, Duron."

He was confused.

"Allison, what are you talking about? You're not making any sense," he declared.

Duron watched as Allison paced back and forth trying to explain why she was apparently breaking up with him and not heading out for the wonderful evening he'd planned for them.

"You know how I grew up, how my family struggled just to make ends meet. I always said that would not be me and I have always had this dream of having it all. As a little girl, I would dream of my prince charming coming in to steal me away from my miserable childhood and making me feel safe. You did that for me and I love you and appreciate you for that. You are the nicest, kindest, sweetest man I have ever known and I felt things with you that I never thought I would feel for any man."

She paused and so far, he heard all good things, but he knew she wasn't finished when she still couldn't look him in the eyes as she continued.

"Just say it Allison. The suspense is killing me here. What's going on?"

He watched as her eyes finally lifted up to look right at him with more pain than he'd ever seen before. He knew whatever she had to say wasn't going to be good.

"Duron, I've met someone. I didn't seek this out, it just happened," she said in a solemn tone.

"What? You met someone? You met someone when and what just happened?"

He couldn't believe what he was hearing.

"I met someone a while ago and..."

Duron cut her off.

"Wait, what do you mean a while ago?" he asked, almost pleading.

Time stood still while he tried to understand what he was hearing.

He watched her hesitate before continuing.

"I met someone a few months ago that I've been seeing. I really tried to fight it at first, but my insecurities took over and I let myself get pulled away from you and I'm sorry. I'm sorry because he pressured me into making a decision about being with him or with you and I chose him, not because I love him, but because he's what I need in my life right now."

Duron felt like a house had just collapsed on him. Did he hear her correctly? Did she just dump him on the night that he was going to propose to her? Did she just dump him for another guy? What the hell?

"What are you talking about?" Duron said, confused.

"I know this may sound shallow, but he has so much more to offer me right now and right now is when I need it. I know that you will have a bright future, but I have a chance to have it all now."

Duron pounded on the shower wall bringing his thoughts back into the present remembering the hurt and pain of her words. He didn't know what to say to her in response because he was too stunned by her admission. What he thought he heard her saying was that she didn't have time to wait for him to climb the ladder of success. She had an opportunity to start out at the top now and she was going to grab that chance while she had it.

That night she proceeded to let him down easy with the *"it's not you, it's me"* speech, while he tried to figure out what happened since he'd seen her the night before when they were on the same page and happily enjoying each other. As he stood in front of her dazed and stunned, she explained to him why the relationship was over and why she was moving on when someone knocked on the apartment door behind him.

Following the knock, he heard a man's voice call *'Allison baby, it's me.'* Allison was obviously caught off guard because she looked uncomfortable as she tried to decide if opening the door at that moment was a good idea. It was obvious she knew who was on the other side, especially since the visitor had called her baby.

When she didn't move to answer the door, he started to do so, since it appeared Allison wasn't going to move to do it. Before he could, she reached around him and grabbed the door handle, opening the door to the person on the other side.

Duron recognized the intruder right away as the new quarterback for the professional Atlanta football team. He looked from the guy standing in the doorway, then back at Allison and realized what this was all about; *money.* She wasn't just moving on with anybody, she was moving on with a sixty-million-dollar, star athlete.

As the shower started running cold, Duron shook off all thoughts of the one woman who had turned his life upside down. He tried to remove any thoughts of the wedding announcement of her upcoming nuptials to the football star she'd left him for and finished his shower. His thoughts carried to the night before at his attempt through his excessive drinking to drown out the visual of the one love of his life walking out on him and soon would be walking down the aisle to marry another man.

He now had to go downstairs to deal with his sister who, at twenty-seven, was four years younger than him, yet who tended to baby him. The hurt still ran deep, but he had moved on and vowed, he would never fall in love again. Allison taught him that women didn't appreciate good men, no matter how much they said finding one was impossible. He also knew that it was her loss because if it was money that she was after, in the year since she'd left him, he'd made double what her football start fiancé was making. He was glad that she did leave him because he would have hated the thought that she was going to be with him because of money. It was obvious they weren't on the same page because he was looking for love.

After toweling dry, he slipped into comfortable clothing to join his sister for the inquisition he knew was about to take place. He couldn't avoid it, so he brushed off any hesitation to face her questioning in hopes she'd leave, while understanding that he was dealing with Allison's engagement with no problem.

2

Heading downstairs, Duron found Loren exactly where he knew she'd be, in his kitchen raiding the refrigerator.

"Don't you ever eat at your own place? Every time you come here, I feel like I've been hit by a food burglar," he said joining her.

He looked on as she shoved a bagel with cream cheese, butter and jelly in her mouth.

"Of course, but food seems to taste better when it belongs to someone else," she replied.

"Ok, so why else are you here, Lo?" he asked, calling her by the nickname that only he used. "If it was only to see if I'm good about Allison's wedding, I am. You can feel free to leave at any time," he said.

"I'm not leaving and I told you I came to check on you and my main reason was because of the announcement, but to also see you because I haven't seen you in a few days."

Duron wasn't buying it. He knew she came by about the wedding, but something else was lingering in the air. He knew his sister and she was leaving something out of the conversation.

"Right and again, why are you here, Lo? It's too early for a visit, even from you on a Saturday, even if you say it was just to check on me, so what else is it?" he asked.

Loren paused before hitting him with the other reason for her early morning visit. She hated that Duron knew her better than she knew herself. Even when she tried to hide something from him, it was impossible to do.

"For starters, I did come to check on you after I saw the wedding announcement, as I already said. I wanted to be sure you were okay after reading it because I know what Allison meant to you. I remember what that skank did to you and I wanted to cheer you up with my presence just in case you wanted to be down about it," she said.

She smiled hoping to get a smile from her brother and lightening the moment for what she really wanted to talk to him about.

"Skank? Really? What are you ten years old? Do people even still say skank anymore?" he joked.

Duron laughed and Loren was happy and laughed along with him. She wanted to see her brother smile even though she knew the hurt still ran pretty deep. She'd never seen her Duron in love before and what Allison did, cut him deep.

"Don't worry about me, sis, I'm good. That's so far in my past, I don't even remember being involved with her," he said, lying.

Loren knew better, but if he says he's good, then she's good too.

"If you say so," Loren said, fixing a second bagel, lathering it with all the fixings.

"Now that we're passed all this, do you want to tell me what else brought you here this morning?"

Here goes nothing, she thought.

"Okay, well I need a big favor."

Duron looked over at her with one raised eyebrow. Whatever the favor was, it had to be a big one, just from looking at her body language. She as nervously twitching and she stopped eating.

"Favor? What kind of favor and how much is it going to cost me?" he reluctantly replied.

Loren exhaled. Leave it to Duron to think everything had to do with money. This favor did, but not in the way he was thinking.

"It won't cost you anything, but a little bit of your time," she said.

When she didn't continue he said, "Spill it Lo, what do you need?"

"My sorority is holding our big annual fundraiser and we decided to do another bachelor auction and I was wondering if...."

Loren never finished her sentence as Duron raised his hand to stop her next words, knowing what was about to come out of her mouth.

"No," he shouted, to be sure she got the message.

"No? But why D? Wait, you didn't even let me finish what I was going to say" Loren said in her baby sister, sad voice.

"Don't try it with the voice that only worked when you were ten and I already know what you're going to say and my answer is still no. You can whine all you want, but you know better. I can't take part in that."

Loren pouted harder.

"But, D," was all she got out again having her words cut short.

"Hell no, I am not going to participate in your bachelor auction," Duron exclaimed.

"D, you know you are considered one of the most eligible bachelors in Atlanta and I won't even speak on the reputation you and your friends have developed getting the panties. I mean, do you know that the women of Atlanta consider it an honor to tell their friends that the *panty dazzler Duron* gave them multiple orgasms all in one night? I hear those hazel eyes of yours have panties dropping all over town. Not that I want to hear any of that, but can you imagine the amount of money local charities and community organizations will receive when the ladies hear the *'Dazzler'* will be up for auction? I mean, think of the possibilities," Loren said. She felt like she was fighting for her life, pleading her case like a lawyer in a courtroom.

"First of all, we are never to discuss my sex life, ever. I'm serious Loren, there are some conversations we're not going to have. Second, I already told you I am not participating and my only reason is because I don't want to."

"Not even to help me out?" Loren asked, pressing harder.

Duron ignored her words and her look. He heard the chuckle in his sister's voice after her snide comment about his sexual prowess. He had a very healthy sex drive and he felt no shame about that fact. The women all knew the score and they walked away with the satisfaction they were seeking when they hooked up with him. It was always a plus for all parties involved.

"No and I don't care what the ladies call me. Keep in mind, it's never to come out of your mouth again," he said chuckling.

Ignoring him, she pushed.

"What else do they say? Oh yeah, Duron Knight comes prepared with all the principles of pleasure, in a night no woman would ever forget, all without them ever minding that you make no promises of love or forever," she added.

He shook his head at her candor. At times like now, it wasn't appreciated.

"Lo, it's not happening and I'm ignoring any further quips about my sex life. I don't leave a trail of broken hearts behind me. Every single one of those women know the deal going in. What does my supposed reputation have to do with your bachelor auction that I'm not participating in?" he asked, grabbing the next bagel Loren had placed in the toaster.

"Come on D, I really need you to do this for me. Ever since you, Tyrone and Mike graced the cover of *Black Enterprise Magazine*, the talk has been about the three handsome, very unattached, up and coming bachelors of Atlanta. If you do this auction for me, I know this fundraiser will be our best ever. In considering what guys to ask, my sorority sisters had you on top of the list and they made me promise to get you to say yes."

He looked at her at the exact moment she hit him with the puppy dog eyes that has melted his heart since they were kids and caused him to do what she wanted.

"You shouldn't have made that promise without talking to me first," he said.

"I know and I'm sorry," she pouted even more, pushing out her lower lip to add credence to her request.

He shook his head, looked away and realized he was going to need some strong coffee for this conversation. He loved her and would do anything for her, but a bachelor auction, he wasn't too sure about. Fixing his coffee and taking a seat at the black marble topped island, he let Loren continue with her pleas for his participation, knowing he was going to give into her in the end. Sadly, he always did. He was that big brother that would do almost anything for his sister and this wasn't going to be an exception. He also didn't plan to make it easy for her either.

"Ok, let me hear it. Tell me, what does being in this auction involve?" he asked.

He didn't miss the grin on her face when she realized she was about to reel him in.

Excitedly she continued, "Okay, here it is. You dress in one of your finest tuxedos and single women from the Atlanta area will bid on you for a dinner date for an evening."

She held up her hand to stop Duron before he could ask her any questions, before she had a chance to lay it all out.

"The hand, Loren? Really?" he asked.

"Let me finish before you throw a million questions at me. Yes, before you ask, it's for dinner only. Anything beyond that is two consenting adults making an adult decision and I don't want to know anything about it. The bachelor auction is for a paid evening of dinner at one of the finest restaurants in the Atlanta area. The dinner will take place within the next sixty days following the auction and a list of approved restaurants will be provided after the auction. Everyone, except the bachelors, pay two hundred dollars a plate to attend."

Loren watched Duron take in all that she'd just told him about the auction. Since she knew begging always worked with him, she was planning to hound him until he gave in.

"Please, help me out with this D. It's only dinner and you know we support a lot of great causes. Think of all the good my sorority has done over the years," she added.

Duron wanted to disagree, but Loren was right. Her sorority was known for the scholarships they provided each year to underserved young women looking to go to college. They also supported dozens of other community programs and charities. One dinner to help her wouldn't hurt and he hoped he wouldn't regret the decision he was about to make.

"Ok, sis, I'll do it for you and try not to gloat because you've won me over again. I don't know why I let you talk me into craziness all the time. You have two other brothers and yet, I'm always on the other end of your shenanigans," he laughed.

He watched as Loren came around the kitchen counter and gave him a big of gratitude for his agreeing to take part. Only for her would he do this. One day he'd have to learn to tell her no and mean it, but today wasn't that day.

"Thank you, thank you D. I knew I could count on you and trust me, I would ask Brian, but his head is in the sand these days and I don't know why. As for Jake, no married men allowed. It's a bachelor auction remember?" she quipped.

Remembering she had a flight to get ready for, Loren grabbed her things and headed for the door before Duron thought harder on it and changed his mind. It was time for her to make hasty exit.

"I have to jet so that I can finish getting ready for my flight. I'll email you all the details about the auction, including all the dos and don'ts."

Duron tried to keep up with Loren's rambling as she moved quickly to gather her things to hightail it out of his house, as if she thought hanging around any longer could result in a change of heart on his part. Yeah, she knew him well because he was already second guessing his decision to participate. He was using long strides to keep up with her even in high heels.

"Do you ever wear flat shoes or tennis? I think the last time I saw you in something shorter than a stiletto was when you ran track back in college," he said. "It's six in the morning and you're dressed like you're about to walk the runway," he added.

"I hate flat shoes and heels make me feel sexy. You know how I like to do," she said flippantly.

"TMIS, too much information sharing, Lo. I don't want to hear anything about my baby sister trying to feel or look sexy. I prefer you looking like a tomboy, so I don't have to jack some fool up for trying to get too close to you. Let me find there's a dude interested. He'll change his mind quick," Duron said.

Loren turned with her hands on her hips, flipping her hair at him.

"D, stop playing. Like you, I am not a child, but a very grown woman doing grown woman things and the overprotective brother routine can cease and desist right now," she declared.

"Whatever. Like I said, let me find out there's some dude. Be careful in Boston," he said.

When they reached his door, Loren stopped and turned to him again.

"Oh, did I forget to mention that I need you to pick me up Sunday from the airport?" she asked.

She gave him a hug before turning and heading out of the door, not waiting for his response. She already knew he'd be there to pick her up. If she knew nothing else, she knew she could always depend on Duron to have her back. Before she reached her car sitting in the circular driveway in front of his house, she called back to him.

"Don't give that wedding announcement thing another thought. I never liked her and she wasn't good enough for you anyway."

That was the last thing he heard her say as she hopped into her red, two-seater sports BMW and sped off out of his community.

Duron went back to his kitchen to finish his coffee and bagel while trying to clear his mind of any more thoughts of Allison and her upcoming nuptials. Nothing about Allison needed to take up any more space in his head. She made her choice and he wished her well. Not really, he thought, but it sounded like the right thing to think. In truth, he didn't wish her well. She could have handled her business better than that.

He checked the time and seeing the hour was still pretty early, he had time to get in his daily five mile run before stopping by his office to catch up on some work.

Loren's last comment did make a lot of sense and she was right. He wasn't going to dwell on Allison and her betrayal anymore. She wasn't good enough for him.

3

Taija looked around her living room at the many cards and gifts she'd received at the going away party the staff at her company had given her the day before. It was a sad, yet happy occasion. They were sad to see her go, but happy to see her move on to the next level in her career. She loved her life in Boston, but it was time to get back to familiar stomping grounds and she was more than ready.

Her bosses had tried everything to get her to stay, including a raise and the opportunity to head her own department. The lure was enticing to stay at the large financial firm she worked for, but the pull to leave was stronger and thankfully, it wasn't due to any unhappiness at her job. She loved the work and the people, but opportunity awaited her and she was ready to grasp it. Taija was appreciative over how much they valued her as an employee and if she hadn't had her mind set to move, she may have given the option to stay a little more thought.

Atlanta, Georgia was calling her and she couldn't wait to see all of the friends and sorority sisters she had only been in touch with via telephone and email. Just the thought of going back to the city that meant so much to her made her feel like dancing around.

After spending a few years in Boston, she began seeking job opportunities in Atlanta and had received quite a few great offers. It wasn't until her boss realized they were not going to be able to talk her into staying, that he reached out to a good friend of his who owned an Atlanta based Fortune 500 company and had put in a good word for her, did the offer come in that she could not pass up.

A knock at the door startled her, shaking her out of her thoughts of the road she'd taken in her life so far. Remembering she was expecting her executive assistant and friend Victoria from work, she shook off her thoughts and rushed to open the door. She was excited that they were going to the gym to exercise and spend some girl time together before she moved. Fitness was very important to her and it was the only way to keep her hour glass figure with all of the junk food she couldn't seem to stay away from.

"Victoria!" Taija said, excitedly when she flung the door open.

As soon as Taija said her name, Victoria started crying almost uncontrollably.

"Oh, Victoria. Don't you dare start that crying all over again. We cried enough yesterday at my going away celebration and if you cry, you know I'm going to cry too, and I don't think I have any tears left," she said.

Taija reached out, giving Victoria a hug hoping it would stop the flow of tears.

"I know," Victoria said through tears she wiped from her eyes.

"It's not like we're never going to see each other again."

"I know. I'm going to miss you so much. You were not just my boss, but one of my best friends, especially at work. Plus, I'm not crying just because you're leaving," Victoria said.

Taija stepped back and looked quizzically at her, not sure of what else Victoria was talking about.

"Why else are you crying then?" she asked.

"I'm also crying because stink breath Ron is temporarily taking over your position and I now have to smell that funk every single day! Well, that is until they find someone to take over your position permanently," she quipped and doubled over laughing.

They were laughing so hard, tears were flowing even harder, not from sadness, but from laughter.

"Girl, you are so crazy. Just do like I always do knowing he's around and put an air-freshener on your desk along with a jar of mints and offer them to him every time he stops by," Taija joked.

"Gotcha," Victoria said.

"Come on in while I get my things for the gym," Taija said interrupting their merriment. "You are silly. I am so ready to get this workout on today. I've been doing a mini workout while packing all of these boxes. I didn't realize the amount of stuff I'd accumulated since moving to Boston. I can remember purging before getting here so that I wouldn't have clutter all around. Now, I feel like I need to purge again," Taija declared.

"You should let me help you purge and allow me to keep anything you throw out, especially some of those designer bags and shoes you have. I swear, I've never met a woman with more shoes and matching bags than you. Do you have anything without a designer name on it?" Victoria asked.

Taija gave Victoria a sly look.

"Girl, I do not own all things designer. Somewhere in the bottom of a drawer or in the back of a closet around here you'll find something that's not name brand. I'm

BACHELOR NOT FOR SALE

going to get my designer workout gear on," she said as she left the room to grab her gym bag.

She was really going to miss Victoria. She had made quite a few friends during her time in Boston, but none were as much fun as Victoria or who was appreciated more for being a true confidant. They'd hit it off from her first day with the firm and had developed a sisterhood bond that she enjoyed since she didn't have any real sisters of her own other than her sorority sisters from college and the one's in the alumni chapter she'd joined with her move to Boston.

She wanted only the best for her friend and was silently hoping that her ex-boss would keep his word and promote Victoria. Taija had given her a glowing recommendation for a new position that was opening up in the firm and Taija knew that Victoria had more in her than just her position as an executive assistant. Now that she'd finally finished college and had graduated, it was time the company did more for her and Taija made sure she had a hand in seeing that done before she left. She was looking forward to the call from Victoria sometime within the next several days, telling her about the promotion. She wanted so badly to tell her about the possible job change, but also wanted to let the bosses present the opportunity for advancement to her, letting it be a surprise.

She grabbed her gym bag and returned to her living room to see Victoria eyeing one of the designer bags she boxed up.

"I should have known you would find something in a box to try and claim as your own," Taija said catching her off guard.

Victoria ignored her and continued to admire the

expensive bag.

"I think this one wants to stay in Boston with me," she said.

Taija shook her head, knowing it was a bag that Victoria had admired a few times before. She guessed it wouldn't hurt to part with just one bag.

"Fine, then it's yours, but only that one. Don't look for anymore. Close the box back up and let's get to the gym before I change my mind."

She laughed at the speed at which Victoria stowed the bag under her arm while sealing the box that contained other items and walked to the door without saying a word. They truly were sisters, Taija thought following her.

Sitting in the passenger seat of Victoria's car as they pulled out into traffic, Taija stared out of the side window feeling melancholy, knowing she was going to miss Boston and her friends.

"Why so quiet Taija?" Victoria asked curiously.

Victoria must have noticed her sullen mood.

"No reason. I was thinking about how much I'm going to miss being here, but it's time I made my home where I really want to live and stop running away from my past. I've been held prisoner by it long enough."

"Taija, I know you've told me all about your ex-boyfriend, but are you really sure you're ready to move back to that area? You've told me about many of your relationship demons and what you went through. I don't want to see you start worrying about what will happen if you run into him again. Under normal circumstances, you may not because he doesn't live in Atlanta, but you still have friends in common in that area and I would hate to see any of them bring up old, bad memories for you."

Victoria was right, but it was definitely time to stop running. She ran away to Boston, trying to escape all that her ex had put her through and now going back to an area that has meant so much to her despite her past was exactly what she needed to do.

"Don't worry about me. I'm going to be fine. I'm not hung up on him or the past anymore. You know I've dated some since I've lived here in Boston and nothing has held me back except for the fact that I let work consume me. Running into him won't be a problem for me. I'm over it and I'm over the past hurt," Taija admitted.

"Good, because when I come to visit you in Atlanta, I want to still see the wild and crazy Taija that I've come to love like a sister and I expect to hear about all the men you have to beat off with a stick. I know you had no problem turning down the tons of men who are always all over you here, but I hear the men in Atlanta are just down-right gorgeous, irresistible and packing. I swear there must be something in the milk in Atlanta," Victoria joked.

Taija turned and laughed when Victoria started fanning herself.

"Both hands on the steering wheel and try to keep your hormones under check. A man is a man and the men in Atlanta are no different than the men right here in Boston."

"Yet, you didn't tap a whole lot since you've been here. You know me, I'm tapping every large package that I can get my hands on and I do mean that literally, too," Victoria said jokingly, but with enough seriousness that Taija knew she was speaking the truth.

"Just because I'm not tapping everything walking like you are, doesn't mean I didn't dabble a little. Besides, you spend so much time with your best friend, Turner I was beginning to wonder if you had anything going on with him. With him around you all the time, I was sure he'd either be trying to tap you or he'd be blocking."

Victoria shook her head as she weaved in and out of traffic.

"Turner and I are just friends, Taija and you know it. Hanging with him has never wrecked my flow. You've hung out with us before and you've even torn up the dance floor with him and it never stopped men from making a move on you. You were the one who didn't bite when the men came calling," Victoria laughed.

Leave it to Victoria to be all up in her love life, just like a true sister.

"Hey, I'm keeping my options open," Taija said.

"Maybe it's because you have your eyes already set on one man in particular who just happens to live in Atlanta. I remember you showed me the cover of Black Enterprise magazine with those three gorgeous hunks on the cover. The way you were looking at them made me think you were waiting for one of them to jump right off of the front page of the magazine and devour you."

"You really know how to exaggerate girl! I did show you that and yes, he is hot. His name is Duron Knight and he's the brother of one of my sorority sisters, Loren. You have to admit that brother is fine!" Taija exclaimed.

Victoria looked over at Taija as they stopped at a red light and noticed her blushing.

"He?" Victoria asked. "Is he the reason you're blushing right now?"

Taija realized she had singled out Duron and Victoria caught it.

"I meant to say them and I am not blushing," she said

trying to cover up her slip-up.

"I know exactly what you meant, but I'll let you slide this one time. All three of them are three of the best-looking men I have ever seen. I want you to know that I see a little blushing going on with your mention of Duron by name. Just make sure you tell me every juicy detail about him that I have a feeling you're looking to explore. I noticed that you always give your magazines away to others around the office after you've read them, but not that one. It never left your office and if someone asked to read it, you gave them a look that said to not even ask."

Taija shifted in her seat realizing she was being put on the spot. She made a serious show playing with the air conditioning knobs in the car to try and avoid the conversation and to also get rid of the heat that had suddenly surfaced in the car.

"I never did any such thing and you know it. It just so happens that the issue of the magazine in question had a lot of great articles in it that I wanted to keep," she said, lying.

She looked over at Victoria to see if her lie had worked. She smiled when she again, had been caught.

"Blushing again," Victoria said, "and turning on the air conditioning isn't going to help. The brother is fine. You'll need an igloo to cool down after checking that brother out."

"Yes, he is," Taija said. She looked at Victoria in shock when she realized she responded out loud and not just in her head. The slick grin on her face let Taija know that she'd been heard.

"He? I thought we were talking about them?" Victoria said, smiling.

"Stop trying to confuse me." Taija smile at how frazzled

she was. She stammered her reply.

"Hey, I'm not the one twitching in my seat at the mentioning of the brother, nor am I the one singling out one of them in particular though all of them are fine and sexy as hell."

"Oh, I.. I mean they are fine, not just him. I meant to say they and I am not blushing," Taija tried to clear up.

The light turned green, making Victoria go back to her eyes being on the traffic.

Taija was glad the conversation had stopped. She hated to admit it, but Victoria was right. The mentioning of Duron Knight had caused her to slide around in her seat to diminish the aching feeling at the apex of her thighs because it was true. Even though they were talking about how good looking all three men were, she couldn't help but focus her attention on Duron. There was something about him that made her think of sweaty nights, hot steamy showers and long sessions of love making, all while staring into his dazzling hazel eyes.

She could tell she was blushing, but there was no need in admitting it to Victoria. She was only admiring him from a distance and had no plans of trying to connect with him, though he did live in Atlanta. She was sure the women of Atlanta were already keeping him busy.

She remembered meeting him years ago when she and Loren, his sister and her sorority sister, were students at Spellman college. He turned heads every time he came to campus to visit his sister and her head was no different.

Duron was handsome beyond description and seeing him on the magazine cover had her feeling like a cat in heat. She was fascinated by his hazel eyes, never seeing such a color on an African American man before. They had reached right off of the cover, right out to her. She didn't know too many brothers with hazel eyes that were not the result of colored contact lenses. She knew his were natural. When she'd first met Loren on campus and noticed the same colored eyes on her, Loren told her of her father's ancestry and that the hazel eye color had been passed down through many generations, but not all of the family line had them. In her family, besides Loren's dad, only she and Duron had eyes that color. She had two other brothers that had dark eyes like their mother.

Victoria started talking and broke into her thoughts.

"So, when I visit you in Atlanta, I'll take one of the other two since clearly, you have hidden plans for Duron and there is no need to even think of denying it. It's not hot in here and as soon as I mentioned him, you started sweating like we're in the middle of a rain forest."

"I don't have any hidden or unhidden plans. I do admit the brother is fine, but I'm sure with as good looking and successful as he is, he's quite occupied when it comes to the ladies. I've had enough of ladies men and not looking to be involved with another one," Taija admitted.

"Girl, who said anything about getting involved. I'm saying get you a little or even a lot. I could write a steamy novel just from looking at his picture and I know you've fantasized about him or you would have stopped twitching in that seat by now. I hope I won't need to have my seat cleaned after you get out," Victoria joked.

Taija was going to miss Victoria. They always had the best conversations, especially about men. She smiled and didn't comment. Victoria was right about one thing, since seeing Duron's picture on the magazine cover and reading his story of his climb to success, he was more than just a handsome face and sexy body and she was intrigued. She wouldn't think too much about it though. A man as fine as Duron Knight had to be in a relationship or he had a woman for every night of the week.

Reading his biography, he was a great catch and there was no way he was still single. Even if he was, she was going back to Atlanta to work, have fun and reconnect with her friends and sorority sisters, including Loren. Maybe she would or maybe she wouldn't run into Duron, but if she did, she wouldn't sweat it. She'd had enough of playboys and it was time she focused on her and not on finding a man.

"Just get us to the gym before we both burst into flames in this car," she said, trying to take her thoughts off of the sexy business executive and back on trying to keep her body in tip top shape.

"Hey, I'm cool over here. Why don't you turn the vents on you before you combust all over my beautiful leather seats," Victoria quipped.

Taija could do nothing, but shake her head.

"Apparently we both are in dire need of some male attention if we're getting this excited over some pictures in a magazine," Taija said.

At the same time, they both said in their best Chris Tucker voice, "And you know this man!"

4

Taija was trying to do too many things. She was finishing up her packing while trying to prepare to make an appearance at a friends' wedding in Boston. She wasn't sure she would make it on time for the ceremony, but she would make it to the reception.

After spending a few hours with Victoria at the gym the day before, they decided to hang out at a local club that night.

Taija had selected one of her favorite navy blue jumpsuits and added a pair of four-inch navy and gold stilettos from her outrageously large collection of shoes. It wasn't until she began packing her shoes up that she realized the number she had. Shoes were her fetish along with her penchant for sexy lingerie. She was in her element as long as she had those.

She and Victoria had to have danced with every man in the club. Every time she thought she'd get a break and rest her feet, she had been asked by another man to dance and by the time the club had closed, she and Victoria had only been sitting for a few minutes. Victoria wanted to send her off with a night out that they would remember.

Now, as she moved around slowly trying to get ready for the wedding, her last event in Boston, she felt like the walking dead. She knew she needed to get herself together.

She was expecting to see a lot of her sorority sisters at the wedding including Loren, who was traveling from Atlanta. The friend getting married had pledged along with she and Loren in college and it would be the first time in a few years that she'd seen Loren and she was excited. They had lost track over the years, but with her move to Atlanta soon, she was hoping to reconnect.

Loren had been the first person she'd reached out to about her move back to Atlanta. They may not have been in touch over the past few years, but they did occasionally email each other.

While continuing to pack and get dressed, she felt a great sense of excitement at the possibilities available to her with her move back to Atlanta. At twenty-seven, she was moving up in the finance world. She had just signed a major contract to work in corporate finance, leaving the senior accounting position she currently held in Boston and had held for the past year and a half. She really missed Atlanta because it was where she'd spent her college years at Spellman and where some of her closest friends still lived.

Taija thought back to the day she decided to move to the frigid cold temperatures of Boston to get away from a soured relationship. She needed to put some distance between her and her cheating ex-boyfriend. Now, she was heading back to Atlanta, more mature, less accepting of mess from men and ready to take the finance world by storm. Putting the rest of her packing to the side for now, she had to rush to finish dressing.

After adding a little make-up to her face and checking herself in the mirror, she admired her canary yellow wrap dress with matching heels. She loved how all of the hours she spent in the gym on a weekly basis paid off. Grabbing what she needed, she rushed to get to the reception on time.

~~

Taija made her way over to the table at the wedding reception where her sorority sisters were sitting. She was excited to catch up with everyone, especially Loren.

She'd made it to the wedding just in time to catch the end and was glad everything had gone off without a hitch with beauty and class. The reception was located in the same hotel where the wedding was held and guests only had to take an elevator to the top floor to attend the reception.

Walking up behind Loren, who was sitting at a table watching others dance, Taija lightly placed her hands over Loren's eyes.

"Guess who?" she said excitedly.

"I know who, even without guessing." Loren smiled and stood up to greet her.

"It's good to see you. How was your flight into Boston?" Taija asked.

"It was great. Even the guy who talked my ear off the entire flight wasn't as annoying as I thought he would be. So, are you still looking forward to moving back to Atlanta next week?"

"Yes, and I'm very excited. I miss living there. Besides, it's too cold for a sister here in Boston," Taija laughed, faking a shiver as if she were freezing over the Boston reference.

"It'll be great having you back. The nightlife is the best and the men are still the finest. Have you found a place to live yet or are you still planning to stay in a hotel for a few weeks while you look? You know I have a spare room that you're welcomed to use until you find something."

"Thanks for the offer, but I had a realtor find me a very nice house that I'll rent for a while until I have more time to look for the perfect house. Luckily, the company I'll be working for included moving expenses and a signing bonus so that I wouldn't feel strapped with the move," Taija explained.

"It'll be nice having you in the area again," Loren said. "The girls and I always talk about the one missing seat when we go out, not having you with us. As soon as you get back, we're going to get together and really catch up with the old crew," Loren said.

They spent the next half hour catching up until Loren needed to make an exit. She had setup a dinner meeting with a potential client for her interior design business and needed to prepare for it. She needed extra time to get the samples together the client requested and if things went well, she would soon have a big influx of cash from signing the contract with a major firm to do the interior designing for their chain of restaurants that span all across the east coast.

"I'm going to say my goodbyes to the bride and groom and head back to my hotel. I set up an appointment in Boston tonight I need to get to. Call me when you get to Atlanta and I'll come by and help you get unpacked. I hope you plan to come to the bachelor auction the chapter is having this year. It's time you got back into being an active member. There'll be lots of the old crew from Spellman there that you haven't seen since you moved to Boston. Everyone will be excited to see you again and besides, you may see a bachelor that's just for you," Loren said.

Taija smiled, but didn't want to tell Loren she didn't think so, as far as the bachelor was concerned. What kind of man would participate in a bachelor auction anyway? Were they desperate for a date? She wasn't interested, but she may think about attending to support the sorority's event. She had big plans for staying focused on work and right now, men had to take a back seat.

After Loren made her exit, Taija settled in to enjoy the rest of the reception. She loved weddings. When she was younger, like so many other young girls, she'd planned out her own wedding from the dress to the reception. Unlike her ideas as a young girl of what her wedding would be like, her reality was not the same.

Years ago, she had been in love and thought that she was on her way to her dream wedding, only to discover that the man she thought was her prince charming had actually turned out to be a cheating toad. Sitting at this reception and watching all the smiling faces of happy, joyous people pricked her youthful longings for the same type of life. She looked over at Alisa, the bride, and could not help but be a tad bit jealous. Alisa had found the man of her dreams, something Taija thought she herself had found a few years ago, but that happily ever after didn't happen for her.

She knew her mood wasn't a good one and had become melancholy after several single men at the reception asked her to dance and she turned them down one after the other. She found herself doing something she said she wouldn't do and that was to think of what she went through in her failed relationship with her ex. She had been happier than she ever thought she could be until it all came crashing down around her. Her heart had been ripped right out of her chest, stomped on and kicked away and as much as she'd like to show everyone that she had moved on, it was clear to her that she had not.

Lingering thoughts of the hurt were surfacing at the wedding reception when she saw how happy her friend was and the good time everyone else was having. Maybe it was a combination of exhaustion and jealousy that was causing her mood to change from happy to sad.

She shouldn't feel this way, especially in a room full of life and laughter and especially dancing, something she loved to do.

Taija began questioning her decision to move back to Atlanta. Though she would not be living in the same city as her ex, she knew that they could possibly run into each other and she wasn't sure she was ready for that. She knew she no longer held feelings for him, but she also knew that seeing him would bring up bad memories and embarrassment and she wasn't sure she was ready to deal with either.

"Are you sure you wouldn't like to dance?" a nice gentleman asked her. Taija looked up into his handsome face and remembered he'd asked her to dance a few songs ago and she'd turned him down. She needed to get herself together and shake off the sullen mood.

She smiled up at him.

"Actually, I would like to dance," she said, taking his extended hand. She saw no reason to not enjoy the joyous occasion and she wanted to no longer give a cheating man space in her head. She'd left him and his cheating ways behind when she moved to Boston.

After dancing through a few fast songs, then a few slow songs and dancing with a few other men who asked, she knew it was time to say her goodbyes and get back to preparing for the next phase of her life.

After getting her car from the valet, Taija settled in for the ride back to her house. She took the scenic route home driving through the neighborhoods she would miss. She knew that she'd be back to visit Victoria sometime, but with all of the packing she'd been doing, it made things seem so final.

By the time she pulled up at home after driving by many areas in town that meant so much to her, she was once again brooding about the reasons for her drastic move to Boston. She'd run away, is what she'd done. She'd run from the hurt, anger and embarrassment of a relationship she thought was the highlight of her life.

She exited her car, went into her house and looked around at her life packed up in boxes. Seeing everything made her think of what her life would have been like if she had not moved to Boston. She knew she would have still ended her relationship, but she wouldn't have felt like she was running away from her life like she did when she moved.

Seeing a few more things that could be packed up for the move, she quickly showered and changed into sweats and grabbed a few more boxes of shoes from her closet that needed to be packed.

While taking the last box of shoes from her closet, she opened it to see what pair were inside only to discover a box of keepsakes from her relationship that she thought she'd thrown out. She flipped through some of the cards, photos and trinkets and wondered why she still had them. She hoped that one day she'd have the kind of love she thought she'd had before and keeping remembrances from something old wouldn't be good for walking into something new.

Still she couldn't resist going through some of the contents of the shoe box and remembering what was supposed to be but wasn't.

At one time in her life, the person she thought was her mister perfect turned out to be the complete opposite.

She remembered five years ago, when she'd first met her ex, Keith Mathers, years before he became famous as a star NBA basketball player. There was a time when she felt like their relationship was just as important to him as it was to her. She loved and trusted him with everything in her, yet on more than a few occasions, he had proven to not be trustworthy.

She knew what he was doing, but turned a blind eye to it hoping it would go away. No matter how many pairs of thongs and panties, not belonging to her that she would find at his place or the number of late night calls and text messages he would not return in her presence, Taija ignored them all. They were all signs that something was going on behind her back that he was trying to hide.

Once he signed on as an NBA player, all of his love and devotion to her had been replaced by the large number of women who were willing to do anything to get his attention and he seemed more than willing to oblige them because he loved the attention. Once women discovered who he was, they were on a mission to bed the promising ball player by any means necessary, whether he had a girlfriend or not.

Keith, thinking with the wrong head, always fell prey to every trick thrown at him and when it came to explaining things to her when he messed up and got caught, he saw himself as the victim of his current circumstance as a star and claimed to be weak, but that he would never do it again. That turned into one lie after another.

One day she walked in on him at his condo with some bimbo with huge breast implants. He was riding her as if she were the winning Kentucky Derby race horse. Just as she was about to interrupt them, another naked woman walked out of his bathroom and joined him and big boobs on the bed. She wanted to scream, shout and throw things, but decided against that knowing how volatile the situation could become. She knew he wasn't expecting her to show up since she'd planned to be out of town with her mother visiting family. She saw the action taking place right in front of her and she kept her calm. She cleared her throat and when Keith realized he had once again gotten caught with his pants down and off, he knew they were finished.

Taija hadn't blown her top or acted like a crazy woman. She told him the relationship was over and she turned and walked out. After the events of that day, she'd spent several months ignoring and avoiding his many calls and texts and the bimbos he'd been with wasted no time posting pictures and videos with themselves and Keith, which led to embarrassing situations with her family and friends. When the opportunity came for her to take the position in Boston, she saw her chance to put some distance between them. Her mother wasn't happy about the move since she lived in Florida. She'd thought about moving to Atlanta where she'd gone to college, but decided that was still too close to Keith and opted instead for the job in Boston. It may have put Taija further away from her mother, but it gave her to new start she needed in an area that was far enough away from Keith that she'd get some peace and the chance to start fresh.

Speaking of her mother, she promised she would call her when she got home from the wedding.

Her mother answered on the first ring as if she were sitting, waiting on the phone to ring.

"Hey, mom."

"Hey, daughter of mine. I've been waiting on you to call me. How is the move coming along?"

"I'm almost all packed. I'm trying to decide what to take with me in my car and what to put on the moving van. The moving company promised me a time they would arrive in Atlanta with my belongings, but just in case they are delayed for any reason, I want to be sure I have a few days' worth of items in the car with me to get me through. If I need to, I'll buy what I need. How are things going with you?" Taija asked.

"I'm doing fine. I'm making plans to take a trip to Bermuda soon for some much-needed rest and relaxation. I'm going with some ladies from work who want to try a *'Stella getting her groove back'* kind of trip, so this should be lots of fun," her mother chuckled.

Her mom at fifty-five, never let much grass grow under her feet. Though she tried to not let on just how excited she was to go on the trip, Taija knew her mother had a little 'Stella' in her, too. That's a part of her mother that she never wanted to hear about or talk about. Some things about her mother she wanted to leave a mystery.

She could recall a few not so good conversations with her mother, who tended to date men closer to Taija's age than her own and she didn't like the last guy her mother was involved with.

Her mother deciding to go on this trip surprised her. Perhaps her latest fling was now a distant memory which would be music to her ears. She decided not to bring up her mother's proclivity for much younger men or the current state of her own lack of a relationship, though her mother never had a problem butting into Taija's life. She did know, however, her mother's usual butting in was coming before the call was over.

"So, since you're moving back to Atlanta, do you think you'll run into Keith at all?"

Taija smiled knowing the question was asked in record speed. Normally her mother waited until the end of their phone conversations to ask her questions about Keith. Her mother never let an opportunity go by without bringing up Keith and trying to weigh if she'd lightened up on her hatred of him and what he'd taken her through.

Her mother thought Taija was crazy for walking away from him. She'd told her a little straying by a man was expected. Taija didn't agree and thought that there is never a time when a woman should be a doormat, as far as she was concerned. Men were given too many passes by women, without consequence, for being unfaithful and using the excuse that it's just how men are as a reason to justify their behavior. Not in her book. That was a sore subject between Taija and her mother and she knew it was best to quickly respond and change the subject before it became heated.

"No, mom. I don't see myself running into Keith in Atlanta. We do have several friends in common who live there, but he lives in Florida. He doesn't have time to be concerned about my moving back to Atlanta. I'm sure he has moved on by now and I have no doubt that there are quite a few groupies keeping him occupied or he's possibly involved with someone by now."

"I was wondering if maybe he has changed. You could give him a call and see where his head is these days. I don't hear about him in the media with a lot of women like in the past. Maybe he has changed and you could give him another chance. I think he really loved you before and still does now, but you know how athlete's lives can be. They are tempted every day. By now, he may realize what he missed out on when he cheated on you and you broke up with him."

She and her mom never agreed when it came to Keith. Her mother always said that she should learn to overlook some things and not lose him or that he would be a great provider. Being a great provider was not enough for her. She wanted unconditional love and commitment from the man she professed her love to. She wanted someone who would be willing to sacrifice being with anyone else for her. She didn't give up on the hope that her prince would find her one day. She would be patient and wait until what is for her, finds her.

Dealing with her mother delicately, she replied, "Mom, it's not going to happen because I've moved on and you should too, especially when it comes to my love life. Trust me, there is no room for Keith ever again. I woman should never have to put up with what he took me through and I would never, ever go back to that," Taija explained.

Before her mom could continue the conversation, and say how upset her last statement made her, Taija rushed her off of the phone. She already knew how things would end and she wasn't in the mood for it.

"I'm only trying to help," her mother said.

"Mom, I need to get this last bit of packing done and tie up some loose ends. I have a very busy week of moving ahead of me. I'll call you when I get to Atlanta. Love you, bye."

She hung up before her mother could find a way back to the conversation she wanted to stay away from. She knew one day soon, her mother would bring up how abruptly she ended the call, but at least she didn't have to deal with it tonight. Right now, she only wanted to focus on moving and how her life was about to change for the better with her move back to Atlanta. That, she was excited about.

5

Duron figured it was a good time to stop by and visit his mother after Sunday church service. He had no doubt she was still worried about his reaction to seeing the wedding announcement since Loren mentioned they had both been trying to reach him after seeing it.

He entered his parent's home just as his mother was coming down the steps. She lit up when she saw him come in.

"Hey, mom! How are you?" he said giving her a hug.

"I'm fine now that my baby boy has stopped by. How are you? Are you staying for dinner?" she asked happily.

"Yes, I'm staying for dinner. I'm coming from picking Loren up from the airport. She's back from Boston and she said she'll be here for dinner later, too. I thought I would come and hang with my favorite girl all day," he said.

He watched his mother smile broadly. She loved when he called her his favorite girl, though he knew she wished he would find his very own favorite girl. He hoped she wouldn't bring it up today. He loved his mother, but her constant reminders to him that he was still single and not married like she'd like him to be annoyed him. Those thoughts also brought up old memories for him and her about the one time in his life when he was ready to settle down.

Loren mentioned to him when he picked her up at the airport earlier that she told their mother he saw the wedding announcement in the newspaper and that he appeared to be handling it well. He didn't want to get into an in-depth discussion about relationships with her, but he did want her to see for herself that he was fine. Allison is in his past and he'd like to leave her there. He wanted to keep things as light as possible as he followed her into the kitchen where the best southern cooking smells were making his stomach growl.

He started a conversation about something other than his ex.

"What do you know about this bachelor auction Loren asked me to take part in?" he asked, lifting the tops from all the pots and getting a good whiff.

Duron still had reservations about participating and he was sure Loren mentioned to her that she was planning to ask him, with coaxing from their mother of course.

"She did mention it to me and I told her to ask you. It's harmless. Besides, I hear there are some lovely young ladies who attend these."

The look on Duron's face did not shock Barbara Knight as she looked at her son who was surprised by her admission. She knew he liked to live a private life, but she always taught her sons to look out for their sister and help her when she needed it. What she did realize was another topic was needed and fast.

She turned to stir the food in one of the many pots on the stove.

"Have you talked to either of your brothers in the past few days?" his mother asked.

"Yeah, I talked to Brian yesterday and Jake this morning. Why?" he asked.

"Your father is working on this year's hospital benefit gala and he wants to be sure he can count on his sons for support. This year's event is going to be at the end of the summer and he expects it to be the biggest year for donations since he began having them."

Duron sat at the island in the kitchen to watch his mother work her magic while they talked.

"You know we always support in any way we can and we'll do so this year, too. I'll see them both later this week because we're meeting for dinner at this new supper club that opened in Atlanta a few months ago. We'll put our heads together to see how we can lend a hand to dad this year, so don't worry, mom. We got it covered and of course, I'll be making a huge donation this year," Duron said.

He saw the relief on her face when he reassured her that he and his brothers would not let her or their father down.

He and his two older brothers, Jake and Brian, always put family first. Brian, at thirty-four was three years older than Duron and Jake was thirty-six, the oldest of the bunch. They have always been close and made themselves available whenever their father, Earl, needed them.

Giving her son a slight nod of acknowledgment of his response, she thought of how much she loved her sons and loved how they had a wonderful relationship with their father. She'd taught all of her children that family was everything.

She looked at Duron when he turned away from her to glance at the newspaper on the counter. She saw sadness in his gaze that she didn't like. As much as she wanted to ask him how he was feeling after seeing the wedding announcement in the paper for Allison, the woman who broke his heart, she decided to stay in the safe lane and address it only if he brought up the subject. Asking him about work was a better conversation topic, knowing how much he loved talking about all of his latest work projects. Maybe it would remove some of the cloud she saw over his mood today.

"So, how is work coming along these days? Your father mentioned to me that you're in the midst of another major development project?"

Duron sat up straight, ready to share all of his exciting work news with his mother.

"Tyrone, Mike and I are excited about this new project. We're designing a new business park and this is the first project we're working on that will include the use of our own construction company to do the actual building. Once we combined forces, adding in the construction side of the business along with the designing, it moved us into a whole new market for acquiring contracts. We're able to attract even more business, especially once people saw the work we did on the design and construction of our own office building. That spotlight in *Black Enterprise* helped a lot as well with connecting us to a market of people who've inquired about our work. Pioneer A&D is off and running and competing with some of the top companies in the country. Your baby boy is out here making big things happen, Ma," Duron chimed.

Barbara turned and smiled at him with unshed tears in her eyes. All of her children made her proud of their accomplishments.

Her oldest, Jake was a doctor, working alongside his father and her other son Brian had a career as a college professor. All of her children had good, honest careers including her daughter Loren who was an interior designer. She was happy when they worked together like Loren often did lending her expertise to Duron's company when projects were completed and were in need of interior design ideas.

Even though the mood had lightened some, she knew they both wondered who would bring up the elephant in the room first. She made the decision for them because she wanted him to let go of any heartache he may be feeling knowing Allison was about to marry the person she'd left him for. She wiped her hands on her apron and came closer to him.

"Son, I know how much you hate for any of us to bring up the past and as much as I'd like to avoid an obvious conversation, how are you feeling after seeing the wedding announcement in the paper for Allison's upcoming wedding?" she asked.

Just the mention of it was leaving a bad taste in Duron's mouth. He didn't know why discussions about that woman still had a lingering impact on him.

"Yes, I saw it and I'm fine. That was over a long time ago. You and Loren should not be worried about me. She made her decision and I've dealt with it and believe me when I say, I've moved on, case closed," Duron said.

He could see from his mother's facial expression that he had not convinced her.

"I know," she said. "I try not to worry, but that woman hurt you and you know I didn't like how things ended with you two. I can't help but worry about you after seeing the announcement and wondering if it would bring up any bad memories for you. That was a bad time and you've done so well moving beyond it. If you say you're okay with it, then I'm okay, too."

She smiled, gave him a kiss on the cheek checked on her dinner. Seeing that everything was okay, especially her son, and that she believed he was fine, she dropped the subject.

"Well, dinner will be ready in a little while. I'm going to get some things done for your father regarding the gala. If you get a chance, can you see what's wrong with the television in the family room? Your father called himself redecorating and had to unhook all the wires. Some apparently got crossed, besides the ones in his head because it no longer works. I don't know why he thinks he's a handyman," she laughed.

Duron laughed along with her. He and his brothers were always fixing something their father said he had fixed, but had not.

"Sure, mom. I'll check it out right now," he said.

His cell phone rang as he was getting up. He glanced down and was glad to see that it was Mike.

"Hey, Mike. What's up man?" he said.

"Hey, D. Nothing much for a Sunday. I'm calling to let you know that we changed the time for the meeting with Jacinta from nine in the morning tomorrow to noon instead."

Jacinta, Inc. was the name of the company they were under contract with to build the new business park that was sure to draw major business to the Atlanta region.

"That's cool. Everything is all set. That gives us a little time to talk through it together before the presentation at noon. That's also good because I can let Sarah know she doesn't need to come in as early as planned since the meeting will be later," Duron said. Sarah was the executive assistant who kept the office running like a well-oiled machine for them.

"Cool. I'll give Tyrone a call to let him know. I think he was coming in extra early to set up. One last thing I wanted to check with you about. Is your sister really busy with work projects at the moment? I want to get her help with decorating my house when construction is complete," Mike said.

"Man, you know you can call her to ask her yourself. I know she has some things going on, but she'll always make time for any of us if we need her to. When I talk to her later, I'll let her know you need to reach her," Duron said.

"That works," replied Mike.

"Don't forget dinner at my parent's house this evening if you want to stop by. Loren will be here then and you can talk to her about your project yourself if you want. Either way, let me know."

"Thanks for the offer, but I have plans this evening. Tell everyone I said hello and I'll be at the next Sunday dinner for sure. I miss your mom's cooking."

"You're right about that. I'm sitting here now in the kitchen wondering how long dinner will be because I'm starving and everything smells good. I'm going to hang around here for the rest of the day and will probably stop by the office before going home to look over some figures the accountant emailed me for that proposal from that firm in Chicago. Soon, we'll have more projects than we can handle," Duron said, all smiles.

"All work and no play are making Duron a very dull friend. Do you realize all you talk about is work?"

Duron knew that was true, but it was all he could do right now to keep his mind off of Allison and the fact that she was getting married soon. He didn't want anyone to know he was still thinking about it.

"Yeah, whatever man. My work ethic is contributing to you, Tyrone and me being some very rich brothers," Duron exclaimed.

"Hey, I'm not complaining; just stating the fact," Mike said.

"Listen, I saw you heading into the office early this morning and I know you. Whenever you go into the office on a Sunday morning, it's to distract you from something that's bugging you. I'm hoping it's not about that announcement I showed you. I did that because I thought you should know before someone brought it up catching you off guard."

"What is up with everyone and this announcement. It's happening and not my deal anymore," he said, trying to convince Mike and himself that he was over conversations about her.

"I hear you, but just in case it's on your mind, stop thinking about it. She wasn't the one for you. I noticed how much you drank after I showed it to you. Shake it off, bro," Mike encouraged.

Duron felt the sting. He wished everyone would just let it go. He knows they all knew how in love he was with Allison and how deeply she'd hurt him by her betrayal. He also knew they were all only looking out for him and he could appreciate that.

"Already forgotten about man. I'm good."

"Check you in the morning then," Mike said.

After the call, he shook off all thoughts of Allison and headed to fix all the crossed wires he was sure to find after his father's attempt at reconnecting them.

6

Taija had been back in Atlanta a few weeks and finally feeling settled in. The house she decided to lease until she found one to purchase had turned out to be everything she hoped it would be. Now that she was back, she was determined to put down some roots and buying her first home was a good way to start.

She looked around at all of the decorating she was able to get done in a short amount of time, accomplished only with Loren's help. Loren, using her expertise as an interior designer, had been a big help in turning her new place into a home that felt like her own.

It was Friday night, the night of the big bachelor auction and she'd promised Loren she would attend even though she was tired from a long work week and wanted to relax with a few glasses of her favorite peach wine. This was the end of her first full week of work since returning to Atlanta. She had put in extra hours at the office getting acclimated to her new surroundings and getting to know the key people in the international finance department she was now the manager of.

The last thing she felt like doing was going back out to her sorority's bachelor auction. She herself, would be making a nice donation to the cause tonight, without planning to take part in the actual auction. She was just getting back into town and the last thing she wanted was to go on any kind of date so soon, not even one in the name of charity. Though hesitant, she was looking forward to spending some time tonight reacquainting herself with many of the friends she knew would be at the auction.

She was able to catch up with a few of them recently during a ladies night out Loren had put together celebrating her move to Atlanta. She felt right at home seeing everyone again. Before she changed her mind, Taija got up and went in search of something sexy and glamorous to wear. Besides, she could get her first look at who were considered some of the most eligible men in Atlanta, just in case her ideas on dating changed. She was actually feeling a little spontaneous tonight.

Going through her closet, she still had not decided what to wear. It was a formal affair and she had a few formal pieces she could choose from. Going to formal events was something she missed when she'd left Atlanta. The city was known for its many high-profile events and she had found herself at more than a few of them. Being in a relationship with a high-profile ball player back then afforded her the opportunity to rub elbows with high society.

She didn't miss the people as much as she missed the chance to get all dolled up. Choosing just the right gown, it was time to get dressed and check out some of Atlanta's finest bachelors. As she eyed her favorite red gown, one of the colors of her sorority, she knew it was the perfect attire for a night of elegance. She searched for the perfect pair of heels to match and laid everything out on her bed while she picked through her jewelry for the perfect pieces to give the gown the dressing it needs.

Taija's eyes caught a glimpse of the fundraiser announcement that had a list of the bachelors and their photos. They were thirty of the most handsome men she had ever seen. One bachelor in particular really stood out. That bachelor was, Duron Knight, Loren's brother. She had been shocked when the announcement came in the mail and she'd opened it to his hazel eyes staring back at her. She hadn't been a part of the benefit planning and decided to not go to the last few meetings since she was focused on unpacking and getting settled.

Her pulse accelerated just looking at a picture of his handsome face. She couldn't wait to see him in person. From the full body photo, she knew he was tall from the few times she'd seen him in person and she loved tall men. Looking at him, it seemed like he was reaching out from the page for her and she was being pulled in by lust. The palms of her hands felt balmy and she felt a little sweaty just as she had the day she and Victoria were talking about him in the car. If she had this kind of a reaction to him from a picture, she could only imagine what his very presence would do to her. His sexuality leaped off the pages of the magazine stimulating her. She really needed to get back out into the dating game. Clearly, she was overdue for some male attention.

Had it really been that long since she had enjoyed the feel of a man that the mere sight of one in a magazine gave her the same reaction she endured when she met a gorgeous man face to face? Yes, she thought to herself, this wasn't just any man and she knew it. This was the man who starred in a few of her erotic fantasies. When she'd talked to Loren a few times, she was tempted to ask her if her brother was involved with anyone.

She rushed to get dressed to get to the event on time, smiling and knowing that it was going to be some night.

~~

Duron was preparing to get dressed in his tuxedo for the auction, thinking back on the day he'd spent at the office being ribbed by his buddies about his participation. They'd found all kinds of jokes to hit him with. Ignoring them, he knew he was doing this for a good cause and to also help his sister.

Rather than head all the way out to Buckhead to his home, he decided to get dressed at the condo he owned on the top floor of the office building he, Mike and Tyrone built and owned. They each had a condo on the top floor, which they'd built with the idea in mind that as they built up their business and entertained late night business meetings, they could stay at the condos for the night. They were also able to hold informal business meetings in the condos for a more relaxed atmosphere that the office didn't provide. He was the only one, so far, that had also built a house, though Mike was in the middle of the construction of his.

Mike and Tyrone had decided to live in the condos while Duron wanted a place where he could get away from the office when he wanted some breathing room. He loved his condo, but his house was his pride and joy. That house and the cabin his family owned in the mountains were his two places of solitude. He had a feeling he would need some solitude after tonight's festivities.

What was he thinking, he thought to himself as he made one final check of his appearance and headed to the auction. He knew he was participating because his sister asked, but he had to have been drunk when he agreed to it.

A bachelor auction? Though his friends made fun of him, he knew he wasn't doing it to get a date. When it came to women, he had more than he needed at times, but still he enjoyed them immensely. There was nothing more beautiful in the world to him than a beautiful woman and he was sure there would be plenty of them at the auction.

He casually dated, but nothing exclusive and he made sure women always knew the score before he got involved with them. He was only out for mutual satisfaction and since he always delivered, he never had any problems when it came to women. They got what they came to him for.

As he made his way down the elevator at the condo to the parking garage, he silently hoped he would be auctioned early so that he could high-tail it out of there and get home. As much as he would like to spend time getting to know a few of the women in attendance, tonight he wanted to get through the event unscathed and feeling good about helping to raise money for needy organizations around Atlanta.

As he arrived at the Georgia World Congress Center for the auction, only a few blocks from his condo, Duron thought that there had to have been something wrong with him when he agreed to be a participant. He gave the valet his keys, took his ticket to retrieve his car later and looked around at all of the people arriving. The event was going to be huge if he was going by the large number of people arriving.

Once inside he discovered even more people in attendance and knew that there were at least five to six hundred people in there. He could imagine what Monday morning in the office was going to be like, explaining to Mike and Tyrone about how the evening went. He only hoped he'd still be able to look his friends in the face after allowing himself to be auctioned off. He just had to remember it was for charity and he'd make it through. He figured a day or two of more jokes from Tyrone and Mike would be worth the contributions that would be received from the auction. They were always teasing each other and it was all in good fun since the day they'd met years ago.

During their days at Howard University, they were known for being players and any one of them could have brought in a pretty penny tonight. He'll remember that if he ever lets his sister talk him into this again, he had a few other guys he would draft to participate.

The main room where the auction was being held had been transformed into a space worthy of a black-tie affair. He noticed that there were lots of gorgeous women and he knew what he was looking at was a player's paradise. There were also a significant number of much older women. It was said that each year, some cougars or ladies who enjoyed the company of much younger men, pooled their money to bid on the hottest young man at the auction. He wondered who that would be this year. He couldn't wait to see who their eyes and dollars were set on.

"Hey, you clean up nice, big brother. I haven't seen you this sharp since Jake's wedding a few years ago," Loren said.

Duron was so focused on checking out the scene and all the women, that he hadn't noticed his sister coming up behind him until she referred to how sharp he looked at their brother's wedding to his beautiful wife Kim a few years back.

He took in her beauty as he leaned down to give her a kiss on the cheek and wanted to be sure to set her straight.

BACHELOR NOT FOR SALE

"I don't know what you're talking about. I dress this sharp at least once a week. Did you know that GQ magazine called after seeing my spotlight in Black Enterprise magazine and they said a brother as fine as me needed to grace their cover too?" he said joking.

Laughing at him, Loren looked him over and thought of how the ladies were going to go crazy over her handsome brother. His custom-made black tuxedo fit him like he was born to wear it. The gold and diamond cufflinks added an extra touch of richness to his look.

The last time her sorority held a bachelor auction, he was in a relationship with that she-devil Allison. Back then, he would never have agreed to participate because Allison was the jealous type.

Her friends had been falling all over themselves trying to get close to her brother for years. She knew he was handsome, along with her other two brothers, but sometimes her friends drove her crazy at how they would go gaga whenever Duron was around. Tonight, she was hoping it would pay off well. There were a lot of people, especially children, who would be able to benefit from the proceeds of the auction.

"Whatever man," she snickered. "As long as your sharp looks bring in some money tonight, I'll agree to anything," Loren quipped.

"I got you," he said.

To her, Duron looked a little uncomfortable. She looked up at him and saw the light glaze of sweat on his brow.

"Okay, it's not really that warm in here tonight, so why are you already breaking out into a sweat? You're not sick or anything are you?" she asked.

Duron looked at her sideways.

"No, I'm not sick," he replied.

She knew what it was.

"Oh, then nervous, are you?" she asked. She smiled as she waited for him to reply.

Duron looked down at his sister's five-nine stature even in four-inch-high heels. Since he was six-five, he towered over her.

"You know how much I like privacy, especially when it comes to women. I'm comfortable in business crowds, but this is different. Feeling like raw steak in a lion's den is not my idea of a fun time. Besides, what's with these cougar stories I keep hearing about? Something you failed to tell me about? I had to hear about them from other people."

Duron reached up and tried to loosen his tie just a bit so he could breathe a little better.

"Oh, you've heard about that have you," Loren smirked.

"Yeah, and they better not try it with me. I'll never hear the last of it from Tyrone and Mike," he said.

"Well, it's not so bad. They are actually pretty harmless. Not all older women are cougars, but the ones that are, definitely come out in rare form. They love the young prey. Nothing inappropriate happens, unless you're down for that type of thing."

Duron looked at her as she tried to suppress a laugh. He could tell she was trying to goad him.

"Well, I prefer that if any woman is going to pay to have dinner with me and is as old as our mother, that it's actually mom whom I'm dining with. You know me, I prefer my ladies a lot closer to my age with all the body parts not yet fighting with gravity."

Loren punched him in the arm and laughed.

"Stop being so cruel. You know that's not right," she said, laughing anyway.

"I know and I'm just teasing you about it. You know my thoughts about women of any age, they are all beautiful. You seem to want to tease me, so I thought I'd toss in a comment to shut you up. No such luck I see," he said.

Loren reached out and hugged him. She loved Duron and she loved that they had a close relationship. She decided to tease him a little more.

"Well, you know if you get the right one, she might ask you to call her mommy," she joked.

Before Duron could reach out and grab her, she laughed and moved out of his reach to head toward her sorority sisters who were greeting everyone. It was almost time for her to get the evening started.

He hollered after her before she was out of ear reach.

"Be lucky that I don't want to ruin your beautiful gown or I would take you outside and dunk you in the nearest fountain to not only wash out your mouth for saying such a thing, but to cleanse your mind from even thinking it."

Duron had to laugh at her. He felt sorry for the man who would eventually have to deal with her and her quick wit. That would be some relationship, he thought.

They both laughed as Loren headed off.

Duron went to find his seat and prepare for what he was sure was going to be an interesting evening.

7

"Ladies and gentleman, if you could all take your seats please," Loren said from the podium. "Now that dinner is about to be served, we want to begin the evening festivities. We would like to thank everyone for coming out tonight for our fourth annual fundraiser. This year, we are once again thankful to be able to host another bachelor auction. The last one a few years ago was a huge hit," she said.

Applause rang out loudly around the room, with a few catcalls added in for good measure.

"If you will refer to your programs, you'll see the names of all thirty bachelors being auctioned tonight, along with their personal bios, which I have no doubt you will find very impressive. The ladies with the highest bid on any of the thirty men will enjoy dinner at a very exclusive restaurant in the city with her bachelor. As an additional incentive, we also have ten giveaways for a week at a spa resort in the Colorado Mountains that have been donated. The spa packages are worth over two thousand dollars. Everyone who bids on and wins their bid will have their name placed in the basket for the drawing. You can also have your name submitted if you win your bid for our silent auction tonight. All of the items available for our silent auction are also listed in your program. The items are here for you to see and touch tonight, so be sure you get your bids in."

Duron was proud of Loren and beamed with pride over all that she accomplished, including a prominent position of leadership within her sorority. This fundraiser was a major undertaking. He was proud of her success as a business woman as well owning her own interior design business. He was more than happy to finance her dream when she told him how unhappy she was working for someone else. He knew she would make it work and his investment had paid off. Not only did she pay him back every cent within the year even though he didn't expect her to, she was also looking to already expand her lucrative business.

"Ladies, the weekend spa getaway does not include the company of the bachelor you may win tonight. Tonight's bid is for the charity dinner only, so let's keep it clean. In other words, watch your expectations," Loren jested.

Everyone laughed when a resounding, *aww* was heard around the room.

"Please take some time during dinner to read up on our bachelors and be prepared to get out those checkbooks because your bachelor awaits!!"

The room went crazy with cheering and applause. Duron had to laugh at that himself. He knew he had no plans to entertain going with anyone to a spa in Colorado, though he was sure some bachelors would. What had he gotten into?

Just as Loren turned to exit the stage, Duron noticed the waiters were beginning to bring the first course of dinner to the tables.

As soon as Loren reached the last step and headed toward her table, something gorgeous and sexy in red caught his eye. His mouth went dry at the sight of the most exquisite woman he had ever seen. He looked at her from head to toe as she exchanged a hug and words with Loren.

The fire red form-fitting gown, that left one shoulder bare and hugged her very curvaceous body was not trashy, but was in fact very classy looking. He was hoping she would turn around so that he could see her face. When she finally did, he had to hold his breath. She was just that breath-taking.

She and Loren were about the same height. He shifted his gaze from her face to her feet in order to get a good look at her from the bottom up. He loved women in high heels. There was something about the way a woman's legs looked sitting high up and he loved that it made them look even sexier and more desirable.

Though her red gown was full length, the slit up the side revealed sexy, well-toned legs. Letting his eyes travel further up her body, he loved how shapely she was. Her hips flared out and going further up her body with his gaze, he saw how her small waste led straight to his favorite part of a woman, large, magnificent, rounded breasts that were screaming to be set free. He gulped when he realized he needed to breathe.

The woman had long, dark brown natural twists that fell in curls around her shoulders. She smiled just as Duron reached her face and her smile lit up the entire room. His gaze fell on her lips, covered in lipstick, the same hot red color as her gown. His attraction was instantaneous. Not only were his eyes caught up in her, but his body quickly hardened at the sight of her. He watched her as she said a few last words to Loren, then ventured off.

To him she had a walk about her that said grace, beauty and self-assurance. Finally taking his gaze off of her, he looked around the table, where he sat with other bachelors and noticed that every male eye was focused on her as well and he understood why. Trying to catch another glimpse of her as she passed through the crowd that was once again moving about, he didn't hear the waiter speaking to him.

"Sir? Was that a yes?"

Duron snapped out of his trance.

"Were you talking to me," he said.

"Would you like a salad sir?" the waiter said again.

"Yes. I'll take a salad."

Throughout dinner, he kept his eye on the beauty in the red gown. He was once again so focused on her, he didn't notice that a group of ladies had appeared in front of him at his table. The minimum age of the group was probably sixty. He had a feeling, he was staring back at the infamous group of cougars. If any of these women bid the highest for him, he would never be able to live through the constant jeering he would receive from his friends.

The spokesperson of the group spoke up first.

"Well, hello Mr. Knight. My name is Eve and these are my friends," she gestured to the others with her.

He looked from her to the other women accompanying her.

"Hello ladies," he acknowledged.

"We plan to pool our money and bid on you, so that you and I can enjoy a nice dinner tomorrow together."

Being the perfect gentleman, Duron simply smiled in response, not providing a comment.

He watched as she came closer to him so that she could whisper.

"Do you know who I am?"

"Well," he was able to get out before being cut off.

She didn't wait for him to respond.

"I happen to be very well off and would love to enjoy your company for a little more than dinner," she insinuated.

She then leaned in even closer to Duron's ear so that no one else could hear her next comment.

"I'll see you after the auction and I want you to marinate on the fact that I'm not wearing any panties," she said in an Eartha Kitt type voice.

She turned to leave with her friends as she waved and winked at him.

To say that he was shocked by her boldness would be an understatement. Women never ceased to amaze him and it didn't matter their age, some were just over the top.

Shaking off her comment, he knew that he'd only committed to dinner and that it's for a great cause.

When the women left his table, one of the other bachelors sitting with him leaned over.

"Hey, man. Those women really are harmless. At the last auction, I was the prize target for them. They won me that night because they pooled their money together. It's not so bad and they can be quite feisty if you like that sort of thing."

The bachelor, who Duron noticed from his name tag, was named Terry, continued on.

"Hey, if you are into that, let me tell you, they can be very, very generous, if you know what I mean. Last year, I ended up hooking up with two of them and in the dark, it's all the same. In the end, you make them happy and send them on their way hummin' a happy tune. As for me, I ended up with an all-expenses paid trip to Vail, Colorado. Like I said, they can be very generous," Terry said.

Duron thought to himself, there is one in every crowd. Opportunists are everywhere.

He thought the guy was finished until he continued talking.

"On the other hand. Have you seen that angel from heaven in the red gown? If you haven't, you're the only one. I can't seem to tear my eyes away. Besides being beautiful, she has a body that could stop traffic. I'm hoping she's here to bid tonight because I'd go anywhere with her."

Duron knew who he was talking about and what he meant. As for the older women, he would pass. If he wanted a trip to Colorado, he'd take himself at any time.

Finding the woman in red again was not a problem. She stood out in the crowd. Duron watched her as she made her way around the room, greeting and welcoming people to the event. It was a must that he has his sister introduce him. His body wanted her badly and before the night was over, he had plans to have a way to contact her. He didn't come to the event to try and pick up anyone, but there was no way he was letting a woman as gorgeous as she was, get away.

Duron's line of sight was interrupted when saw the older woman who had approached his table pass across his view. When she winked at him as she had done before, he knew he needed to come up with a plan. He needed to find a way to make sure the cougars were outbid. He meant no disrespect against the older women and the dinner was only for charity, but it was clear to him the woman had something else in mind and no matter what he'd heard about what some of the older women were looking for, he didn't want to have to disappoint them by turning them down. He would rather avoid it all together if he could. His eyes continued to follow the path of the woman in red and he wondered if she was planning to bid on any of the bachelors. He was thinking all sorts of things he'd like to do with her besides sit across from her at dinner.

He excused himself from the table and headed over to talk to Loren before she continued in her duties as mistress of ceremonies for the night. Maybe he could get some information about the mystery woman before the auction started and he could get more information about how to avoid hurting anyone's feelings. He wanted to keep things strictly business.

Duron reached Loren's table, where lots of chatter was going on until he cleared his throat. In an instant, all conversation stopped and all eyes were on him. For a moment, time stood still as nine pairs of eyes stared at him without blinking.

Loren looked to see who had arrived that could stop all conversation. When she saw it was her brother, she understood. This type of thing happened all the time, especially with her brother dressed as if he were at a magazine photo shoot. Women were attracted to him like this on a daily basis.

He was handsome and the women found those hazel eyes of his irresistible. Over the years, she'd had the same problem with men when it came to her own hazel eyes that matched his. To bring life back into the time standing still moment, Loren introduced her brother to everyone at her table.

"Ladies, for those who don't remember, this is my brother, Duron. I think most of you met him when we were at Spellman. He's one of the bachelor's tonight. Duron, this is everybody!" she exclaimed. She then quickly ran off everyone's name to him.

"Hello, ladies. It's nice to meet you all," he said.

"Who could forget those eyes," one woman said as she grabbed her chest as if she were having a heart attack.

"No one and surely not me," another said.

"It's nice to see you again, Duron," yet another woman around the table said.

"So, you're being auctioned off tonight. I may have to check my account balance to withdraw all of my money and I wasn't planning on bidding tonight. You, Mr. Knight, have just changed my mind."

Duron watched as the woman turned to Loren.

"Girl, why didn't you tell us your brother was up for bid tonight. I haven't looked in my program yet to see who was being auctioned."

Duron watched as Loren shook her head at her sorority sister. He knew that in her mind, she was thinking of how many conversations she'd had about her brother and how good looking he was. She'd always told him how she would turn down friend after friend when they asked to be introduced to him for more than just a hello. She wanted no parts of what and who Duron did behind closed doors and she knew that was exactly what all of her friends had in mind when they asked.

"If you didn't know about the list of bachelors you must have been living under a rock. Every single bachelor for tonight is so fine, you'll be picking up your tongue all night. How about you pick it up right now and stop looking at my brother like he's steak on a platter," she quipped, laughing at the reaction from them all.

"Girl, am I drooling? If not, I should be," another woman at the table said looking at Duron as if she had x-ray vision and could see right through his clothes.

"You are certifiable," Loren said, making fun.

Another woman chimed in. "Then we're all certifiable. Stop acting like you don't know how women react to how sexy your brother is. He is what dreams are made of."

Loren was done. As usual, every woman at the table was making crazy eyes at Duron and she'd had enough.

"Okay, stop it. This is my brother and to me he's a toad," she joked.

Duron turned his attention to Loren and shoved her for making the comment.

She smiled up at him.

"You know I'm kidding big brother. What brings you over here?" she asked.

He turned his attention back to the ladies at the table.

"It was nice meeting you ladies. I need to steal my sister away just for a moment," he said, not wanting his conversation to be public.

Loren stood up and walked with him to a secluded part of the room.

When she turned to look at him, the smile he sported at the table was gone and he looked uncomfortable, fidgeting.

"What's the matter, D? You look like you've seen a ghost or something," she said.

Duron needed to lay it on thick if he was going to be able to convince her to help him out.

"A group of ladies came over to the table. They all looked to be close to mom's age, though I think the youngest may have been around sixty-ish. That one sort of claimed me. She looked at me like I was a cure for eye wrinkles. What have you talked me into with this auction?" he asked. He was nervous and would only let Loren see it.

Loren, tried hard not to laugh. She'd never seen her brother shy away from anything or anyone. He was surer about himself than anyone she knew.

"D, they are harmless. I told you they've done that before and remember, it's just dinner. You can handle dinner, can't you?" she said.

"It's not the dinner I'm concerned about. You know me, I never want to hurt a woman's feelings and I think she has more in mind than just dinner."

Loren looked at him with her hands on her hips, surprised at his reaction.

"Wait are you scared? Not you!" she exclaimed.

"You know better than that. I'm not scared of anything. I'm trying to keep things professional and from what I hear, they're used to the guys taking them up on their offers for more than dinner. I don't want the fact that I won't have that reaction to them to affect your auction," he explained.

"Don't worry, D. I'm telling you they are harmless and they know how to back off when someone's not interested. They are older members of the sorority and are completely harmless. I think the issue is that a lot of the guys have been interested, not only at the auctions we've had in the past, but at others that have taken place around town over the years. Like I said, Duron, I'm serious, it's just dinner and no other expectations. I'm sure you can handle that with no problem and do it with class even if they win the bid on you."

Duron didn't care how Loren tried to sugarcoat what was going on, he wasn't having it.

"You know me, Loren, I'm more concerned about making sure you have a successful event, so I wanted no drama."

"Then we have no issues, I'm serious. It's dinner, conversation and then it's over. You got that right?" she asked.

"I'm sure he can handle dinner," a voice to the left of him said.

Duron and Loren both looked at the same time to the voice and his heart stopped beating when his next breath got caught in his throat. Standing a few inches from him was the beauty in red he had been eyeing all evening.

"Hey!" Loren acknowledged when she walked up.

"You can handle dinner can't you Duron?" she asked.

He noticed one thing he couldn't tell from seeing her from across the room before and that was her brown sparkling eyes. She was the most beautiful woman he had ever seen and with the number of women he'd known in his life, that's really saying something. Forgetting there was a conversation happening with his sister, Duron found his voice again.

"Yes, I can handle dinner. That woman had more than dinner on her mind. I'm trying to be respectful, but I'm not interested and I'm not use to being auctioned off, but yes, I can handle dinner," he said calmly. Everything about his words were calm, but inside anxiety was in control.

"Hello, I'm Taija - Taija Charles," she said.

Duron reached out to shake the hand she had extended to him.

"Pleasure," he said, not able to take his eyes off of her.

"I'm one of Loren's sorority sisters."

Taking her small hand into his, he felt what could only be described as an electric shock. He could tell by her reaction that she felt it too when he felt her hand quiver in his.

"It's nice to meet you Taija. You look exquisite in red," he added. "Absolutely stunning."

Taija felt electricity in the air she'd never experienced before and looking into Duron's hazel eyes was more mesmerizing than looking at them in any publication. The magazine didn't do him justice at all and she remembered how her body reacted to seeing his picture on the cover. Seeing him in person, she felt like she was about to internally explode. She couldn't take her eyes off of him and it was obvious he was having the same reaction.

Loren noticed the instant sparkle happening between Taija and her brother as she stood looking from one to the other with them looking as if no one was in the room except the two of them.

She interrupted the intense moment.

"Taija, you may remember seeing him when he visited me at school a few times. If not, I know I've talked about him a million times."

"I remember seeing him, but only from a distance. I do, however, remember you talking about your brothers all the time. I've also heard and read a lot about him especially in the magazine spread about his company that's the fastest growing architecture firm in the country. He's also very popular in the Atlanta area I see. Every woman I encountered tonight has made a comment about him, some which are unladylike for me to mention again," she uttered quietly and smiled.

Saying the words and remembering the remarks some ladies were making about what they'd like for him to do to them was setting the section at the apex of her thighs on fire. Where was a nice cold breeze when you wanted one, she thought to herself.

"We must have only seen each other from a distance because if we were close up like we are now, there is no way I would have forgotten you," Duron said.

Taija was excited at his boldness. The attraction was definitely mutual.

"I'm glad to finally put the name to a face close up and a handsome face it is. It's nice to finally meet you," Taija said finally releasing Duron's hand from the handshake.

Looking again from her brother to Taija, Loren could sense that three was a crowd.

"Well, D, I think you'll be fine and I'm going to head back to the stage to get things started. Taija, don't let my brother run off," Loren said.

Taija looked right into his eyes when she replied to Loren.

"Don't worry Loren, if he tries to run off, I'll handcuff him to me."

Hearing the word 'handcuffs' come from Taija lips had Duron's insides doing all sorts of flips and twists. He quickly had a visual of her handcuffed to his bed while he played around her gorgeous body. He needed to cool himself down before he forgot about the auction and found the closest spot where he could devour her. Now that they were alone, he focused his attention on her and her handcuff comment. He had to bring it up and lighten the sexually charged atmosphere between them.

"So, do you often come to bachelor auctions with handcuffs?" he asked.

Taija laughed heartily which made Duron's body go harder, something he didn't think was possible. Not only was her beauty doing a number on him, but her sultry voice and sexy laugh made his body come alive with want; hot desirous want.

"No, not at all, but if I see a sign of you trying to leave, I know a few police officers that I may be able to borrow a pair from. So, why does your sister think you may try to make a break for the door?" Taija asked.

Duron thought for a moment and decided to be honest. He moved closer to her so that anyone passing by couldn't hear.

"Well, here's the deal. There is this group of older women, some call cougars, who are planning to bid every cent they have on me to have dinner with one of them and I'm not feeling it. I know it's for charity, but these women have more on their minds than dinner, no matter what the rules say. I'm thinking of getting one of my sister's friends to bid on me and I'll cover the amount no matter how much it is. I've heard some interesting stories about this group of ladies and I'm steering clear. I hope that doesn't sound too offensive."

"Not at all," Taija replied. "I've heard about them and they can be pretty crass. I say if you can avoid it, do so," she said.

Before the conversation could continue, Loren was onstage at the microphone asking for everyone's attention.

"Ok, everyone, we will be starting the auction in fifteen minutes, so get your checkbooks out and be ready for thirty of the most handsome bachelors that Atlanta has to offer."

While Loren went through the rules for the auction, Taija took the time to get a good look at Duron as he turned to pay attention to Loren.

She noticed his strong chiseled features, his runner's body and she could tell the tuxedo he wore was covering up the body of an Adonis.

Her legs weakened when she remembered how he looked at her. His eyes were bright and dazzling, especially with the lighting of the room. He now stood in a manner where she could check out his profile. He had very strong and handsome facial features. His smile, when he laid it on her, showed the straightest, whitest teeth she had ever seen. She loved a man who was serious about grooming. She could tell he took great care in his appearance and she liked that.

When Duron smiled his dimples were pronounced and deep and could melt ice at the north pole. His close-cut hair and neatly trimmed goatee put him on the top of her list for the year's sexiest man. His shoulders were broad and even through his clothes, she could tell his biceps were huge. He was definitely all muscle and no fat.

To his credit, Taija could see how any woman, older or younger would love to spend some time with the handsome bachelor. She wouldn't mind doing so herself, but she needed to focus. Tonight, was not about a hookup. She also hadn't come prepared to bid on anyone tonight, but she had an idea.

"So, Duron, what would you say to my helping you out with your dilemma?" she asked.

Duron turned back around to face her, giving her his undivided attention.

Taija shivered at his intense stare. No man should be this good looking, she thought to herself. How does any woman keep her panties on around him, she wondered and smiled at the thought. She shook off her erotic thoughts and turned her attention to the auction.

"How would you do that?" he asked.

"If you still need someone to bid on you, I'll do the bidding for you as long as you cover the bid. I know being in an auction can be awkward and I know you're doing this to help out your sister. I see the predicament you're in, so are you game?"

Duron, happy about her offer, immediately responded, "Absolutely."

She continued on, intrigued.

"So, tell me, is there an amount that I should stop at when it comes to bidding? I don't want to spend all of your money."

Duron grinned.

"Bid until you outbid the highest bidder. I got it covered no matter what the amount is," he said.

"Oh, you got it like that huh?" she asked smiling.

"I do if it means my sister takes in a lot of money for the community charities and if I can get myself out of being on the spot."

Taija smiled back.

"No problem. I can do that. It looks like they're about to call the bachelors up, so you better get going. The bidding will be starting soon and I want to be front and center and ready with your checkbook," she laughed.

Duron gave her the biggest, brightest smile that drew moistness between her legs that she hadn't experienced from just a look from a man in a long time. If this was the reaction her body had just from his smile, she could only imagine some of the other ways he could entice her.

"Thank you. I owe you. Listen, if you win the bid, which I'm sure you will, you don't have to go through with the dinner if you don't want to. I know you're doing this to help me out and I don't want you to feel obligated to have dinner with me, though I'm hoping you'll want to."

Duron was hopeful that the signs he was reading were those of interest because if so, the feeling was mutual.

"If I win the bid, which I'm sure I will, even though it's with your money, I still want to have my paid for dinner. I wouldn't have it any other way," Taija replied.

Duron smiled.

"I look forward to our dinner, Ms. Charles," he said heading off to join the other bachelors.

Taija headed back to her table on shaky legs remembering the way his voice dropped to a deep baritone as he spoke before heading off. She grabbed her bidding paddle as she uttered to herself, let *the bidding war begin.*

Loren looked around the room at all of the hungry women and they weren't just hungry for dinner. They were looking forward to snagging a sexy bachelor for dinner and she was looking forward to the proceeds that would go to help many people in need.

"Ok, everyone lets settle down. We're about to begin the bidding with bachelor number one, Sean Davis."

Sean gave the crowd a smile that made all of the ladies go crazy. Duron listened from behind the curtain as the bidding war started. The ladies were brutal and serious at the same time. He could tell that these ladies came to win. The amounts they were tossing out to get a bachelor surprised him. He had no idea the kind of money women were willing to spend, all in the name of charity. As the auction continued on, they were getting closer to his number.

"Alright ladies, are you ready for the next bachelor?" Loren shouted.

"Yes!" A resounding roar went out over the room.

"Well, I present to some, and introduce to others, bachelor number thirteen, Duron Knight."

At the sound of his name, Duron took to the stage and immediately looked out to be sure Taija was there and ready to bid. He saw her and winked to the crowd, but actually winked at her. As Loren gave biographical information about him to the crowd, a gavel sounded, signifying the bidding could begin. The bidding that started at two hundred dollars quickly reached two thousand dollars. He looked and Taija appeared to be in a bidding war with the cougars that had approached him earlier. They had already quieted all of the other bidders who apparently couldn't bid as high as Taija and the cougars were, so everyone focused on the challenge.

He looked at his sister and if she had any clue of what was going on, it didn't appear on her face. He then heard the word *sold* and didn't know how he had drifted off and not paid attention. He held his breath as the auctioneer gave information on who the winning bidder was.

"Sold, to paddle number two hundred and thirty-seven for four thousand, five hundred dollars. Ms. Taija Charles, come claim your bachelor!"

Duron, breathed a sigh of relief and headed off stage. He knew he wasn't a mean or selfish person, but he really wanted the chance to spend some time with Taija, even if it meant it was due to a dinner won by way of an auction.

As he passed his sister, she whispered so no one else could hear.

"Sneaky! I see you big brother. Do you, D. I'm not mad at you. Ka-ching!"

Duron laughed at Loren's comment and reaction, making the sound of a cash register and happy about the amount of money he helped her raise.

As he reached the table where all bids were settled, Duron walked up to Taija.

"Thank you. I really owe you one," he whispered.

Taija whole body tingled when Duron spoke directly into her ear. Even though she figured the way he did it wasn't meant to be sexual, that's the reaction she felt. For a split second she could see herself spread out under him with him doing all kinds of naughty things to her while she focused on that and the way he parlayed his every action to her. She shivered, which seemed to be the reaction of the night each time he came near her. She calmed her body and responded ladylike, unlike her thoughts.

"No problem and I look forward to our dinner, my bachelor," she said.

They stared at each other for what seemed an eternity until they were interrupted. They turned to find the older woman, the cougar, staring at them with her hands on her hips and with her posse behind her for support.

"You know you were to be my bachelor, but I bow out gracefully. Perhaps, I could give you my number and we could discuss a more private dinner on me in the near future, Mr. Knight. I think I could make your time worth it in more ways than one," she said.

Duron, searched his mind for the right words to respond with to let her down easy. He didn't have a problem with women speaking their mind for what they wanted, he just had other things in mind and those things involved getting to know Taija and not playing a playboy as if he was only all body and sexuality and nothing else. He was about to respond in kind, but before he could, Taija stepped up and replied for him.

"I'm sorry, but this bachelor is no longer up for bid and the man, is not for sale. It was nice bidding with you for the purpose of raising funds for the needy tonight. Perhaps, you could use your funds to bid on one of the silent auction items or perhaps one of the available bachelors since you obviously have the money to do so. The sorority really appreciates your donation of any type tonight. Mr. Knight and I are going to step to the side to discuss the details of the dinner date I won with my bid and we'll bid you and the other ladies a good night," she said.

Duron noticed Taija added a little, 'around the way girl' attitude to her response and he was in love! He liked her more and more by the minute. She was his kind of woman.

In a surprise move, she linked her fingers with his and escorted him off, so that they could discuss the dinner they both secretly hoped would lead to something more.

8

Duron spent the week following the auction, unable to concentrate on anything other than Taija. He was looking forward to the bachelor dinner later in the evening when he would get to see her again.

He was caught off kilter by how intense his attraction was to her. This was not just an ordinary attraction he usually encountered when he met a gorgeous woman. He felt a certain kind of spark, between the two of them the instant they met.

On some level, it disturbed him because he felt out of control with his thoughts and feelings for her, something that never happened. His attraction was normally sexual, but what his thoughts were about Taija was more than that and he looked forward to the opportunity to explore it further.

He was also shocked because it had been a long time since he'd been this excited about spending time with a woman for more than just sex. Most of his dates had been for the purpose of sexual release and the women were always on board for that. He had a few who tried to get clingy, but he easily side stepped any ideas they had of anything other than great sex by reminding them that it was purely pleasure he was seeking and nothing else.

Duron's thoughts regarding Taija were much more dangerous. He could see her seeping into, not only his thoughts, but into his being as well. She was a beautiful sight to behold and when she came to his rescue, he owed her plenty. No woman outside of his family had ever had his back like that before.

The dinner tonight could have gone a whole different way. Duron certainly would have gone through with the dinner no matter who acquired him, even the brash cougar. It was, after all, about the charity and he could remain a gentleman in any situation. With Taija, he was able to help with the auction as well as get himself a dinner date with the loveliest woman at the auction. This was definitely a win-win situation and he couldn't wait to learn more about her.

Being deep in thought, he didn't notice Mike entering his office until he was standing right in front of him.

"What?" Duron said, with a perplexed look on his face when he noticed the big, stupid grin on Mike's face.

"Ready for your dinner tonight? You know, that highest bidder thing and all?" Mike said, humorously.

Duron saw no humor in the situation, but clearly Mike did.

"Actually, I am, bro. I am having dinner tonight with a goddess. She has brains, beauty and a body that should be registered as a lethal weapon and tonight I'll get to enjoy her company. So, in answer to your question, yes, I'm ready for it. Make all the jokes you want."

"Oh, so it's like that huh? So, you were one of the lucky ones? I've heard stories about some of those bachelor auctions that make it seem as if it's a meat market with a room full of desperate women," Mike said.

Duron didn't like his comment and he wanted to be sure he was clear in his response, to remove any negativity that could be in Mike's mind about what the auction was about.

"My sister's sorority puts on a classy event. It's all in fun and the proceeds go to many of the great causes right here in the Atlanta area, some we already give to through the business. I don't know what you've heard, but I can tell you, it was a five-star event that brought out some major checkbooks. If that means a guy gets to spend an evening having a nice dinner with a bachelorette from the great city of Atlanta, then I'm in. No harm done at all. I've heard things also, but I do know that as adults, what occurs as a result of the auction should be about the auction and its cause. Anything further than that, should not be associated with the auction. Adults will do what they will do."

He could tell he made his point when the silly smirk left Mike's face and he nodded his appreciation for the explanation.

"I hear you, bro. I hope you have a great time at dinner tonight and congratulate your sister on what I hear was a great event. I also wanted to check with you before I headed out of town in a few for the rest of the weekend to be sure you were on point with the revisions of the design of the office park. We can't afford to have any more delays if we're going to meet the construction start deadline."

"I've got this. I'll go over all the comments from the last meeting, get some updates completed and we can follow-up when you return next week. Where are you off to?" Duron asked.

"My mother is once again complaining that I don't get home often enough to visit her and laid a guilt trip on me for not visiting her in the past few months. I'm heading to

New York for a few days and I have a feeling she's trying to set me up again with the daughter of one of her friends."

Duron understood his reservations. He had been on the other end of his own mother's matchmaking attempts. What is it with mothers always wanting to find wives for their sons? Bachelorhood has many benefits and he had no problem taking advantage of those benefits especially when they came with large breasts, long shapely legs and a no commitment attitude.

He laughed at Mike's current state of affairs regarding heading to New York to visit his mother, not knowing what he was in store for.

"Better you than me man. When my mother starts trying to set me up, to keep her happy, I play along for a little while, then brush it off after a dinner or lunch date. I tell her later that it didn't work out. That tends to pacify her for a while," Duron said.

Mike turned to leave.

"Yeah, I'll try that since I have a pretty good idea what I'm in store for. Who knows, maybe I'll even get an itch or two scratched before I return," Mike said.

"I should have known you would throw something like that in. Get yours man!" Duron exclaimed.

Throwing his fist up in the air with the solidarity fist pump, Mike said loudly, with gusto, "Bachelors for life club still in full affect!"

Duron laughed so hard, he almost fell out of his chair. He and his two best friends were always staking claim to bachelorhood like it was a badge of honor.

"Yeah, bachelors for life club still in full effect," Duron replied, while shaking his head at the college slogan the three of them would always say when heading out on dates.

Speaking of dates, he looked at the clock on the wall. The hour was getting late and he needed to get going to prepare for his dinner date. He had to get home, shower, change and pick Taija up by eight for dinner.

He smiled to himself at how anxious he was to see her again. He felt like a little boy again sitting in class while noticing the prettiest girl and working up a sweat trying to figure out how to tell her that he liked her.

Earlier he'd sent flowers to her office thanking her again for helping him out and for agreeing to still have the dinner with him even though she didn't have to. When she'd called him to thank him for the flowers, she wanted to know how he knew where she worked. He gave up the information that Loren hooked him up and he hoped that wasn't crossing a line. She assured him it wasn't and that she loved the arrangement he'd selected. His day got even brighter when she told him how much she was looking forward to seeing him later.

Duron grabbed the files he would need to work on over the weekend and headed out. He smiled to himself knowing that having dinner with a gorgeous woman was a great start to the weekend.

~~

Taija was dumbfounded by her own behavior for the past two hours. Anyone on the outside looking in would think that she'd never been out on a dinner date before. Mumbling to herself, *'well it's not really a date. It's more, just dinner.'*

She had clothes thrown all over her bed, having tried on a pile of dresses from her closet and not knowing which to choose from. It was seven in the evening and Duron would be at her place in an hour to pick her up. She was still standing around in her black laced demi bra and matching, barely there, black lace thong. As soon as she picked out a dress for the night, she could then begin the task of choosing which Manolo Blahnik's to wear with it. This night definitely called for shoes by her favorite designer.

Deciding black would be the color for the night, she chose a black scooped collar dress that came mid-thigh and hugged her in all the right places. Though she was not one to advertise with her body, she also believed that since she was blessed with a beautiful body, it should not be hidden.

She could still remember the first time she'd seen Duron on the Spellman campus, visiting his sister. She'd only seen him from a distance, but even afar, he was handsome. Up close and personal now, he damn near took her breath away just with his smile. The dimples did her in every time he showed them. Just the thought of those dimples gave her shivers. She shook it off and continued with her preparations for the evening.

After another twenty minutes, she was finally done with a few minutes to spare. She checked her appearance in the floor to ceiling mirrors in her walk-in closet and had to admit, sexy was definitely the word for the night.

Her door bell chimed letting her know Duron had arrived. She took one last look at herself in the mirror and noticed her own nervousness.

'You sure are excited for someone who is only having dinner as part of a male auction,' she said to herself. She turned to head in the direction of the door.

When she reached the bottom of the stairs, she glanced around to be sure everything was tidy and her eyes landed on the beautiful arrangement of pink and white roses that were delivered earlier in the day to her job in a beautiful crystal vase. She remembered how her hands shook as she opened the card and her heart skipped a beat when she saw that they were from Duron with the beautiful message, *'Lovelies for a beauty. Thank you in advance for sharing your evening with me.'*

Her heart melted and the roses were out of this world lovely. She was delighted, feeling like a teenage girl, and stared at them for the rest of the workday.

Hearing the doorbell again snapped her out of her trip down today's memory lane and she proceeded to the door.

Duron was rendered speechless when Taija opened the door and stood before him looking like what he could only describe as hot! He didn't know she could be more attractive than she had been the night they'd met at the auction. Getting his fill from head to toe, he almost forgot to speak since his tongue felt numb. He needed to find a mirror and check to be sure he wasn't foaming at the mouth. She spoke first before he could even muster up a single syllable.

"Hi, Duron. You're right on time and you look great," she said.

Duron still stunned by her, barely heard what she said.

He took a few seconds to get himself together to come up with some words to respond.

"You are even more beautiful than you were the night of the auction," he said. Never had he seen a woman as mesmerizing as her.

"Wow," he said.

Taija blushed. "Thank you. Would you like to come in for a minute? I need to grab my things."

She was excited that she could feel his approved perusal of her and that let her know that she'd chosen the right dress.

Holding the door open wider, she stepped back to let Duron pass and didn't miss the opportunity to check him out as well. He was superbly dressed in a black suit that looked as if it were made especially for him and was topped off by a crisp black shirt opened at the collar. As he passed by her, she saw something she had not paid attention to the night of the auction. Duron was bowlegged and his walk was making her imagination run wild.

Damn! she thought to herself. *This man is fine.* Her mind jumped to the work she knew he could put in with those legs. Yeah, it had been too long since she'd been with a man intimately. Her mind and body were completely off-kilter and all she could think about was his powerful legs.

She didn't realize she was staring until he spoke again while she was still holding the door open, as if he still needed to walk through.

"Are you okay?" he asked when he noticed time had stood still as neither of them moved.

Closing the door, she headed for the stairs.

"I'll be right back down."

Duron watched her go up the stairs and exhaled the breath he had been holding in. What was wrong with him? He never had this kind of reaction to a woman and he felt like he was experiencing an out of body experience. He couldn't believe he was actually in her presence in person.

Taking his mind off of her for a minute to get his body and mind back in check, he took in the room he was in and was impressed by the impeccable decorating. He also noticed the roses he'd sent her. She displayed them in the center of the table in the room. He was happy the florist had followed his instructions in making sure they sent her an arrangement that contained the prettiest flowers they had.

The sound of heels clicking on the stairs brought his attention back to Taija and what he hoped would be a great time at dinner.

"Ready to go?" he asked, trying to break through the electricity in the air.

"Yes, and thank you for the beautiful flowers you sent today. I love roses."

He opened the door as she turned out the lights and set the alarm. He made sure she locked the door before they headed to his car.

"I'm glad you like them," Duron said as he led them to his car parked in her driveway.

"Nice car."

Taija admired the sleek black car as she waited for him to unlock and open the door for her.

"What series of BMW is this?"

"It's the BMW 650I convertible," Duron said.

"It fits you," Taija stated as Duron slid into his side of the car after making sure she was comfortably seated.

"The black on black is all man," she said.

Duron didn't respond as he looked over at her, not being able to take his eyes off of her beauty. He was so enraptured by her that he couldn't look away long enough to start his car.

Taija noticed something about the air around them that had changed. Though there was a slight chill in the air, the heat between them was at a boiling point. Duron's stare was intense and deep reaching and she couldn't look away from his sexy look.

No sound was heard above the deep breathing they experienced separately and together. It was as if neither of them wanted to look away and continue with the evening they had planned.

Duron finally gathered himself before he asked her if they could go back inside and head straight to her bedroom. That was how bad he wanted her. He broke the stare and started his car, pulling off to head to the restaurant. Thinking about her as he drove off, he knew he was one lucky man.

9

Dinner was all that and a bag of chips as far as Taija was concerned, a term she'd heard earlier on some television show that was on at home as she got dressed for dinner. She loved the slogan and it was fitting for the night she was having. Duron turned out to be more than she could have imagined. Unlike a lot of closed mouth and secretive men she'd been out with, he was open to telling her all about himself over dinner.

She learned that besides his sister Loren, who she knew was the youngest, he had two older brothers who had professional careers, one as a doctor and the other as a college professor. She remembered Loren talking about them when they were in school, but not with great detail. She remembered that Loren talked a lot about Duron because they were the closest and he visited her more often than the other two.

While going into more detail about his brothers, Taija found that his oldest brother Jake was the physician and he worked at Atlanta Medical Center and was married to Kim. They had two children, a three-year-old daughter named Lyric and a four-year-old son named Milo, both whom Duron adored. He lit up every time he talked about them.

His brother Brian was a professor at Morehouse College. Brian was single like Duron, and didn't have any children. She'd also learned that his father, Earl, was chief of surgery at the same hospital where Jake worked and his mother, Barbara, had always been a stay at home wife and mother.

Duron shared with her that he was one third owner of one of the most up and coming architectural firms on the east coast with his two best friends Mike and Tyrone. She remembered reading about the three of them in that copy of *Black Enterprise* magazine. They had graced a recent cover and were pegged as the three to watch out for in the business world. They were making a name for themselves as the triple threat in their field. They had been acquiring some very lucrative contracts over the past year or so once people caught sight of the building they designed and built that housed their company and a few others in downtown Atlanta.

Taija found herself intrigued by Duron, not just because of his successful accomplishments or because of how good looking he was, but because of his zest for life. She loved a man who continued to fight to earn his part of the American pie. She could tell how much work meant to him by how excited he was every time he talked about it.

"So, tell me a little more about you, Ms. Charles," Duron said as they continued to enjoy the last remnants of dinner while enjoying the restaurant ambiance.

Taija was more than ready to tell him her story after he'd shared his life with her.

"Well, I'm originally from Florida, which is where my mother currently lives. I stayed here after graduation from Spellman. After a year or so, I was offered a senior accounting position at a firm in Boston and lived there until recently when I acquired a position in corporate finance here in Atlanta. I've spent the past few weeks unpacking, getting settled in and getting reacquainted with the city. Currently, I'm leasing the house I live in with plans to start looking in the next few months for a house to buy, since I don't plan on moving out of state again," she shared.

Duron loved the soft sound of her voice. He was paying attention to everything she said while also marveling at how beautiful her lips were every time they moved. He wondered if they felt as soft and luscious as they looked. He forced himself to stay focused on what she was saying and not how she was saying it.

"I can understand your love for this area," he replied. "I've lived in Atlanta my whole life and though I have traveled to other places, including other countries, I'll always consider Atlanta home. Besides, my family is here and wherever they are is where home is for me," Duron said.

"If you don't mind me prying a little bit, I remember the interview you did for *Black Enterprise* magazine and they titled you as one of the most eligible bachelors in Atlanta. I take it, you prefer the single life because frankly, I can't imagine every woman in Atlanta not trying to become Mrs. Duron Knight," she said.

Duron chuckled.

"I don't know about the most eligible bachelor title, but I am single and for me that happens to work. I've had a few relationships and let's just say, I think I was meant to be single."

Enjoying how mysterious Duron was being, Taija decided to pry a little more.

"So, were these relationships so bad that they turned you into a bachelor for good?"

Duron smiled at her. He loved that she wanted to know more.

"Not really, just one relationship turned out bad. I was involved with a woman who I discovered was not as interested as I was in what the word commitment meant. I'll just say it left a bad taste in my mouth. What I tend to do now is keep things simple and casual and if the woman I'm seeing can deal with that, then there are no problems," he admitted.

"I can understand that. A cheating mate can be heartbreaking for men and for women," Taija said.

"So, since we are digging, how about you tell me why you're single. A beautiful, intelligent, obviously got it going on woman like yourself, must spend the day beating men off left and right," Duron said.

Taija laughed thinking to herself, if only that were really true.

"I'm single by choice. Bad relationship experience as well. I actually moved to Boston to put some distance between myself and a relationship that was always on a rocky road. He had no problems with commitment like what happened to you, but he never understood what the word faithful meant. He committed to being unfaithful all the time. His wandering eyes led to other body parts wandering as well. I'd finally had enough and space was the only thing that would really make me wake up and smell the coffee and see that he and I were not a match. I took a nice job that was offered to me in Boston, packed up and moved."

Duron became even more intrigued. What man in his right mind would cheat on such a well put together woman? Everything he'd learned about her made him more and more interested.

"He never came to you to try and mend things?" Duron inquired.

"He made contact quite a few times, but it was hard for him to get away and chase after me to Boston. He's an NBA ball player in Florida."

"Oh, you were involved with a big timer. Who is this mystery guy?" he asked. He'd had his own experience with a professional player being on the other end of Allison's infidelity.

Taija hesitated before telling him.

"Keith Mathers, star center."

"I hate to say I can relate," Duron stated. "I was about to propose to my ex and she decided she needed a man with more money because she wanted to live the high life and not wait around for me to become successful. While we were dating, she was being wooed by an NFL player and the rest, as they say, is water under the bridge," he said.

Duron wanted to change the tone of the evening. Though he liked getting the past relationship discussion part of a date taken care of, he wanted to move on to better things to talk about than old relationships.

"There's a lot of that going around, apparently," she agreed.

"Taija, have I said how absolutely lovely you are?"

She blushed knowing he had said it already and she loved hearing it every time. His deep baritone voice did things to her psyche whenever he spoke. The penetrating look he gave her with those eyes that she enjoyed looking into could put a woman in a trance and have her doing anything he asked. She wasn't sure how much longer she was going to be able to handle being in his presence without being all over him because he was deliciously irresistible. There was so much spark in the air between the two of them, she felt like a moth being drawn to a flame, not worried about being burned.

"Thank you," she said, looking down at the table and then back across the table at him, locking eyes.

That was all she could say as the heat stirring up between them began to intensify the moment.

Breaking the stare, as one or both of them seemed to have to continually do, Taija looked around and realized the restaurant had pretty much cleared out.

"Duron, do you realize that there aren't many people left here and that the staff is cleaning up all around us?"

He looked around and then turned back, hitting her with that one-hundred-watt smile of his.

"Yes. The restaurant closed over an hour ago, but I know the owner and he doesn't mind at all. Besides, even though it's getting late, I'm enjoying spending time with you and the time just flew by. I wasn't ready to leave when the restaurant closed," he said.

Taija could relate. It's exactly how she was feeling.

"Neither was I. Thank you for a lovely dinner. It was well worth helping you get out of a bind. I'm happy for all the lives that will be enriched by the money raised from the auction."

Taija decided to go for broke and take a leap.

"I'm even happier that I had the chance to have dinner with you."

Duron felt the same way and hoped her only reason wasn't because of the auction.

"I'm hoping I can interest you in having dinner with me again soon, now that the auction activities are officially over. I really want to see you again and maybe also take in a movie."

"I would love that."

When she looked at him as she replied, she saw the delight on his face and knew it matched how she was feeling. This dinner date was as close to perfect as a dinner date could get.

Duron was relieved when Taija agreed to go out with him because he couldn't imagine not having an intimate night of dinner with her again.

"Great. I look forward to it. Let me get you home before it gets late."

He stood to help Taija out of her chair and watched her move with grace as she stood. This had turned out to be the best date he'd ever had, feeling more comfortable with a woman than he'd ever felt, especially since his attraction to her was more than just about her physical appearance. His want for her was on a deeper level which was unexpected. That's not a way he typically felt when he was out with a woman. Distant and aloof was more his way of operating.

As the valet brought his car to the curb, Duron helped her in and after giving the driver a big tip, he hopped in, ready to take her home, but not ready for their night to end.

On the ride back to her house, Taija settled in on the soft black leather of the seats, closed her eyes and listened to the soothing sounds of Earth, Wind & Fire coming from the speakers. She thought of how easy it had been talking to Duron all evening. With ease, she shared her dating history, which was something she never did on dates, especially on a first date. She never wanted anyone to know what a fool she had been to let Keith treat her like a doormat for so long.

The dinner date had been different than most she'd experienced. Finding things to talk about over dinner on a first date could be a challenge, but tonight flowed like they were meant to be. She liked that and she liked Duron. Opening her eyes slowly and glancing over at him as he drove her home, she took delight in looking at the man she was enjoying getting to know. She did not take Duron's interest in her for granted and was equally interested in him.

Stopped at a traffic light, Duron turned to find Taija staring at him. The lights outside the car were casting a soft glow on her and he thought she looked perfect. He didn't want the night to end, but he didn't want to press for anything. He wanted to take things slow with her and really invest his time in getting to know her and sharing more time together.

Finally pulling up to her house, Duron got out and came around to help Taija out. Escorting her to her door, he waited until she unlocked the door and turned off the alarm before asking her to give him a minute to look around inside to be sure everything in the house was okay.

Taija liked that and smiled before giving him the okay to look around. Every time she thought Duron couldn't get any more charming, he surprises her. No man has ever asked to check her house after a date to be sure everything inside was safe and sound before she went in alone. She knew a true gentleman always made a pass through the house of a woman he'd been out with for the evening to be sure nothing and no one had invaded her space while she was out. She wasn't sure there were many men who still knew to do that. When he returned after a brief check of her house, she watched as he turned when he reached the door and came face to face with her.

"I'll have to thank my sister for convincing me to participate in that bachelor auction. I'm sure you and I would have crossed paths since the two of you are friends, but I'm glad it happened when it did. I can't imagine spending my auction inspired dinner date with anyone other than you. Thank you for a nice evening," Duron said.

Taija knew she was going to make a call to Loren herself to thank her for being so convincing about her attendance at the auction. She couldn't imagine going with her first thought of staying home that evening and missing the opportunity to spend the evening with Duron.

"I should be thanking you for a wonderful time tonight. Everything was great. he restaurant was awesome, the food was incredible and the company was the best part of the night," she said.

After thanking him, Taija's heart took a leap when she took notice of Duron's hazel eyes focused on her lips, watching them as words escaped through them. His gazed seemed to darken giving them a smoky look.

"I'm glad," he said.

It didn't escape Taija that when he spoke, he did so directly to her lips in a voice that made her shiver.

It should be a crime for any man to be as sexy as he was, she thought.

"I'm looking forward to hearing from you soon," Taija said boldly. There was nothing wrong with making intentions clear and she wanted to see him again.

"I'll give you a call to see when you're available for dinner and a movie sometime. I'm hoping next week is not too soon."

"Next week is perfect for me," she said under the unwavering look of pure lust on his face. If he didn't stop looking at her like he wanted to devour her, she was going to melt into a puddle at his feet. The man is scrumptious, she thought as she fought to control the pounding of her heart.

Taija could feel her body heat rising in response to the way Duron was continuing to gaze at her lips. She hoped he was thinking the same thing she was. She wanted him to take the lead and ease the aching need to be touched and caressed that had taken over her. She gazed at his lips and for a moment, she imagined them covering every part of her body, eliciting an ecstasy she was sure only he could derive from her. If he didn't bring their lips together, she wasn't sure she'd get a good night's sleep without a sensual night of self-pleasure the calm her body down.

Duron could feel that the attraction between them was unmistakably amorous and there was no way he'd be able to leave without first tasting her.

Looking from her lips to her eyes, he couldn't resist getting his fill of her. His body hardened as he watched her tongue come out to give her lips a caress and overwhelming temptation to taste her took control of him. He leaned in closer, doing it slowly to give Taija a chance to backup if she didn't want to be kissed. Not seeing any resistance from her or any attempt to move out of his reach, Duron licked his own lips and leaned in for a light kiss on the lips – at least that was his initial idea.

When the light kiss wasn't enough to satisfy him, he deepened it as his tongue sought entry into her mouth. She opened for him as her tongue curled with his for a kiss filled with passion, lust and unadulterated thirst. Duron reached down and pulled her closer to him, pouring everything he had into the kiss, letting her know how much he wanted her. He wanted no doubt between them that he was into her.

Taija felt that any second her legs would give out and she would crumple to the floor from the onslaught of feelings the kiss produced. Duron was kissing her like he was staking claim on her lips. She melted as his lips nipped at hers right before his tongue plunged deeper into her mouth again. Taija held her breath as she savored every pass of his tongue across hers as it searched out hers again and again, feeling rough and smooth as silk at the same time. She felt like jelly when he used his tongue to stroke the roof of her mouth making her body feel like it was about to shatter just from that seductive move. She gave as good as she got by joined him in the intoxicating kiss, wondering where the moaning sound was coming from. She wasn't sure if the lusty sound was coming from him or her.

Duron tried to pull Taija even more flush up against his body, but the hard erection now pressing between the two of them prevented him from doing so. His mind swirled at the same pace that his tongue stroked hers and if he could, he'd push her up against the door to satisfy the need they were both facing. He began to feel the need to breathe, but never wanted to set her free away from him. This was how a kiss with a woman was supposed to be, he thought, reaching up to entwine his fingers with the locks in her hair to meld her lips even tighter with his, letting her know that he had no intention of setting her lips free.

Taija put even more into the kiss when she raked her tongue along the bottom row of his teeth, pulling back a little to lick across his lips before responding to the invitation from his lips and tongue to duel again. No one had ever kissed her so thoroughly before and all she could think about was what other tantalizing and beguiling acts his lips and tongue could do to other parts of her body. Letting her mind run away her body tingled and she twitched trying to relieve the pressure that was building up in parts of her body that recently had only been entertained by electronic sex devices. Her body was letting her know that those things were no match for a sexy, gorgeous, and willing to die in the throes of passion kind of man. This man was making all of her come alive, awakening a sleeping beast. No matter how she tried, she couldn't seem to get enough of him as they dueled to derive even more pleasure from each other. The need to breathe became important when they withdrew slowly from the kiss. They were breathing as if they had just run a marathon.

While continuing to stare into Taija's eyes, Duron leaned back toward her and made one last slow pass of his tongue across the seam of her lips before backing up and drawing in a much-needed breath. His mind was reeling with delight at how responsive she was to him. He knew without a doubt that she would be a tigress in bed.

When Duron broke the kiss, Taija felt the void left by his missing lips on hers. Without thinking, she reached up to touch her lips where his had been. She took in as much air as she could, exhaled it and wondered what happened to the boulder that had to have just hit her. That was one powerful kiss.

Duron's body was hot with need. He knew it was time to leave before he got carried away.

"I better leave and I need to do that right now. I can't remember the last time a kiss felt this good and I'd better hit the road while I still have the energy to leave you," he said.

Duron leaned down and got one last taste from her swollen lips that had that look of being thoroughly kissed.

"Okay," Taija finally said when she could breathe again. Never in her life had she been kissed so completely.

"Lock the door behind me and set the alarm, beautiful. I'll call you tomorrow," Duron said and walked toward his car.

Still feeling the effects of the kiss, Taija cleared her throat as she waited for her body to calm down from the effects of the intimate kiss they shared. She went inside her house, locked up and waved from the window as Duron pulled off. She was thankful that one of them had a level head because her next move was going to be to drag him inside and practically beg for more.

"Whew! What a man!" she said, smiling as she looked forward to not only seeing Duron again, but engaging in more kissing. She loved kissing!

10

The next week could not go by fast enough for Taija. She and Duron had spoken every night during the week and they'd made plans to go out over weekend to check out the latest Denzel Washington movie and have dinner. She wasn't sure where things were heading between them, but she liked where it was right now.

She knew from several conversations with him that he wasn't looking for anything serious or permanent at the moment and that he preferred to keep his relationships casual. She, on the other hand, knew deep down that she did not want to casually date and hookup. She wanted a serious relationship that she could invest her energy into and could lead to a more permanent relationship down the line. She was getting older and the desire for a family of her own was beginning to eat away at her. She knew what she wanted for herself and though it wasn't anything casual, she was finding herself getting more and more interested in Duron.

The impression of the last relationship he had that turned out badly kept him from wanting to have a healthy, long-term relationship. Even through the hurt of her relationship with Keith, she still planned to love again and she could see that happening with a man like Duron. He was caring, kind, passionate about life, open, honest and incredibly sexy – all of the things she loved in a man. She hoped that his thinking about relationships would change and that he would give them an honest try. She knew she wasn't the first woman to want more with Duron. Any woman would lucky to get more.

She had never connected so closely with a man before, especially in such a short period of time, but Duron was just that special. He loved calling her each day and asking her about her day. He shared the ups and downs of his busy week and how speaking with her lightened up every tiresome day he'd experienced. She thought, perhaps, time was what he needed. Since things with them were still very new, she believed time together, getting to know more and more about each other would be the key to either moving forward with a meaningful relationship or just continuing with a casual friendship, something she may be open to if deep down, that was all he could muster up to share with her. She believed time was the key to making everything worthwhile having and she knew that just as he was worth it to her, she was also worth going the extra mile.

Her thoughts went back to the first night they'd had dinner and the explosive kiss that topped off the evening. She was definitely looking forward to more of that. If he could set her body on fire from a kiss, she could only imagine what other parts of his body could do to her. Her body responded to her thoughts with a tingle that vibrated to her very core. If there was a man who could convince her to go along with his thinking and indulge in a casual affair, it was Duron.

They had just shared another phone conversation that lasted for hours, well into the middle of the night. When he spoke, she would close her eyes and concentrate on the sultry sounds of his deep, soulful, seductive voice. The sound of it sent waves of pleasure all over her. His words were lulling her, not to sleep, but into a sexually charged state. Words from his mouth were melodious and her body reacted with every word he spoke making her rub her legs together to ease the need to touch herself and think about what it would feel like to have him talk into her ear while he pleasured her body with kisses she knew would set her on fire. She remembered that tongue of his which should be registered as a lethal weapon. By the time they ended the call, she had to run to the bathroom and though she'd already showered before bed, she removed her night clothes and hopped in the shower to stand under a chilling, cold spray to cool down her overheated body. If they didn't do something more than talk and kiss soon, she didn't know if she'd be able to focus on her day.

~~

Duron had endured the work week from hell and was looking forward to a relaxing night with Taija. They had talked a lot during the week and the more he talked to her, the more he liked her. Never before had he enjoyed being on the phone all night talking to a woman, considering how much he hated talking on the phone. He preferred talking face to face, but he needed to hear the sound of her voice in order to get some sleep.

This thing between them was unlike him because where he always said he would keep his relationships with women on a casual level, since meeting Taija, he'd been thinking differently.

Taija wasn't the type of woman he played around with like other women. He could see himself involved with her on a much deeper level and though he liked the idea of that, he couldn't let go of the trust issues he had when it came to women.

Allison had done a number on him and until Taija came along, he was happy playing the field. He had all the fun without any of the hassles experienced in relationships. He knew he never made it a habit of getting too close to any one woman, but he noticed throughout his day, he couldn't stop thinking about her and every chance he got, he'd pick up the phone to call her to hear her voice. He had experienced enough let downs as far as relationships were concerned that he was not interested in one, but he was definitely interested in Taija.

Relationships were hard work and he had to consider if he was willing to invest in more than a casual relationship with her, knowing she was well worth it, but was he ready for it, was the issue. He'd had a few nights during the week where he'd end up working until the wee hours of the morning after spending most of the night on the phone being enticed by the silky sounds of her sexy, sweet voice. Already he felt like he was beginning to develop deeper feelings than those on a casual level and he wasn't sure which direction to go in.

Duron knew he had a habit of avoiding women when he started developing any feelings beyond those of a sexual nature. He knew most women had issues with men who couldn't commit to anything more than a night of great sex and he tried to elude being drawn into anything that involved feelings. He tried to find women who were looking to have fun like he was, without things getting too serious. The problem was that in the short span of time that he has known Taija, and after the kiss they experienced, he could feel her already getting under his skin. To him, this wasn't good, it wasn't good at all.

Now that their date night was finally here, she'd been on his mind all day. This wasn't a night like the auction dinner where they got together because of an obligation. Tonight, they were on an official date because they were interested in each other.

He smiled, thinking about her as he pulled up to her house as she was coming out of the door. He got out quickly to meet and escort her to his car.

"Hello. beautiful," he said when he reached her.

"Hi, yourself," she replied.

As if it was the most natural thing in the world, Duron leaned down and stole a quick kiss. He hadn't been able to think of anything other than kissing her sweet lips again and feeling the electrifying feeling he'd felt the first time they kiss. Lifting back up, he loved that the feeling was still there.

"I've waited quite a few days for this kiss," he said.

"You weren't by yourself in the wait," Taija admitted. As she prepared for their date, she was putting on a thin coat of lip gloss and thought about the fact that she felt warm and tingling when his lips were pressed against hers. She hoped they didn't have to wait until the end of the date to indulge again. She was thankful that hope had turned into reality.

"You taste amazing."

"Likewise," Taija chimed.

"Were you as anxious to see me as I was to see you since you were already coming out here when I drove up?" he asked with a hint of humor to his voice as they walked the rest of the way to his car.

"Well, my reason for being out here is two-fold. First, I needed to roll the windows up on my car before we left and I figured I'd do that when you drove up to save myself two trips out."

"The second reason?" he asked.

Taija looked at him suggestively.

"My second reason is that I was just as anxious to see you as you were to see me. I heard you pull into my driveway and I wanted to save you the trip from walking all the way to the door."

"Your keys?" he said.

Taija handed Duron her car keys and waited while he unlocked her car doors, inserted the key and rolled the windows up. After locking it back, he handed her the keys.

"Thank you for looking forward to seeing me tonight and know that I will never tire of taking a trip to your door to pick you up. To know that someone as gorgeous as you are would be on the other side of the door, is well worth the trip."

Taija smiled.

"Well, in the future, I'll be waiting anxiously on the other side of the door for you," she said.

"That sounds like a plan to me. Shall we head off to the movie? I think you'll enjoy it because I hear it's very good and I made reservations for dinner at my friend's supper club for later," he said walking her over to open the car door for her to get in.

"Yes, I'm ready and I can't wait to have a relaxing evening. I really need to unwind and let my hair down. Work was crazy today and I've been looking forward to spending this time with you all week, since our first dinner," she admitted.

"So have I," Duron replied when he'd settled into the car. He didn't want to say more, not sure if he could hold back from telling her how much he wanted her.

The minute he pulled up and saw her walking toward her car, his heart sped up and his slacks felt a little more snug than usual. The more he thought of and was around her, the deeper the bearing she was having on him and it was unnerving. He drove in silence to the theater smiling along the way that they were together.

As they drove, they laughed when they caught each other catching quick glimpses.

"I hope it's okay for me to admit how much I like you," Taija said. There was something growing between them and being with him again was distracting, though it was a good distraction. "I know you're all about keeping things casual between us and believe me, I can respect that. I can't imagine how any woman could agree to only being casual with you. You have to know that you're an incredible man that any woman would be lucky if she caught your eye and I'm no exception," she admitted.

Duron looked over at her and then set his sights back out on the road.

"There is something growing between us that I agree is more than just casual and it's a sidetrack to the direction I usually go in with women. You, Ms. Charles are a breath of fresh air and I'm finding myself more than just casually attracted to you. We've gone out once and talked a countless number of times and I find myself drawn to you. I'm happy we connected," he said as they pulled up to a red light and stopped.

Not one for always being aggressive, Duron brought the tigress out of her that had her reacting without thinking.

With no thought at all, Taija leaned over and when Duron realized her intent, he leaned closer as well, allowing her to take control of the kiss that was inevitable.

To her delight, the moment she touched her lips to hers, Duron didn't take full control like most men liked to do. He, instead, allowed her to take the kiss wherever she wanted it to go and knowing they only had a few seconds before the light would change, she gave it her all tasting him, caressing his lips with her tongue before they each parted and the kiss deepened. It was slow and sensual and held the promise of so much more if that's what they both wanted. It wasn't until a honk from the car behind them startled them that they broke apart, with neither of them looking away.

"Too bad we're in traffic," Duron said. "You taste delicious," he added and drove off.

"I see this is going to be some night," Taija said as she settled back into her seat. She had a need to touch him and his wonderful, full lips were reaching out to her like a radar. She couldn't resist indulging even if she tried. With Duron, no woman would ever resist kissing him.

11

"The movie was great," Taija said after they were seated in their prime seats at the supper club Duron had selected, waiting for the live entertainment to begin.

After the movie, he told her that they were having dinner at a supper club one of his friends owned and operated and that she would love the food. Once they arrived and were immediately seated, their orders were taken and before long the most delicious looking meal was placed in front of them.

They were feasting on parmesan encrusted salmon for her and a porterhouse steak with all of the trimmings for him. She loved fish and this ranked at the top of her list as one of the best.

"I'm glad you enjoyed it. I think you'll love the band that's playing tonight. I've heard them before when they first came out and now they're known all over the country," Duron said.

Taija looked around and loved the layout and feel of the place.

"This place is incredible," she said.

"One of my friends owns this place and I'm always recommending it. You probably haven't heard of it since you've been living in Boston, but it's become one of the most popular spots for dinner and live music. Times when there isn't a band, the DJ is the best on this coast if you like to really get your party on," he added, dancing a little in his seat to show her that he didn't mind getting in a few steps himself.

Taija smiled at his attempt to charm her with his moves in a chair.

"I love dancing whether it's live music or a DJ. I love the way good music makes me move," she said.

"I'd love to see you move," Duron said, hoping his comment didn't sound too sexual, but it definitely held a double entendre for him. He wanted to see her move on the dance floor and if he is lucky enough one day, he'd love to see her moving around under him in bed.

He was about to add more when the band came out on stage.

"Ladies and gentlemen, thanks for coming out to support us tonight. We hope you'll enjoy the songs we've selected for you. Feel free to get up and dance or just groove to our beats from your chairs. We're sure that you won't sit still for long," the band leader said.

Duron watched as Taija gave the band her full attention allowing him to admire her silently.

Throughout the dinner, he hadn't been ashamed of his thoughts drifting, thinking about how sexy Taija looked in her casual, rich, deep purple dress. It sported just the right amount of cleavage to leave a brother wondering just how far down the rabbit hole does that dip go. His fetish when it came to women was breasts. Hers, he knew were lovely.

Anyone that knew him, knew that he was a breast man and he could easily see that Taija was, at minimum a double D cup. Her breasts appeared to be firm and were more than a handful which was a major turn on for him.

He loved what she had on and though it was low cut, it wasn't slutty, but sexy as hell. He could tell one thing about Taija and that was, she loved being feminine and sexy in every attire she put on. Even tonight, though they were both dressed down, she was still jazzed up with high heeled shoes. Her purple dress wasn't flashy or dressy, but it was perfect for her and for him. He had been admiring her in it all evening long. Like Loren, it appeared Taija loved high-heeled shoes, too. Each time he'd seen her, she had them on and she looked comfortable in them. He often wondered what the love relationship was women had with high heeled shoes. He loved seeing a gorgeous pair of legs in some heels, but he knew they had to be hurting a woman's feet to wear them all the time. Loren told him she spent too much money on her shoes for them to hurt her feet and assumed Taija was under the same impression. It didn't matter because so far, anything Taija put on, she was just sexy multiplied by ten.

The male beast in him started to rear its ugly head every time he looked at her gorgeous body. Everything about her turned him on. Just the sight of her had his mind going wild and crazy with need. He couldn't stop watching her mouth move with every word she spoke. The lavender colored lip gloss she had on her lips was calling out to him in the worse way. She was not only beautiful on the outside, but her personality oozed beauty as well.

He couldn't help but be enraptured by the full package sitting across from him. The soft jazz music the band was playing began setting the atmosphere for the perfect evening. He wanted to get up and dance in order to enjoy holding her close to him again, but he knew that if he did, he would embarrass himself with the hard-on he would prominently display if he stood.

Duron was jarred from his thoughts when Taija excused herself to go to the ladies room. He stood up to pull her chair out and watched her walk away in her body hugging dress. He was temporarily appreciative of her departure, feeling like a simple fifteen-year-old teenager again, whose hormones were out of control.

As he retook his seat, he noticed that he wasn't the only man watching Taija as she headed to the ladies room. A few men looked right at him when Taija disappeared from view and held up their drinks, saluting him with what Duron knew was an acknowledgement that he was a lucky man to have the company of the beautiful woman they saw and he couldn't agree more. He was one lucky ass guy!

Taija reached the ladies room and struggled to get herself together and reign in control of her body which was reacting to being in Duron's presence again. He was so handsome it was scary. Once again, those eyes were doing a number on her. Sitting across the table from him, her traitorous body was tingling in places that only self-satisfaction had provided an outlet for most recently.

It had been over a year since she'd been intimate with a man and it was as if her body could sense the presence of a sexy, virile man. She'd had to make up an excuse to get away from the table for a few minutes to get her body back in check. The soft music, the candlelit atmosphere and the most handsome man she'd ever been out with overwhelmed her. She thought turning towards the band and taking some of her focus off of Duron would help, but it didn't. Now, if she could just get her mind to go along with the plan of being in check like she was convincing her body to do, she may survive the evening with her panties intact. She had a she-devil within that had been dormant for far too long that was ready to be unleashed. Making a few adjustments and checking her flawless make-up, she headed back into the lion's den.

Duron watched as Taija made her way back to the table and knew he was a goner. He didn't want to seem too eager, but before the night was over, he wanted to have Taija laid out before him like the main course at a buffet, sampling every part of her luscious body, getting lost in the pleasure he knew he would experience only with this woman. If the look in her eyes was any indication, he sensed that Taija was just as much into him as he was into her. He wondered if she wanted more from their evening. As she settled back in at the table, he was once again completely focused on her and his desire to feel her close to him again.

"I hope you're enjoying our time together tonight," Duron said when they couldn't take their eyes off of each other.

"I am having a wonderful time."

"Would you like to dance?" he asked.

"I'd love to," she replied.

Taija waited for Duron to come around to her side of the table. As she stood, she placed her hand in his as he found a place on the dance floor that was already full with dancers. When he turned, she went willingly into his arms, place one hand on his chest and the other on his shoulder. She exhaled with a pleasant sigh when Duron's arms circled her waste.

As they swayed to the music, Taija kept her eyes on Duron's and wondered if he felt the heat building between them as much as she had. Her body was on fire. She could feel Duron's hips move silkily along with hers to the beat of the band playing. Feeling bold, she moved the hand that was on his chest to grip his other shoulder and the Duron pulled her closer. To complicate things even more, the band started playing a song by Stephanie Mills that she loved called, "Something in the Way You Make Me Feel". There was something in play tonight that was making it hard for her to play innocent on their date. She and Duron moved in sync with the music, she wound her hips along with his, making the moment less about the music and more about the sensual haze between them.

I love the way you move, is all Duron could think about as Taija moved to the music with him. Having her this close to him felt naturally right. He kept his eyes on hers and hoped she was reading the signs of how much he wanted her. The way their bodies were moving together, he knew they would be perfect together in other ways, too. The moment was something out of a sexy romance novel. He didn't know about a happy ending, the way those books often ended, but he knew he would love a happy ending to their night. There was no way he would admit to being able to leave her at her door again tonight. He wanted to go inside her house and inside of her.

Thinking about where their night could lead, he felt a part of him harden and knew the moment Taija felt it, too. There was no escaping the impact she was having on him.

What he loved most was her reaction. A lot of women would move away or act like they didn't feel the hardened flesh between them, but Taija did something he wasn't expecting. She smiled a smile that let him know she loved what she was feeling.

The song was over too soon as the band leader took to the microphone to talk more about the way the evening would flow. Duron escorted Taija back to their table just as the waiter asked if they would be having dessert.

Taija had other plans that didn't involve dessert at the restaurant. She wanted dessert and much more, but not where they were. One thing she had never been before was brazen and bold when it came to her needs. Duron was used to women who gladly went along with his plans for a no commitment night of passion, but what was growing between them was more and she wasn't sure he'd put his same suggestion out on the table that he typically would. She respected that he was respectful of her and allowing her to set the tone for what was happening between them, but with what she felt when they danced, there was no way she was letting the night get away until she was able to experience him up close, personal and naked.

She shook her head not to Duron about dessert and the waiter walked away. She looked at her watch, then looked back over at Duron. She smiled knowing he was trying to be a gentleman and yet she could see his struggle with containing what he really wanted to say. His body throbbing against her while they danced said everything.

She hoped that he was not the type of man to be turned off by bold woman because she was about to get as bold as any woman in heat could get.

"So, are we done with dinner, because I'm thinking dessert at your place or mine?" she said.

Holding his gaze, she wanted to let him know that he wasn't hearing things. She meant exactly what she said and what the words insinuated.

Duron held Taija's intense gaze seeing lust looking back at him. He was sure she saw the same intense look in his eyes as well. Not missing a beat, Duron didn't need to look at his watch to decide what his response would be. At that exact moment, the waiter brought their check, interrupting their moment. Without missing a beat, he reached into his pocket, withdrew enough money to cover the check and a very large tip, placed it in the waiter's hand and slid his chair back. He went around to Taija's side of the table to help her up. When he reached her, he bent down to help her slide her chair out and whispered close to her ear, making sure the intent of his desire was as clear as hers was.

"Let's discuss whose place in the car. At this point, I would say whoever's place is closest, but I'll let you make the decision. It doesn't matter whose place, as long as I can get you alone," he said.

Taija trembled at the determined, huskiness of his voice and prayed that she would make it as far as either of their places. She was feeling delightfully impassioned and her body's reaction to the sexy, deep husky way he whispered those words in her ear made her breast feel heavier and moistness developed between her legs almost soaking the barely-there thong she was wearing. Her mind became occupied with thoughts of what could be in store for the night. As far as she was concerned, it was time to leave the restaurant and the sooner the better. Her mind stayed on what was next as they walked to the car.

Once they were seated in his BMW, Duron turned the car on, locked the door and realized he couldn't wait another second before he got another taste of those luscious lips he had noticed the instant they'd met. Once again making eye contact, he tried to gauge where Taija's thoughts were. When her gaze went from his eyes straight to his mouth and her tongue slipped out and lightly licked across her lips, the strain in his pants holding back the bulge became almost unbearable. His mind went crazy with desirous, pure animalistic need.

"I need to taste you, Taija. I'm not sure I can drive a block without first getting a taste of those sweet lips. I've been thinking about them all night and it took everything in me to not give everyone in that restaurant a show," Duron said.

No one spoke and a mere second later as she moved a fraction closer to him, Duron took the lead, leaned in and captured her lips in a mind-blowing kiss, allowing him to release the pent-up frustration he'd been experiencing all night holding back his true need for her.

Taija could not help but wonder if she were experiencing a dream. The touch of Duron's lips to hers and the slow invasion of her lips with his tongue encouraged her to open to him as he took the kiss up a few notches. The kiss was electrifying and explosive and she thought if it did not end soon, she would be experiencing her first orgasm from a kiss.

She put her all into it and gave back to Duron as much as he was giving to her, matching his tongue, lash for lash, as it made travels around the inside of her mouth, setting her core on fire and sending a tingling shock to the apex of her thighs. His made her realize how much she needed release and only he could provide what she needed.

Someone moaned and Taija thought at first it was Duron until she realized the moan of immense pleasure was coming from her.

Duron deepened the kiss even further and reached up to cup her face in his hands as he made love to her mouth right in the front seat of his car.

If this were not a public street, she may have been tempted to lay her seat back and take a trip down memory lane of her college days of sex in the front seat of a car. That's how badly she wanted him.

Another moan and Taija knew that one had come from Duron. He was getting just as carried away as she was. They were in this together, she thought.

Duron was enjoying kissing Taija so much, he didn't want to stop, but knew he had to so that he could get his body back under control and drive where they could finally be alone. He slowly withdrew from her lips, but not before licking the top and bottom of her lips, then across the seam, giving Taija a hint of what was in store for her as the evening progressed.

"Wow. Your kisses are tormenting me inside and out. You are even more sexy now that your lips have that thoroughly kissed look about them. Where to sweetheart? My place or yours?" he asked finally starting the car. He needed to find a bed and quick.

Taija couldn't speak. The kiss had rendered her without the ability to speak. She had never in her life been kissed so systematically complete before. His tongue did nice, nasty things to her leaving her with the promise of unrestrained passion and pleasure to come as soon as she told him where they were going.

"Yours if that's okay with you. I don't want to intrude on your space, but I would love to see where you live, but if you'd rather not, my place is fine too," she said.

Duron replied with one word as he headed toward their destination.

"Done."

12

Duron and Taija drove in silence to Duron's house. A few times Duron looked over at her as she stared out of the window and wondered what was on her mind. He was glad when he didn't see any hint of reservation about the evening on her face. She appeared to be totally relaxed which was a good sign. Things appeared to move at a fast pace after they danced, but he wanted her to know that she was still the one in control of the direction of the rest of their evening. The last thing he wanted was to seem pushy or overbearing. He absolutely wanted to be inside of her as much as he needed to breathe his next breath, but the call was and always would be hers.

"Are you okay? Having any second thoughts?" he asked.

Taija turned her attention to him.

"I'm wonderful and a for having second thoughts, none. My only thought is I'm wondering how far away do you live!" she said and laughed.

Duron laughed along with her, glad that there wasn't any tension in the air. It had been a long time since he had felt such a connection to any woman in this way and he had been anxious to explore the connection all night long.

"I like the sound of that. I'm just checking and I want to be sure you know that tonight is in your hands. I want you, there's no doubt about that, but if there are any reservations on your end, we pause. Good with you?" he asked.

"I'm good with that," Taija said and laid back more comfortably in her seat, enjoying the feel of the soft buttery leather.

Taija closed her eyes, focusing on the soft music wafting through the speakers, closing her eyes calming her overzealous body. When she opened her eyes, they were pulling into a gated community, with row after row of beautiful homes in an area where she knew the houses were priced around a million dollars. Each one they passed was more beautiful than the next. Even in the dark, she could see the majesty of each design.

"Beautiful," she said.

Duron had been focused on getting them to his house, he almost missed that she'd said something.

"Did you say something?" he asked.

"Yes, I was saying how beautiful this area is. I'm looking at all of the houses we are passing and each one we pass is more beautiful than the last."

Duron had thought the same thing when he'd been house hunting and came upon this development.

"Yes, I love this area and I love that I was able to build my house here. I've been here about six months now and I love it. The neighbors are great, very friendly and everyone respects each other's privacy. The large lots allow for the ultimate privacy which was the selling point for me."

They pulled into the driveway of a huge red-brick home with large white pillars in front. Reaching for the garage remote above his head, Taija watched as they pulled into the second bay of his three-car garage. Once in the garage, she could see that the garage bay to the left held a white

Lincoln Navigator truck and the bay on the right housed a sleek looking red, white and blue Harley Davidson motorcycle.

"You have a great collection of wheels," she said, admiring each.

"This is only the start. I'm hoping to purchase some older cars and restore them. I acquired a love for that from one of my friends, Tyrone. You should see his collection of cars. I'll soon need a much bigger garage. With all the land I have, I'm thinking of having four extra attached garages built around the side. I'm a man who loves his toys and wheels are becoming a new love."

"Even at night from the outside, I can see that your house is magnificent. Thanks for bringing me here," Taija said.

"Thank you for wanting to come here. Let's go inside and I'll give you a tour."

Duron was proud of the modern design, something he had designed himself. He was happy to be able to share his space with her. He didn't want to scare her off by telling her that she was the first woman he had brought to his home as far as a woman he was seeing romantically. He didn't want her to think anything major of his decision to bring her here. He actually surprised himself that he didn't head downtown to his condo where he usually took his dates.

Generally, if he were spending an evening with a woman, he preferred to either go to her place or entertain at his condo. He considered this home his private place where he came to get away from everything and everyone. He didn't give a second thought to bringing Taija here and hoped this first time wouldn't be the last time.

When she said his place, he knew he could have easily driven to his condo, but with her, the thought of going there didn't cross his mind. He wanted her in his private space. She was becoming someone different than the women he usually went home with for an evening.

"Can I get you a drink?" Duron asked as they entered his kitchen.

Taija took in everything she could see from the entry from the garage.

"Just water if you don't mind," she said.

"Sure. Why don't you come on in to the great room and make yourself comfortable while I get us both some water."

As Taija entered the room that contained a large flat screen television on the wall resting above a fireplace, she marveled at how spectacular and steely everything about his house was. She looked at the sofa which seemed inviting and took a seat practically melting into the plush brown leather. She felt comfortable in his space and looking around, everything looked a lot like him.

As Duron joined Taija in the room with bottles of water in his hands, his eyes were immediately drawn to the gorgeous pair of legs that seem to go on forever as he watched her comfortably seated with her legs crossed. Thank goodness he had a cold bottle of water in his hands.

"Let's get you a tour" he said after taking a big gulp of his water and then reaching out to help her stand as he handed her one.

"Thank you," she replied. "Where are we starting? I can't believe you live in this gigantic house all by yourself," Taija said as they walked.

"Let's start at the top and work our way to the bottom. They headed toward the steps that led to the top floor. She listened while he explained that the top level had four large bedrooms and five bathrooms. As they went from room to room, she fell in love with every room which was more splendid than the last. She was also able to get a brief look into Duron's room and felt a chill. It was a good chill, the kind that made her imagine herself laying on his large bed. It was the kind of chill you felt when you happened upon the spot where your body's dreams could come true.

They then headed back downstairs to the lowest level where Duron had a movie theater and game room, which he aptly called his man cave. The level also boasted a small gym, laundry room and a mini-kitchen. When they headed back up to the level they started on, she was treated to a tour of his magnificent living room, dining room and the extra-large kitchen that she instantly fell in love with. It was the kind of kitchen any cook would love and she was sure it mirrored any kitchen a professional chef would have.

"Do you cook?" she asked while checking out the marble counters and restaurant style stainless steel appliances than hung from the bakers' rack that dropped from the ceiling.

"Yes. That was something my mother made sure all of her children could do before we moved away from home. She didn't want us starving or expecting that she would be cooking every night and we would all drop by for dinner. I love to cook. I'll have to do that for you sometime," he said.

Taija smiled at him as she rubbed her fingers across the shiny marble.

"I'd like that," she said, following him as he led her back into the room where she sat when they first came in.

She remembered catching a glimpse of the large fish tank earlier, but this time she went straight to it, loving the sight of the biggest, brightest, most colorful fish she'd ever seen. A big, bright royal blue fish caught her attention. She leaned over to get a closer look at it.

"What kind of fish is this? It's so beautiful."

Duron walked up close behind her to look over her shoulder into the tank.

Taija felt heat radiated from his body with his closeness and she struggled to get her next breath out.

"It's a royal blue Tang fish. If you've ever seen the movie, *Finding Nemo*, you would recognize it as the fish Dory in the movie," he explained.

Taija laughed at Duron's reference to a child's movie. She didn't want to admit that she loved that movie too.

"Finding Nemo?" she asked with humor.

"Don't laugh at me. I've seen that movie enough times with my niece and nephew to know it by heart. I also spotted the same fish at the Atlanta Aquarium and as soon as this house was completed, I knew I wanted a tank."

As he was talking, Taija could feel the heat of his breath on the back of her neck, sensitizing her skin. Her breath caught when Duron reached up to caress her shoulder just below where his breath had been. His hand felt good, like it was created just to touch her. He had the perfect touch. When he leaned down and placed an open mouth kiss first on her shoulder then on her neck, she leaned her head further in the opposite direction giving him room to explore her neck further. When his hands smoothed down her arms and encircled her waist, she leaned back into his embrace to enjoy the closeness. She gave a little squeal when she leaned back, bringing her body flush against his and realized his groin was pressed intimately against her behind, letting her feel just how aroused he was.

Duron was not shy or ashamed at his body's reaction to her and giving her a little grind, he let her know that he was enjoying not only his reaction to her, but her response to him as well. He knew words were needed and that he should choose them carefully.

"I don't want to pressure you in any way Taija, but I want you," he whispered sweetly in her ear as he captured the bottom part of her lobe between his teeth before quickly letting it go. He hoped she still felt the same way.

Taija released a long breath of relief that they were on the same page.

"I want you, too," she whispered. "I have since the moment we met, but tonight, something broke loose and my body longs for you," she added.

"Good, because I want to make love to you until we both pass out from exhaustion. I want to be so deep in you that we won't be able to see where you end and I begin. I'm starting to feel like a junkie needing a fix whenever I'm around you. What I don't want is for you to think that sex is the only reason I wanted to be alone with you tonight. Though I do want you, badly, I am a man who knows how to control his urges and I would be happy if we went into my movie theater, popped some popcorn and watched movies for the rest of the night. We could just sit and talk all night and get to know each other even more. I know that I have wanted you since the moment I first laid eyes on you. I can't explain this feeling, but I know I want to explore it with you if you're feeling the same without any indecision," he said.

Taija could feel herself being drawn in with every word Duron spoke. Her body was now doing all of the thinking for her. She wanted him just as bad.

"I'm here and I know why I'm here and believe me when I say that I'm not having any doubts," she said.

Duron held her closer against him.

"I have to be honest with you. I know we've touched on this in several of our conversations and I want to be sure I'm giving you every opportunity to see where I'm coming from and say you're not interested if that's how you feel. I like you and there is no doubt that I want you, but I don't offer forever or serious relationship commitments," he explained.

Duron placed a soft kiss on the side of Taija's neck and her gasp told him she loved the closeness they were sharing and he hoped his explanation of where they stood wouldn't scare her away. She definitely seemed like the committed relationship type and he never wanted to discount what she was looking for. He knew he needed to stop because he didn't want the physical need they were both experiencing to overshadow the seriousness of what he was saying.

"I understand, though I believe you underestimate how incredible you would be to a woman if you had more to offer. We all have our lines we don't want to cross and tonight, I'm fine with where the line is drawn," she said.

"Taija, what I can do is offer you pleasure beyond your imagination and my promise that I will always treat you with the utmost respect. I just need us to be on the same page, so that no one gets hurt at the end of the day. I am enjoying getting to know you and I want that to continue. I don't want anything to occur tonight where we don't know what the expectations will be after tonight," he elaborated.

"I want tonight to be all about you. I would like to give you the kind of evening you want and whatever satisfaction you need and desire."

Taija turned around in his arms. Looking again into those magnetic hazel eyes, she knew exactly what she wanted and needed. In the heat of the moment, she found her voice.

"I want you, too, Duron. I'll admit that through dinner my fantasy of being with you was driving my mind and body crazy with desire. Every time I looked over at you, all I could think about was how it would feel to have you touch me and kiss me. I thought about how your body would feel under my touch. What I want and need tonight Duron, is you. Tonight, I want to feel," she said.

They stood staring at each other for what seemed like an eternity. Thinking back to the kiss in the car, Duron needed to feel her lips again, right now. He knew the moment Taija looked again from his eyes to his lips as she did in the car, that he was done for.

He leaned down and took her lips ever so sweetly. This kiss, unlike the one in the car and the one the week before that were intense and blazing hot, was soft, slow and just as thorough. When his tongue ventured inside her mouth, slowly and sweetly, he knew the effect it would have on her and he wanted to give her a taste of what it would be like to be with him.

One thing about him is he never rushes because giving and receiving the ultimate pleasure should be done painstakingly slow. They weren't going to be in a hurry. He wanted to take things nice and slow. Deepening the kiss even more, but still keeping it slow, he reached up to lightly grasp her head drawing her closer to him imitating on her mouth how he would soon be making love to her body. The passion between the two of them could cause a twelve-alarm fire as he experienced mini fireworks behind his eyelids. It was time to take this to another room where they could get more comfortable.

Breaking off the kiss, Taija looked up at Duron and realized he was struggling to catch his breath just as she was.

"Goodness, Taija. Kissing you is intoxicating. I feel like I can't get enough of you. Come on. Let's take this upstairs."

Taija nodded and when Duron reached for her hand, she entwined her fingers with his as he led her up the stairs to his own personal heaven on earth.

13

As they entered Duron's massive master suite, Taija once again took in the majesty of the setting that she'd only gotten a glimpse of earlier. The room was a den of pure masculinity.

In the center of the room against the back wall was the biggest bed she had ever laid eyes on. Due to his height, she should have figured he would need a large, customized bed. It was all black with large posts on all four corners and was covered with a black and gray down comforter with pillows that matched. All man, was her first thought when she saw it. The room was sexy even if that wasn't the look he was going for.

Duron had only turned on a small light upon entering the room, but Taija could see that there was an illusion of a spotlight shining down on the bed. She looked up to find what she did not see on the tour. She could see straight up to the brightly, star and moonlit sky. There were slanted glass panels above the bed where the moon shined through, creating a glow that centered right on the bed. She thought, how amazing it would be to go to bed each night with the stars right above your head and no ceiling to block the view.

"What an incredible view of the sky. How do you block out the early morning light or the bright sun from coming in through the panels?" she asked.

Looking up at what Taija was referring to, Duron knew exactly what she meant. Those glass panels were his favorite part of the house. It was the first thing he knew he wanted when he began the design.

"I have a switch on the wall, on both sides of the bed that control panels that slide out to cover the glass, putting the room in total darkness. There's also a remote control on the nightstand that does the same thing. I never close them at night because I love the view. If you'd prefer that I close them, I can. They can also close using a timer that I've programmed. I designed that addition myself," he said.

She wouldn't think of closing off the starry night.

"No, leave them open. The view is lovely," she said as she turned to see Duron leaning against his dresser, staring at her, his muscular legs crossed at the ankles and his hands gripping the dresser's edge. His piercing stare and insatiable look on his face made her feel incredibly beautiful and wanted and she wouldn't dare look away. He was mouthwatering sexy and saying he looked like an Adonis wouldn't do him justice.

As he never wavered from giving her his full attention, Taija scanned him from head to toe and noticed on the passage with her eyes down his body, his massive chest was beckoning her to touch him. She could hardly wait to see him shirtless. She wondered a countless number of times what he looked like under his clothes. She could feel him through them, but she longed for the real thing, skin to skin. She continued her perusal down his body and began to tremble when she was able to see the outline in his pants of how turned on he was and the imprint was huge, massive and beckoning to her. She pondered what had she gotten herself into. She had never wanted any man the way she wanted this man and he appeared more than ready to provide whatever she wanted and needed in the biggest, longest version possible. Her mouth watered and her sex jumped.

Duron noticed a hint of nervousness in Taija's body language and was wondering if she was having second thoughts because he certainly wasn't. Standing before him was the most beautiful sight and she looked right being in his room, near his bed. Though he could hardly wait to strip her of ever stitch of clothing she wore, he wanted to savor every moment and become acquainted with every part of her scrumptious body. He saw the way she was looking at him and knew from her facial expression that she appreciated what she saw. It was time to seek out pleasure.

Taija watched as Duron moved away from the dresser and came in her direction, not stopping until they were standing in front of each other. Without uttering a word, he went straight for her lips. Again, the kiss was purely electric, sending sparks through her body. He must have felt it too because as he deepened the kiss, he tightened his grip on her waist pulling her flush up against him. She could feel her breasts as they molded to his chest. She felt her nipples harden against the inside of the bra she wore. They were so hard, they threatened to poke a hole right through the confining lace. She had never felt more turned on in her life.

Duron wanted to ravish Taija right on this spot and not let up until he had his fill. is desire for her was overwhelming and he knew that if he didn't soon get her closer to the bed, he would lift up the hem of her dress, unzip his pants and take her standing up. He held back his animalistic instinct to mate with her on the spot and slowed things down.

While his hands roamed over her arms, her back and down to grip her behind to bring her even closer, Duron licked a path from the corner of Taija's mouth, around to her ear. When she threw her head back, overwhelmed by the passion of it all, he took that as an opportunity to explore her neck with his lips and tongue, leaving a wet trail as he caressed her. When he blew where he had just licked, he felt her go limp in his arms. He loved how responsive she was to his every touch.

Taija was so overwhelmed by the sheer torture and pleasure of the way she was being worshiped with his amazing tongue that she didn't realize he had backed her up to the bed until the back of her legs came in contact with the mattress. When she would have sat down, Duron held her up and reached for the back zipper of her dress to remove it from her body. She looked up at him then and could read in his eyes all of the things he wanted to do to her and she was ready.

As Duron peeled the dress slowly down Taija's arms and watched it drop to the floor, his eyes traveled first down towards the dress now resting on the floor and then back up her body to take in her beauty. Looking at her standing before him in silver, strappy stilettos, a whisper of a strip of a lavender thong and matching bra, his mouth went completely dry. The sheer magnitude of her beauty was unmatched to anything he could have imagined. Standing before him was a goddess who wasn't shy and who he knew took great care of her body. He made a silent promise to himself that he would take good care if it, too.

"You are gorgeous, Taija. Even more than I could ever have imagined. I'm glad I didn't know what was under that dress you were wearing when we were in the car. I would have been tempted to find a secluded spot and relive my late teenage years," he admitted.

Taija realized Duron had been having the same thoughts that she had been having. They were so in tuned with each other it was scary.

"The way you are making me feel, I would not have minded at all acting like a couple of teenagers, crawling in the backseat of the car. The way you make me feel from how you look at me, to how you kiss and touch me make me want to go along with anything as long as the end result leads to where we are now," Taija said in a sultry voice, one she had never heard in herself. The moment was bringing out a lot of newness for her.

Duron didn't know what to say in response. This woman was unlike any woman he had ever encountered before. He locked ideas away in his head for another time when they could do a little car exploration. For now, the bed was more inviting to him than it ever has been with anyone else.

He looked deep into Taija's eyes.

"I really want to take this slow, but I'm not sure I can. My body is hot for you beyond anything I've ever experienced before," he said.

To prove his point, Duron took Taija's hand in his and guided it down the front of his pants to his huge, bulging member. He allowed her to feel for herself just how much he wanted her. He watched as her eyes glazed over at the thought of what it was going to feel like to have him inside of her body, stoking embers that had not been stoked by a man for some time. He remembered her telling him that she had not been intimate with a man in about a year, so he knew he was going to have to be sure that her experience with him was one she'd be glad that she waited just for him.

Taija's want for Duron went to a level that she'd never felt before. Without any help from him, she stroked him up and down through his pants. She loved the feel of him as he seemed to grow longer, thicker and harder under her ministrations. She couldn't wait to get her hands wrapped around him in the flesh.

Under her touch, and loving the feeling, Duron drew his breath in and held it, fearing if he released it, he might embarrass himself and things would be over before they got started. Though he enjoyed the feel of her hand intimately stroking him, he needed to stop her.

"Baby, as good as you are making me feel right now, I need you to stop or I'll lose all control I'm trying to have here. You are making it very hard for me to do that as long as you keep doing what you're doing," Duron said through clinched teeth as he tried to hold onto some semblance of his sanity.

He looked from Taija's face down to where her hand continued to stroke him. He looked back up into her eyes and could see that she was just as affected by her caress of him as he was.

Taija looked up at Duron and felt powerful that she could draw such passion from him and have the touch that made him hard as steel.

"Yes, I can see you are having quite a hard time here; rock hard in fact," she said with a voice laced with seduction.

Hearing the sultry sound of her voice, Duron's pulsing erection jumped against the palm of her hand. His reaction made her lose all of her self-control.

Not being able to resist the temptation of seeing the chest Duron was hiding under his shirt, while he continued to kiss her and explore her flesh with his hands, Taija pulled his shirt up and out of his pants and with nervous hands, unbuttoned his shirt, pushing it from his shoulders. Looking deeply into his eyes, she let her hands explore his chest loving the feel of his strong muscles under her fingers. She could tell he worked out vigorously because as she looked at his chest and stomach she saw no sign of fat. He was all chiseled muscle, as she suspected.

Laying her head on his chest, she took a moment to gather herself. Being with him was overpowering and so far, they had only kissed and caressed. She smiled knowing much more was on the way.

"As much as I love how we're going really slow with this, I need you Duron," she said.

To prove her point, she took his hand and placed it between her legs allowing him to feel how hot and wet she was for him. When he stroked her there, she moaned out something that sounded like a plea.

Hearing her plea and feeling her on the edge, Duron stepped back and removed the rest of his clothes allowing Taija to get a good look at the part of him that would soon be inside of her providing pleasure beyond measure. She gasped at the sight of how long and thick he was. Her body was reacting to what she was seeing making her feel alive and invigorated, ready for him to invade her body.

While Taija continued to stare at his hardening flesh, Duron reached to remove her bra. Now that he was here with her, he needed to see her breasts. Breasts were a weakness for him and hers did not disappoint. When he released them, the large globes with dark brown nipples felt wonderful in his hands. They were big and heavy and more than a handful. In his hands, they felt as if they were made just for him. He kneaded the fleshy mounds, loving how they seemed to grow even larger under his touch. The nipples pebbled under his strokes when he gave them a little pinch. As he did, Taija uttered a mewling sound of delight, told by pleasure-filled look on her face. He was glad because he had much more in store for her.

Duron looked down and saw her barely-there thong, the last piece of clothing that separated him from seeing her in all of her glory. He kept his eyes on hers as he used both hands to slide the thong down her shapely legs, lifting one leg, then the other to first remove her shoes then the thong. Before standing to his full height again, he looked from her face to the area in between her legs that was now level with his face. Being this close, he could see her Brazilian waxed sex and he couldn't and wouldn't resist getting one quick taste with a swipe of his tongue. He leaned in, gripped her hips to steady her and connected his tongue with the sight before him.

Caught off guard by the onslaught of feelings Duron was stirring in her, Taija had to grip his shoulders to keep from collapsing in a heap on the floor when she felt his tongue reach out and caress her most sensitive area. Feelings she had never felt before took over her senses and she felt like she was in another world. She saw stars beginning to form in her head. She knew if he continued, she would shoot off like a rocket while standing before him.

Noticing the change in Taija's breathing and the slow grind of her hips drawing him in closer, Duron stood and made sure she was watching him as he licked the essence of her that was on and around his lips.

"You taste delicious," he said.

That was perhaps one of the most erotic sights Taija had ever witnessed. That one move of his tongue licking her juices that were on his lips had her wanting him desperately. She wasn't sure how much longer she'd be able to wait to have him in her.

Duron reached around her and pulled back the thick down comforter and lifted her body to place her in the center of the bed. Before joining her, he reached into the bedside stand and withdrew condoms so that he was sure to protect them. Keeping one, he laid two more on the night stand, knowing he would need them before the night was over.

He then turned back to Taija who looked perfect in his bed. He joined her on the bed, covering her body with his and sliding the condom under the pillow for the moment. Before he sheathed himself, he wanted to explore her body from head to toe. He started with another fiery kiss on the lips before venturing down and around her neck.

"Duron, I need you baby. I don't think I can wait any longer," Taija said gasping for air. Her body was on fire.

She found herself moving and shifting to find release. She tried to control her movement, but her body apparently had a mind of its own.

Duron needed this and he could tell Taija needed it as well. He wanted to get to that sweet place just as much as she wanted him to be there.

"Let me please you sweetheart," he whispered. "I don't want to rush this. I want to taste you all over."

Shivers ran through her body as he continued his assault on her ear which just happened to be her hot spot.

Those were the last words Duron spoke as he released her ear and moved further down her body. When he reached her breasts, he took first the left nipple between his teeth and bit down slightly before wetting it with his tongue and blowing on it to cool it off. He planned to spend a lot of time throughout the night getting acquainted with her delicious breasts. This was only the beginning, he thought.

Fondling and caressing the right one, he was basking in the feeling of how it felt in the palm of his hand. Wanting to give her right breast just as much attention, he leaned over and took her right nipple into his mouth, showering it with his lips and tongue just as he had done the other one.

At this point, Taija's was about to explode. She wasn't sure how much more assault on her body she could take before she did. The way Duron was pleasing her body was more than she could ever imagine. She loved how he was paying special attention to her breasts, which were very sensitive. She used to be self-conscious about the large size of them until she became a woman and began to understand the pleasure that could be drawn from just the right amount of attention. Duron was doing incredible things to her body and she never wanted it to end. The pleasure was so electrifying, she felt herself thrashing about on the bed. She wanted the feeling to last forever.

She thought she would have a heart attack when Duron reached the apex of her thighs, spreading them far apart. She opened her eyes briefly, just in time to see him position himself as if he were about to settle in for a feast. She caught that sexy glint in his hazel eyes when she realized that was exactly what he had planned. Just as his tongue ventured out to swipe her sensitized nub, Taija stopped breathing. A feeling so deep and uncontrollable over took her as spasm after spasm of pleasure speared through her. As Duron worshipped her with his tongue, she could no longer hold back as an orgasm more intense than anything she had ever felt before hit her. She could not control the scream of pleasure that escaped her lips as her orgasm went on and on. It seemed never-ending. The orgasm was heightened when he placed his finger inside of her, replacing his tongue.

Duron looked up briefly after replacing his tongue with his finger. He wanted to see the look of pleasure on her face.

"That's right baby, get what you need," he said.

When she continued to ride out her orgasm, he went back in for more with his tongue, adding it along with his finger for extra added delight. He didn't let up even when he felt her crest again at the peak of her orgasm as wave after wave assaulted her body. His tongue continued making love to the most intimate part of her body. It was his plan to make sure she never regretted being with him tonight and to his delight he was accomplishing that task.

Duron got a high from how responsive Taija was to this brand of lovemaking. He believed in using every part of his body to please a woman and not just with his penis. It gave him great pleasure knowing he could make her feel this good. Following her body's second crest over the edge, he watched her body relax as he made his way back up her body, kissing it as he made his way to her lips. He needed to kiss her, to join their lips once again.

When he leaned in to kiss her, Taija wound her arms around his neck and gave as much as she was being given. She started running her hands all over Duron's body while continuing to relish the kiss.

"That was incredible," she said when she was able to speak again.

Duron knew how she felt.

"There is much more in store for you baby. I told you it would be a night you will never forget," Duron said.

Before she could speak again, he leaned down with his mouth and sought out her tongue. As he did so, he could feel her body grinding up into his, letting him know that though she'd just experienced two orgasms back to back, she wanted more and he was ready to oblige.

"Are you ready for me?" he whispered into her mouth while continuing to kiss her. He ground his erection down onto her so that she could see how ready he was for her.

Taija couldn't speak even if his tongue had not been in her mouth, so she nodded to let him know she was on board. He waited no longer. He reached for the condom he'd placed under the pillow.

Under hooded eyes, Taija watched Duron as he placed the condom over his massive organ. If she didn't know any better, she would have thought that they didn't make condoms large enough to accommodate his size. She wondered if her small size would be able to handle him. That thought brought her a little hesitation and at the same time, it brought her body great joy of what she was about to receive.

After placing the condom on, Duron leaned back down to join their lips once again as he slid in between her legs. He gripped her legs lightly under her thighs, widening them.

"Look at me Taija. I need you looking at me as I enter you. I want to be sure you not only feel me, but that you see me too."

Taija opened her hooded eyes that were straining to stay closed in order to concentrate more on the feeling of Duron, but she did as he asked.

As he wrapped her legs high around his waist, he reached down to cup her behind to lift it higher to receive him as he guided himself into her body. As his tongue slid deep inside of her mouth, the lower part of his body slid into hers and into ecstasy. He had to enter her body slowly because her sex was grasping him like a glove. He didn't want to hurt her as he worked himself in inch by inch, making room for his huge flesh in her small body. Her body was still wet from her two orgasms so he used her body's essence to lubricate his entry, as not to cause her too much pain due to his size. She felt so good that he wanted to surge into her body, but he knew that would only benefit him so he continued grinding in further and further. When he finally slid all the way in to the hilt, he didn't move, giving her body time to adjust to his size. He wanted to be gentle. The feeling was so vast, he was afraid this was going to be over fast. He fought the need to take her with aggression and the sweat he felt forming on his forehead was a sign that his body was internally fighting itself.

"Duron, this is exactly what I've been craving since the moment you and I met at the auction," Taija said breaking into his concentration. "Don't hold back. Give it to me baby," she whispered in his ear.

"I'm trying to take things slow and not hurt you baby. You are so tight. I'm trying to let your body get accustomed to my size."

"I know and I promise you I'm fine," she moaned.

When he did not move, she moved to let him know she was okay.

Duron felt Taija push up onto him while he tried to control his movements and gritting his teeth to show as much restraint as he could.

"If you keep moving like this, I'm not sure how long I'm going to be able last," Duron said with a strain in his voice.

"I can't stop. I have to move. You need to move, too. I need you baby, please," Taija pleaded.

When she said that, Duron knew all bets were off. Desire, unmatched to anything he had ever felt, started taking over him as he started to move inside of Taija's body. He started off with a very slow stroke and slowly picked up the pace when she started to respond to him aggressively matching his thrusts stroke for stroke. All he could think was that this was exactly where he was supposed to be. With this woman, inside this woman, giving her as much pleasure as he could muster while she gave him satisfaction beyond anything he could ever imagine, Duron took their lovemaking to another whole level.

"Taija, baby you feel so good," he whispered while he stroked her to higher heights.

Duron wanted her to know what she was doing to him.

Taija's body was responding to the pleasure that was pouring from Duron's body into hers. She had never felt so full and so complete in her life. Duron's flesh, filling her was doing things to her that she could never have thought possible. He felt incredible and she could feel herself about to plunge off of that ledge once again as her body sought out that ultimate pleasure. She could barely contain herself as her body lost all control as she wrapped her legs tighter around his back, using her hands to stroke his arms and his back letting him know that she was happily on board for the ride of her life. He had set the pace and she couldn't be more pleased with it. He was giving her just the right amount of pleasure as she began to anxiously seek out release.

"Duron, baby, I need.....oh my, I....I...need...ohhhh."

Duron quickened his strokes as his body felt Taija once again on the verge of another powerful orgasm.

"Let it go baby," Duron whispered as he continued to pump into her body again and again going as deep as he could. She was milking everything he willingly gave her whatever she wanted.

His words, his voice, the of him plunging in and out of her body sent Taija over the edge again into an explosive rupture. She rocked into him hard pulling every last bit of pleasure she could from his body. Duron knew he had to have died and gone to heaven when he felt Taija use her muscles to grip his hardened member as her climax flowed from her to him. He finally let loose and followed her over that edge as his own climax claimed his very soul. He had never in his life been with a woman who made him feel this way. As his own orgasm hit, he reared back and let what felt like a roar escape from him as he groaned out his release. Holding in or suppressing his holler was not an option. The sensation was nothing he had ever felt before and it seemed to go on forever and ever. To him, nothing else existed, but he and Taija and the enjoyment pleasure of the moment.

As they both surged to earth from shattering orgasms, neither spoke and the only sound in the room was of them trying to catch their breaths.

Feeling overwhelmed, Duron couldn't say a word. He continued placing soft kisses across Taija's sweaty face and around her neck, giving her his very own version of thank you, until he could find the energy to speak.

They stayed in this position, with Duron laying on top of Taija for a while until his mind started working again and he realized with his size, he had to feel like dead weight on her. He moved to extricate himself from her body when she drew him back in, not wanting to release him yet.

She loved the feel of him being this close to her. He was such a thorough lover that her body felt like a lump of clay. She held on to him tighter, letting him know that she didn't want him to move from on top of her.

"Taija, baby." Duron whispered to her in between kisses. "I'm too heavy to be on you like this."

Taija, mewled like a little kitten.

"You're not too heavy. You feel good just like this." Taija was rubbing her hands up and down his back, loving the feel of his body still being intimately connected to hers. She never wanted to move.

Not wanting to break the connection, but not wanting to continue with his weight being on her, Duron rolled over so that Taija was on top. He drew her in closer while she laid her head on his chest and snuggled. They laid in that position until Duron could see that Taija's breathing had slowed down and she had fallen asleep. He didn't want to wake her so he slid her off of his body slowly and onto the pillow on the other side of the bed.

After getting up to discard the condom, he rejoined her, drawing her up against him so that they could spoon. Feeling sleep about to overtake him as well, he joined her in slumber.

~~

Duron was having the best dream. He was dreaming that Taija was placing kisses all over his chest while reaching down to stroke him slowly until his pliant flesh was rock hard. As he came slowly awake, he realized it wasn't a dream at all. Taija, had in fact, woken up and was kissing his chest looking right into his eyes. It was still sometime in the middle of the night because it was still dark when he looked up through the skylight in the bedroom. Even in the darkness he could see her intent. She looked like a woman on a mission and enjoying herself.

"Ready for another round I see," he said. Duron placed his hands behind his head and enjoyed her touch.

"I wondered how long it would take for you to feel me and wake up," Taija said. She was ready for another round and then some. She woke up with her body feeling marvelous.

Duron watched as she continued to kiss her way down his body. He felt his sleeping body coming awake.

"I'm definitely woke now," he said.

"Well, since you're clearly up again," Taija said looking her fill of his body, "and I do mean literally up, I have my own plans for this sexy body of yours."

She looked down his body and saw that part of him that had brought her so much pleasure earlier, once again rise to the occasion.

Duron was certainly going to oblige her.

"I'm here for the taking sweetheart," he said.

He watched Taija enjoying her movements around his body, getting acquainted with every part of his flesh. When the pleasure started to be more than he could stand, he reached for another condom on the night stand and proceeded to not waste another moment. They made love for the rest of the night, only having an hour to rest before the sun came up.

After a quick nap, Duron woke in the morning feeling drained. It was a good kind of drained. His body had gotten a much-needed workout and the cause of his drained feeling was snuggled up against him still sleeping. He watched Taija sleep, knowing that following their all-night lovemaking session, she probably needed the rest. Deciding to let her sleep, he slipped out of bed to take a shower and head downstairs to cook some breakfast for them.

After making coffee and some omelets, he entered his bedroom and didn't see Taija in bed. Hearing water running, he knew she was in the shower.

Soon the bathroom door opened and she came out wearing only a towel, looking sexy. Duron's body stirred to life once again.

She made eye contact with him and thought of the night they'd spent together. Her body could still feel his touch.

"I hope you don't mind that I used your shower," Taija said, looking at him like a seductress.

Duron couldn't speak. His mind was already on if he could use some kind of kinetic energy to get that towel to just drop.

"Is that for me?" Taija asked, pointing towards the tray

of food he'd placed on the bed.

Watching her come towards the bed, he forgot he had prepared breakfast for them. His sex stirred at the sight of her, making him forget everything else.

He needed to focus.

"I figured you may be hungry with the appetite we worked up. I thought sustenance would be a good idea to build your strength back up."

Climbing back up on the bed with Duron joining her, Taija first attacked the coffee then tasted a forkful of the spinach omelet.

"Mmmm. This omelet is so good. I guess you can cook huh?" she said smiling.

Duron was glad she was enjoying it.

"I can do a little something, something," he replied.

Taija looked at him with pure sex in her gaze.

"So, you can make magic happen in the bedroom and the kitchen huh?"

"Your pleasure in any room is how I aim to please, baby."

Duron leaned in for a kiss to start his morning off right. The kiss was turning fiery and heading into dangerous territory. He broke off the kiss before he completely forgot that he wanted her to eat.

"Eat Taija. Time for that later."

14

The next few weeks went by in a blur. Duron was happy with the amount of time he and Taija were spending together. The type of friends with benefits kind of friendship they started out having was gradually turning into something more. When they weren't together or talking, he was thinking about her and what activities they could do so that he could spend even more time with her.

They took in movies, plays, spent countless evenings at his house or hers talking, renting movies enjoying having quality time.

Dating other women, as Duron had been known to do, was a distant memory. He had reached a comfortable place in life enjoying being with Taija and only her. They made love in every room in both of their houses and the sex was exciting and adventurous, never boring. They were blissfully happy and though neither one of them brought up the term "relationship", they sort of slipped into the relationship realm naturally.

In the back of his mind, Duron could feel that Taija's expectations of the relationship they were developing were growing and though she was the most exciting woman he had ever met in his life, old wounds always had him looking for the other shoe to drop. For now, things felt right. Things between them felt so right to him that when his parents decided to have a cookout, he invited Taija to come along. He hadn't done that since being involved with his ex-girlfriend, so his family would be shocked to see him show up with her. Only his sister knew about all the time he and Taija had been spending together and she was delighted. He knew the rest of his family would be delighted with her, too. If nothing else, Taija was an incredible woman, the full package.

When Loren was clued into what was going on with the two of them, she was over the moon happy that they had gotten together. Though she pushed him for more details and for him to admit that he was into her for more than just a casual fling, he wouldn't give in to her. She and Taija may be friends, but he wanted to keep what happens between them, between them. If Taija wanted to share anything with Loren, he was okay with that, but she wouldn't hear much about it from him.

After sitting through his last briefing of the day with his partners and one of their new clients, he couldn't get his mind off of the woman who was occupying his thoughts day and night. It was still pretty early in the day and he didn't have anything else that was a priority and he felt a pull to go see Taija. He knew she was busy at the office and he hoped she wouldn't mind his stopping by. He knew her transition to the job in Atlanta had been causing her a lot of stress lately. She was enjoying the job, but it was a lot more challenging than her previous one.

He left his office and took the short drive to her office.

"I'm here to see Taija Charles," he said to the guard in the lobby of her office building.

"Sure, sir. Take the elevators to your left to the eighth floor. The receptionist on that floor will show you to her office."

Duron thanked him and added a little more pep in his step as he made his way to the elevator that would take him to Taija.

When he reached the receptionist, who alerted Taija to his presence, he was escorted to her office where she sat behind her desk, finishing up a phone call. His heart swelled when she smiled when he entered. He would never tire of seeing her beautiful face. When she completed her call, she got up and came around to greet him with the kind of kiss that he had come to enjoy. He noticed that she was in her workout gear, not work attire.

"Is today dress down day at work or something?" he asked.

Taija looked down at herself, realizing she still had on gym clothes. She'd had a free morning and due to much stress at work, she'd decided to work out at the gym on the lower level of her office building. When she returned to her office, she'd spent time returning phone calls and had yet to go into the adjourning bathroom in her office to shower and change back into her work clothes.

"I went to work out this morning after a stressful meeting and haven't showered and changed yet. I was just about to do that when you arrived. So, what brings you by today?" she asked.

"I wanted to see you and to see if you wanted to partake in an afternoon delight of lunch with me," he said.

Taija loved how spontaneous Duron could be. Over the past several weeks that they had been seeing one another, she had experienced his spontaneity on more than a few occasions.

"Of course. Let me get out of these sweaty clothes, grab

a shower and I'll be ready to go," Taija said.

Duron watched the sway of her hips as she made her way to the shower in her office. His thoughts turned back to one morning a few weeks back when he entered his bedroom and Taija had been in the shower. He wanted to join her then, but she had just turned off the water and gotten out. The sight of her always turned him on and seeing her today was like seeing her for the first time. His body's response to her was instantaneous. He heard her turn on the shower and wondered how adventurous he could get her to be. He walked over to her office door, told her secretary that Taija asked if she could hold all of her calls and visitors. When her secretary smiled at him, knowing his intent, she acknowledged as he closed and locked the office door. He wanted Taija bad and he wanted her now. He began removing his own clothes as he headed for the bathroom to join her.

Taija knew the moment Duron had entered her office bathroom. She had just been thinking about him being naked and wet in her office shower. She wasn't sure if he would ever be willing to take the risk of sex in her office, but the thought turned her on. The water pounding on her over-sensitized body was arousing. That wasn't the normal affect until she'd started seeing him. Now, every time she was naked, she would close her eyes and imagine his hands being all over her while her hands roamed all over his gorgeous body. Even now, she tingled knowing that her fantasy was about to come true.

She waited to see if he would do what she figured he had on his mind when she'd excused herself to take a shower. She never missed that lustful gleam in his eyes.

When Duron slid the shower door open, the look on

Taija's face that said she had been waiting for him to join her. He watched the show of emotions on her face as she took in his naked body. He watched as her nipples pebbled, making themselves ready for his touch. When she moved back making room for him, he knew he'd made the right choice joining her. The sinful look on her face told him everything he needed to know.

No words were said as he entered the stall, closed the door behind him, and immediately took Taija's mouth in a hot, searing kiss. They had been together intimately so many times that Taija knew what Duron's body needed and one thing he loved to do was to kiss her. She gave into his heated kiss as he lowered to lift her body up and turned so that her back was against the wall of the shower stall.

"Tell me there isn't an office on the other side of this wall because I have a feeling if there is, someone is about to get a show via sound through the wall," he said lowering his mouth to savor one of her nipples.

Taija couldn't believe he was talking. She wanted to feel him inside of her and could barely wait the few seconds it would take for him to sheath himself let alone have a conversation about sound proof walls.

"No one's on the other side. There's a maintenance closet on the other side of the wall that's only used over night when the crew is here cleaning the office. At this point, I wouldn't care. Now that you're standing here in my shower all naked and wet, I would be willing to risk it," she said breathlessly.

Duron smiled.

"That's all I needed to hear sweetheart," he replied.

All talk ceased as his mouth met hers again.

Wrapping her legs around his back while plundering her

mouth with an insatiable kiss, Taija remained patient while Duron lifted her higher on the wall so that he could place the condom on. She looked down, watching him as he did so, enjoying the view of his stiff flesh as it rose to prepare to deliver the ultimate pleasure to her.

"Quick and dirty?" he asked, knowing they shouldn't prolong the sex since they were in her office.

"The quicker and dirtier the better," she replied.

"Hang on baby, it's about to be a wild ride," he exclaimed just before spreading her legs a little wider and lowering her down onto him.

The feel of him entering her caused them both to sigh with satisfaction. Apparently, this was something they both needed.

Duron braced his legs with a sturdy stance so that he could sustain them both and without much pretense he surged in with one long thrust. The immediate invasion into her body caused her to shriek and that little sound urged him on. To keep her shrieks from being heard by anyone, he closed his mouth over hers and swallowed any further sounds either one of them would make as he pushed into her over and over. His thrusts were hard and deep just the way he'd come to discover she liked. He held onto her with one hand under her behind while he braced himself against the wet shower stall wall with his other hand. He entered her strong and powerful, moving them closer to ecstasy.

As Duron entered her over and over, Taija did everything to suppress the scream that was aching to exit her mouth. The cold wall of the shower felt good on her back as the heat from Duron's body radiated the space in front of her. He was making love to her like a starving man and only she could satisfy his craving. The intensity was so great that the friction of his up and down stroke sent her into bliss where he soon followed her. Where they both would holler their joyous release, Duron deepened the kiss with her to swallow both of their screams of pleasure.

As their breathing returned to normal, the only thing Taija could think was that she loved Duron's idea of an afternoon delight.

15

"What should I bring to your parents' house on Saturday for the cookout Duron?" Taija asked as they enjoyed lunch at a bistro not far from her office.

They had finally made it to lunch after the quickie in her office. After using her office bathroom to freshen up, they were starving by the time they'd reached the restaurant.

"Bring something for what?" he asked.

"I don't want to show up empty handed at your parents' house. I wouldn't want to be rude showing up with nothing to add to the meal. I wouldn't want them to think my mother didn't raise me right," she said.

"Taija, you don't have to bring anything. Believe me, my parents will have everything, plus some. It's fine if you just come and bring me with you," he quipped.

Taija wasn't sure about that. She felt it was customary to bring something when coming to any kind of meal at someone's house. Besides, she was about to meet his parents and she wanted her first visit to leave a great impression.

"Duron, stop it. I can't show up with nothing. I know we're not in some serious relationship or anything, but I still want your family to like me and to get a good first impression of me."

"I'm serious when I say my parents will be excited that

I'm bringing someone, that they may forget I'm in tow. Even if you bring something, they won't remember. The shock of me bringing someone with me will be all that any of them will remember," he said.

Duron leaned across the table to give her a quick, reassuring kiss on the lips.

"You don't have to bring anything but your sexy self. It's all rather casual. My mother loves when we all get together considering how busy we all tend to be. I want you there because I enjoy spending time with you and I know you'll get along well with everyone. Don't feel any pressure to bring anything," he encouraged.

Taija contemplated not bringing something and going on what Duron said, but then thought otherwise. She wanted to go with her first thought.

"Okay, but I think I'm going to pick up a cake or some kind of pie for dessert. I can't show up with nothing but their handsome son on my arm. That's a plus for me, but I want to contribute something. Are you okay with that?" she asked.

Duron laughed, knowing he should let her do what she needed to do.

"Baby, if you want to bring something, then bring something. It'll be fine either way. I'll be by to pick you up tomorrow around two. Wear something sexy for me. A skirt, preferably a short one. I can show you my old room where I learned to master my quickie technique as a teenager," he laughed.

Taija could not help the loud laugh that escaped from her lips. With his amorous appetite as a man, she could only imagine what he was like as a horny teenager with those sexy eyes drawing girls to him like a moth to a flame.

"Okay, you caught me off guard with that. Cute, but it's not happening, babe. I am not getting busy in that house with your family there. We'll save the skirt for later at your house."

"Well, if that's the case, I say ditch the skirt all together, and the cookout and let's just get to the part where we are at my house with you and the skirt and nothing on underneath. I bet you were one of those cheerleaders in high school who teased all of the boys in short skirts."

Taija huffed at him.

She wouldn't tell him she was head cheerleader back in high school and every boy flirted with her.

"Maybe, maybe not. If you're trying to smooth talk me into sex at your parent's house, stop it and we won't be missing the cookout. I'm meeting them for the first time and I don't want anything to happen that could tarnish their image of me. Besides, I'm looking forward to it and there will be no slipups and certainly no quickie sex. I will not let your mother think the worst of me for keeping you away from a family gathering. Never, lover boy. I'll see you tomorrow at two."

~~

Duron sat back at his parents' house during the cookout, watching how easily Taija seemed to fit right in with everyone. His brother Jake's wife Kim and Taija connected as if they were long lost sisters. His niece, Lyric and his nephew, Milo, fell in love with her and he could see she loved kids. Watching her interact with his family made him realize how close the two of them were becoming. Her presence with everyone felt like a natural occurrence. He knew they were indeed in dangerous territory because the lines seemed to be blurring between where he initially wanted them to be and where they were going. He knew it wasn't fair to hold his relationship in limbo because of his past. He knew Taija wanted more and even though he wanted to fight it, he wanted more as well. He had a lot to think about as far as the future of what they had going on. His brother Brian interrupted his thoughts when he walked over.

"Hey, man. I like your girlfriend, Taija. Besides being down right fine, she has a great personality. You picked a winner. I don't see what she sees in you, though," Brian jested.

Duron swiped at him and missed as they laughed together. He didn't miss how Brian slipped in the word girlfriend.

"She's not my girlfriend, Brian. Taija and I are just friends. It's actually my typical friends with benefits type of situation. It's nothing serious," he said.

"Really? I don't know about that because I haven't seen you bring around any of those tarts you bed on the regular. This thing with Taija must be different if she's here with you laughing it up with everyone," Brian said.

Feeling uncomfortable, Duron knew things were different the moment he asked her to come with him. It was out of character for him, but Taija was someone he wanted her family to get to know. Beyond that, he hadn't thought much about it.

"Listen to me when I say, it's nothing serious. She's nice and I like her, but we're not in a serious situation. Don't try to find something that's not there," Duron said.

Brian looked at Duron questionably.

"Duron, are you trying to convince me or you? I've seen how you've watched her all day long. You have the look of a man in love, not just a man enjoying a friend with benefits situation."

Just as Duron was about to further explain, Jake walked up to them.

"What are you guys deep in conversation about?" he asked.

Brian spoke first.

"Duron is trying to convince himself that he's not in love with Taija and that he's just enjoying her friendship with benefits. Now, you and I both know that Duron has never brought a friend with benefits home before, so this is definitely more than that even if he won't admit it. I know this is not his typical benefit situation. Lately, whenever I call to talk to him, I haven't heard anything about another woman. He catches me up on the latest with him and Taija. He's always offering information on what movie they saw or what band they went to see. Jake, you know he is normally quick to tell us how the sex was with his latest fling, but nothing about Taija when it comes to how good she is," Brian said.

Duron gave Brian a look that said back off.

"Watch it, Brian," Duron said curtly. "You'll get nothing about my personal business with Taija. That's not up for discussion."

Jake chimed in.

"Since when? Brian is right, you are really feeling this one. I haven't seen you like this since you know who and when the three of us are together, you're always ready to tell us about the latest woman and the bedroom acrobatics. That's not the case with Taija? Yeah, this must be serious," Jake said.

Duron knew who he was referring to when he said 'you

know who'. He was talking about Allison.

"Both of you give it a rest," he said impatiently. "I said there's nothing there and that means there's nothing there. I told you, we're just friends."

"If that's the case, then how's the sex?" Brian asked. He jumped back a few steps when Duron suddenly stood up looking like he was about to pound on him. Brian threw his hands up in a defense position.

"Whoa bro, you know I'm only teasing you. Just admit you have some real feelings for her. Any other time, after you nailed a broad or two, you'd be forthcoming about how she was in bed. Don't blame me for asking what I usually ask. Blame yourself for being sensitive. I'm smelling love in the air. What about you Jake?" Brian asked, edging Duron on more.

Duron's sudden anger was subsiding because Brian was right. Any other time, he'd be willing to share with them his sexual escapades, but they were getting nothing about his time with Taija. It was too special to him and though he wouldn't admit it, Brian was right, she was something special to him and he needed to sort out what that was.

"Brian, leave him be. We have all seen how he looks at Taija since she's been here and we all know he's been missing in action lately because he spends all of his free time with her and only her. That's not just a friend look. Believe me, I know. I had that same look when I fell in love with Kim. If he wants to deny it, let him," Jake explained.

Duron hated when his brothers goaded him into a conversation he would rather not be in. He wanted the conversation about his private life to end.

"Both of you don't know what you're talking about, so why don't you just keep your observations to yourselves.

I've said what it was and that's that," Duron said, adding more base to his voice than was needed. He was more frustrated at himself for not realizing his family, especially his brothers wouldn't see through his usual declaration of nothing going on.

Brian, the most outspoken never missed a chance to butt in.

"I know one thing. I've seen how she looks at you and her look says she's in love with you. How are you going to handle that when clearly, she's all in, bruh? Remember what it's like to be in love with someone and they don't love you back? If you say it's nothing, then it's nothing. If it's more than nothing, then don't let what happened in your past affect what's happening in your life now. According to Loren, she's a winner and a keeper."

Duron knew Brian was right. He had known it for a while. Taija was seeing him as more than just a friend with benefits and he's gone along with it because he liked everything about her. He started getting that vibe from Taija that perhaps she was in love with him, but had not said so because of his assertion that they would never venture into that type of relationship when all along, that's exactly what was happening. He could kick himself. He didn't want to hurt her, but sitting back and listening to his brothers and really taking a look at what has been happening with the two of them, they were definitely acting as an exclusive couple, something he didn't want – or did he? He wanted her, but he didn't want anything too serious that would come crashing down one day, as with his past relationship.

"Leave him alone Brian," Jake said again. "If the man says he's not in love, hey, who are we to say otherwise. We are just his brothers. We're only the two guys who know him better than he knows himself."

Duron didn't want to comment, he wanted to let it go.

"Listen guys, I'm going to get Taija and head out. We have plans for this evening. I'll see you both Tuesday evening at the gym for some pick-up basketball, right?" Duron asked looking from one brother to the other.

Jake and Brian knew when to back off. Duron was the touchiest about his personal life, so they dropped the conversation about him and Taija.

"I'm in," Brian said.

"I'm in, too. Kim is off and I told her we had a pick-up game that night and she's good with it. She's been working so much lately that she wants some alone time with the kids."

Duron got up to leave. What he didn't see was his brothers shaking their heads at him.

Brian offered his opinion to Jake first.

"This is going to end badly, Jake. I know it."

"I think you're right, but he's a big boy. He'll figure it out."

Taija and Duron helped his family clean up and then said their goodbyes and headed back to his place for the night.

Taija noticed Duron was unusually quiet as they drove through traffic. She tried to engage him several times in various conversation topics, but when he answered with short, curt responses, she could tell something was on his mind. They had enjoyed a nice day with his family. He appeared to have a great time until it was time to leave and they were alone again. She decided to give up in engaging him and let him have the quiet he clearly wanted. She sat back quietly and enjoyed the ride as she thought back over the wonderful day.

16

When they reached his condo, Taija had the feeling that Duron had something on his mind that was bothering him. She wasn't sure what it was because she thought the cookout had gone well. She loved his family and from their reaction, they enjoyed her being a part of their day. They were open and welcoming to her and his mother was happy that she'd brought dessert. She was happy her four layered cake was a huge hit. Whatever was bothering Duron wasn't going away easily.

His silence, as they made their way first from the car, then up the elevator to the condo was starting to bother her. She was actually surprised they were at the condo. She had spent time with him a few times at the condo since they'd met, but only as a brief stop-through. Usually on a weekend, he preferred to stay either at his house or at hers. He always said the condo reminded him too much of business and she knew through conversation with him that if he did spend the night at the condo with a woman, it was a fling and nothing serious. Duron once told her that she had been the only woman he'd ever taken to his house. She wondered what was different now that he wanted to spend the night at his condo and not at the house. The distance she started feeling from him at the end of the party was now as wide as the ocean. She let it go for now because she couldn't think of anything that would put him in a sullen mood. Whatever it was, he was making her feel like he wanted to be alone, but didn't know how to tell her.

Duron couldn't shake the uneasiness he was feeling. Perhaps it was the conversation with his brothers that was getting under his skin. Was it true that they could look at Taija and see that she was in love with him? Were her feelings for him that obvious? He needed to pull back a little because he'd been so caught up in enjoying her that he wasn't paying attention to how close they were really getting. The silence between them was his fault and he didn't know how to fix it without saying something that would most likely hurt Taija's feelings.

He surprised himself when, instead of heading in the direction of his home in Buckhead, he drove to the condo. He'd taken Taija to the condo a few times, but never to spend the night. He always equated spending time with women at his condo as casual relationships. Maybe his brothers playing with his head made him think that he needed to remind himself that things between he and Taija were supposed to be simple and non-committal. He wasn't trying to disrespect her by putting her in a category with other women he'd been intimate with by bringing her to the condo to spend the night. On its own accord, his mind directed him to the condo instead of his house. Now, he had to think to himself about who he was trying to convince - Taija or himself.

Taija glanced over at Duron as they rode the elevator and noticed a perplexed look on his face like something serious was on his mind. She decided to break the silence and lighten up the mood, hoping to cheer him up.

"Thank you for inviting me today. I had a wonderful

time with your family," she said.

She waited for some sort of response from Duron, but only received a light smile and a head nod.

When the elevator reached the penthouse level, Duron moved to exit and turned when Taija didn't move to follow him.

"Are you coming out of the elevator?" he asked in an irritated voice. The tone surprised him. He'd never spoken to her harshly before.

Taija was losing patience and was beginning to think that maybe she should have him take her home. It was obvious, even from his tone, that something was wrong and he wasn't going to tell her.

"I don't know. Should I? What's wrong Duron? Your mood seems a little somber and I've been trying to figure out what happened that has you in a bad mood after spending a great day with your family."

"Nothing is wrong Taija. Come on out of the elevator," he said.

"Did I do something to cause you to act like this? You were fine all evening until we got in the car. It's almost like a cloud is hovering over you."

Duron didn't know what to say. Nothing was really wrong, but he was coming to terms with how serious his feelings were becoming for her and it made him uncomfortable. Damn his brothers for putting all this love stuff in his head. Once again, his past was haunting his present. He was upsetting Taija and he needed to put the current state of his emotions on the back burner so that it didn't have a negative impact on their evening. He redirected his thoughts, cleared his mind and attempted to put a reassuring smile on his face.

"Baby, I'm fine. I just have a work thing on my mind," he lied.

He pulled her to him, placed a soft kiss on her lips in hopes it would let her see that everything was fine. When she returned his kiss, he knew everything was good.

They proceeded into the condo.

"What about a movie?" Duron said.

"Sure, a movie sounds great. You go ahead and get the movie started, I'll meet you in the media room after I freshen up a little."

Taija knew Duron's favorite room in his condo was his media room. It was the room where he was most comfortable with his big screen television, top of the line sound system and comfortable seating that she knew he often fell asleep on while enjoying a movie. She didn't know what was bothering him, but she wanted him in a relaxation mood.

"Cool," Duron replied, leaning down and placing a hot, wet kiss on Taija's lips.

While he headed to the media room to get the movie started, she had other ideas on her mind. Duron had a work issue that was distracting him and she wanted to change the tone of the evening from worry to one of seduction. She headed into the bedroom with her overnight bag which contained new red lingerie she'd recently purchased with him in mind. Duron loved her in red since the night they'd met at the auction when she was wearing a fiery red gown.

Grabbing a quick shower and donning the new red-hot lingerie and high heeled red bottoms, Taija made her way to the love of her life. That thought stopped her dead in her tracks. No matter how she tried to play by Duron's rule of nothing really serious, she had fallen in love with him. She couldn't deny that fact, no matter how hard she tried in order to keep the peace and play things out the way he wanted. Love happens even when you try to keep it at bay.

Things were going well and they were on the path to something more than just friends with benefits. She hated that term and the stigma attached to it, but because she was into him, she let it linger in the air, not focusing on it and going with the flow. Now that her feelings had deepened for him, she saw their friends with benefits status as an insult to the vibrant, loving woman she was. She deserved to have someone return the love she felt. It was only natural that they would head in an upward direction. She wouldn't push him, but she needed to know if things were going in a more serious direction for him as they were for her.

Checking herself once again in the mirror, she headed in the direction of love.

Duron looked at the clock on the wall wondering what was keeping Taija. Just as he was about to get up to check on her, she entered the room and time stopped. Only Taija had the power to render him speechless and this time was no exception.

She had come into the room in the sexiest piece of bright red lingerie and red stilettos to match that a woman could wear. As she sauntered over to him, his eyes went from her beautiful face to the way the garment was hugging her luscious body. Her breasts were sitting high and prominent like a beacon. When she came to stand before him he was afraid to move and afraid to reach out for her thinking she must be a mirage.

"I thought I would try and take your mind off of your

work troubles for a few hours," she said turning so that he could get the full effect from every angle.

"You look amazing," Duron said with eyes wide open.

Livening up his mood was working, Taija thought. The look on Duron's face as soon as he saw her spoke volumes. Walking up to him, she slid down to straddle his lap, never breaking eye contact. She smiled to herself at the completely turned on expression on his face. The bulge growing in his pants was an unmistakable clue that his mood was turning around and whatever had been on his mind was now replaced with thoughts of her and what was next for them.

"Let me remove all thoughts from your mind that have nothing to do with you and me at this moment," she said.

Taija leaned forward, placed her hands on both sides of his face and captured his lips in a kiss that expressed her desire for him. When she sought entry into his mouth, he opened to her, letting her take the lead. She could feel the heat from his body and combined with her own body heat, they were forming an inferno.

Duron was experiencing his own Shangri-La, his very own heaven on earth. Taking the time to savor the attention Taija was giving him, he let her take control. He knew that whatever she needed would be gratifying for him, too. He wanted to leap off the chair when she started grinding, first from side to side and then up and down, simulating the act of lovemaking.

Taija, more than ready now, reached into her cleavage withdrew a condom for both of their pleasure. Still not breaking eye contact and trying her best to let her eyes tell him how much she loved him, she reached down, unzipped his pants and withdrew that part of him that brought her satisfaction over and over again.

As she slowly opened the condom wrapper and sheathed his hard as steel flesh, her fingers shook with excitement for what was coming next. Not giving him any clue of what she had planned, she rose up, unsnapped the lingerie at the juncture of her thighs and without breaking eye contact, slid down on him taking him into her body as much as it would allow.

Duron was experiencing new sensations that were turning his brain to mush. He couldn't think, all he could do was feel. Gripping Taija's hips, he held on tight for the ride.

"Taija, what are you doing to me?" Duron said huskily, enjoying the slow grind of her hips.

Taija leaned forward until her lips graced his ear.

"I'm making you feel like you make me feel all the time. I don't want you to talk. I want you to close your eyes and feel me."

When he closed his eyes and leaned back, Taija moved like a woman on a mission, slow at first until the natural instinct to move settled in and she picked up the pace.

Duron couldn't breathe. She was consuming his senses with her lovemaking. Each time she rose and slid back down on him, he had to remember to exhale in between to keep from passing out. He felt completely in tune with her as she rode him like never before. They were letting their bodies do all the talking.

Taija increased the pace even more as the friction of their two bodies melded together in the most intimate way caused her to let go and let the pleasure overtake her. She threw her head back and screamed through the onslaught of pleasure that flowed through her body as her released flowed through her. When her action brought Duron along with her on the ride of pleasure, they tumbled into paradise together.

Feeling her body go limp, Taija collapsed against Duron and stayed that way until the muscles in her body could work again. Lying on his chest, everything felt right and perfect to her. She wanted to scream out to him that she loved him, but she knew any talk of love might push him away even after being thoroughly satisfied. He still had a lot of trust issues and she knew how he felt about them getting any more serious than they were. She was ready, but could she convince him that her love for him was deep, honest and true? Could she convince him that he could trust her with his heart and trust her not to hurt him in any way? He may not admit it, but she sensed Duron was struggling with his feelings for her. He may want more, but didn't trust going in that direction again after the past that still haunted him.

Having relaxed their bodies and their minds, they settled in to watch a movie and the wine and strawberries she was able to scrounge up from the kitchen. Neither of them had spoken much after making love. Instead, they relaxed quietly together.

Duron looked over at Taija who was snuggled up against him and pretending to watch the movie. He hadn't paid attention to the movie either. He wanted to find a way to get them back to a place where he didn't have to lie to her about a work project being on his mind, distracting him when the issues he was dealing with was about their relationship. Something was changing between them, but he wanted things to remain the same. Maybe it was time for them to have some fun. He decided to approach her about an idea. He lowered the volume on the television and turned to her.

"Taija, I was thinking after the finishing touches are completed for my latest project at work, I would take a few weeks and take a trip to Paris and I want you to come with me. It's a place I've always wanted to visit and I'm going to need a vacation in between projects. It looks like we'll have another major one right after this one."

What brought that on, she thought. A trip abroad? She always loved the idea of going to Paris and she wouldn't mind a trip there sometime, but were they at the stage where they should take a trip for a few weeks together? Not only that, but she was still the new person on her team at work and taking a few weeks' vacation so soon would not go over well. If he was offering, maybe she should consider it.

"Paris sounds wonderful. I don't know about going for a couple of weeks though. I don't have that kind of time at work right now, but I'll see what I can work out. I'm actually planning to close on that house I told you about soon. I told you the realtor and I agreed the offer on the table was a good one. I think I'm going to take it. I was planning to take some time off to get settled in. I may be able to squeeze out some extra time for a trip," she said.

Duron remembered when she first moved back to Atlanta, she moved into a temporary house while at the same time, having a realtor looking for something more permanent. He had been surprised recently when she mentioned the realtor had found the perfect house for her. Since that deal wasn't sealed yet, perhaps it was a good lead-in for the next part of the conversation. He wasn't sure what it would mean, but he hoped it showed her he was loving being involved with her, but it wasn't a trip to permanency. He was having conflicting feelings about where they were going as a couple, but perhaps a little at a time would let her see that he was trying.

"Speaking of houses, what do you think of instead of buying that house you've been looking at, you move in with me, into my house?"

Taija sat up straight, not sure she'd heard him correctly. Did he ask her to move in with him?

"What?" she asked.

"I think it's logical. We spend all of our down time together either here at the condo, at my house or at your place. We're practically living together already spending every night together, so why not take the next step and do it."

Duron was concerned when Taija looked at him and then went to lay back down and turn her attention back to the television. This wasn't the response he was expecting. One thing he knew was that any of the other women he had been seeing before her would jump at the chance for the small olive branch he was offering in the form of a relationship. Lots of people moved in together and he'd like to go to bed and wake up to Taija every night. They were practically doing that already. When she didn't comment further, he reached over and turned her face toward his.

"Did you hear me what I said?" he asked.

Total shock is what Taija was experiencing. Over and over in her head all she heard was *move in together*. He was saying it as if there should be a simple answer and there wasn't, at least not for her. He was talking about moving in together and they had never talked about where they were with their feelings. She knew what hers were and if he was talking about moving in together, she wanted him to know where she stood.

"Duron, I love you."

If Taija thought shock was what she felt when Duron blurted out the idea of them moving in together, the look on his face when she declared her love for him was beyond shocking. She could contend that he had turned white as a ghost and that's quite a feat for an African American man. When he dropped his hand from her face, she knew she'd said the wrong thing, but honesty is what was needed.

"What?" Duron said.

"Yes, I said it, I love you. I see the disbelief and what looks like fear on your face and yet, I going to say it again. I love you. I have for some time now. I haven't been sure of how to bring it up to you because you're against ever falling in love again or having any type of serious relationship. I need you to know how I feel because you are asking me to make a major decision about moving in together and I don't even have an idea of where the relationship we currently have is going. I agree, we spend most of our down time together and I enjoy every minute of being with you. We have a great time whenever we are together, with whatever we are doing. I've met your family, something I understand you have not done since your last serious relationship. Now, you want to take a trip to Paris with me and you want us to live together. Both of those are major for two people who are casually kicking it. I need to know if we have any kind of real future beyond all of this. I know that what we started out with and agreed to was something casual, but even you have to admit that this is no longer just casual. We are taking big steps and making big plans that couples in committed relationships take."

Taija saw the puzzled look on Duron's face.

"I don't know what to say," Duron said.

Taija wasn't expecting much, but she expected more than him not knowing what to say. She was pouring out her heart and he was stunned.

"I know you still hold a part of yourself at bay, not wanting to be all in because of the past, but you have to let go of that. I am not your ex. I know what she did hurt you to your core, but that's not the case here. I'm not trying to pressure you into anything. That's far from what I'm saying and it's important that you get that. What I am saying is when I decide to live under the same roof as a man, as if we are husband and wife, that's exactly what I want to be - his wife. I'm not saying we're ready for that, but shacking up is not for me. I'm a believer that if a man finds me worthy enough or enough of a catch to want to live with me like husband and wife, then husband and wife is what we should be. I know it sounds old fashion, but it's me," she explained.

"Taija, I know where you're coming from and I understand what you're saying. I was hoping you felt the same way I did about our situation. We're moving in a direction and a good one, but I can't predict the future. I'm not ready to declare love yet, but that doesn't mean I don't care deeply for you because I do. I'm more involved with you than I thought I would ever be again with anyone. I like where things are with us. People live together all the time. That's a level of commitment in itself. I want to live in the right now and right now, I want you with me. I thought maybe you'd want that, too," he said.

"I'm not pressuring you into doing or saying anything you don't want to do or say. I'm telling you my thoughts when it comes to living together. No matter how much time we spend together or how many nights we spend in each other's arms and in each other's beds, it's not living together and I'm not the type of woman to provide a man with his cake and letting him eat it too while I sit, wait and wonder if when he's finished playing house, he'll decide he's done and can easily walk away."

"Walk away? Taija, I'm not going anywhere and I don't understand your objection to our moving in together. I need some time to get to where you are in this. My asking you to move in with me is a big step. I'm asking for you to be patient with me. I thought you would be as open to moving in together as I am. I didn't mean to bring down the evening with this."

Taija turned all the way around to face him.

"You didn't bring down the evening. I think we both see that, though we are enjoying this relationship, we are far from on the same page and that's fine. All relationships have ups and downs. I need you to think about what you really want. I mean really think about it. I'm not saying run out and buy a ring and propose and that's the only way we will be on the same page. I'm saying think about your feelings for me and my feelings for you and understand I'm not the moving in together type. I've never done that and I never will. I'm comfortable having my own space until I do get married one day."

No one said anything after that. It seemed as if neither had much to say and didn't know how to bring life back into the moment. She thought it may be a good time for them to have some space and think about the talk they'd just had.

"Listen, I think I'm going to go home," Taija said. "I

think we need a little breather to take in and understand where we're coming from," she added.

Taija stood up to go get dressed.

"Wait, you really want to leave? Are you upset because you've declared your love and I haven't? Is that why you're leaving? Come on, this is crazy and I get it, okay. You don't think it's the right time for us to move in together. Case closed, we move on, but you don't have to leave."

"I'm not leaving because you didn't say you love me or because instead of marriage you want to live together. I'm leaving because we both need a little space to think about where this relationship is going. Asking me to move in with you lets me know that you are serious about me and about this relationship. I've gone along with the casual covering over our relationship because those were the parameters you set for us, but I cannot suppress my feelings the way you can. I love you. I am in love with you! I want a man who can return that love on the same level and not play house in a way that makes him happy. There are two people in this relationship, Duron. Your feelings aren't the only ones that matter here. I can't make you love me and I don't want to. I want you to see that there is more going on here than a friend with benefits relationship and I need a little more from you, especially if you want me to move in with you. That's major and I'd be making a big sacrifice of what I want for myself. That's not fair to this relationship and it's not fair to me," Taija said.

When Duron didn't come back with a response, Taija turned and walked toward the bedroom. When she returned after a few minutes, Duron was standing at the door holding his keys.

"I really want you to stay and not leave here with this

space between us," Duron said. "If you insist on leaving, I will take you home, but this isn't the end of us. I don't want to lose you over what we talked about. I didn't mean to ruin the evening by bringing up something heavy."

"You didn't ruin the evening. I had a wonderful time, as I always do when we're together. I want to give us both some time to think and we can't do that in the same bed tonight. I don't want sex to cloud either of our judgment."

"Baby, I don't want you to leave like this."

"Duron, I'm fine. This isn't the end of us. I'm not that shallow or uncaring. I said I loved you and I meant it. I can't turn my feelings off and walk away from you. Space is just space, it's not an ending."

To reassure him, she leaned up and placed a soft kiss on his lips.

Duron smiled. "Okay, as long as I know we're still good."

He wasn't sure what had happened that turned the night around from where it started. He hoped it wouldn't impact what they had together. Unbeknownst to her, his heart was beating a mile a minute in his chest. Was he being selfish not thinking at all about how she feels in this relationship? Had he been so set on making things go his way to keep from getting hurt that he never thought to consider what not giving his one hundred percent to this relationship was doing to her? He needed to think.

17

Duron woke early Monday morning with Taija on his mind. He hadn't spoken to her since Saturday. He'd left several messages for her on Sunday, but she hadn't returned his calls. He didn't like how things had turned out Saturday evening with her. Spending this time with no contact with her made him miss her and couldn't imagine his life without her. The revelation that he was in love with her came to him in the middle of the night and he tossed and turned several hours before finally falling to sleep, anxious to start the next day by making amends for the terrible way he handled the events of Saturday.

He didn't accept the fact that he was in love with her because he didn't want to lose her, but taking the time to think about all that had transpired between the two of them since they met at the auction, deep down he knew she'd stolen his heart and he'd fallen helplessly in love with her. Now he knew that was the reason the comments from his brothers disturbed him. It wasn't because they were speaking an untruth, but because they hit his predicament right on the head, seeing right through his façade. He had fallen in love.

Thinking back on how his Saturday went with Taija, he had no one to blame but himself. He moved to slide out of bed, sitting on the edge with his head in his hands scolding himself for possibly ruining the best thing that has ever happened to him. Hearing Taija profess her love for him shocked him, but he should have expected it. He may be one to hold back his true feelings, but he shouldn't have expected her to do the same thing. He didn't know if she expected to hear them in return, but he couldn't do it. It wasn't because he didn't believe it or feel it, but because she did something no other woman had been able to do since Allison. Taija has broken through the barriers he'd placed around his heart and he wasn't prepared for it. He wondered if saying those three words really meant that much to a woman. He had said them before and it didn't get him the happy outcome he expected.

He looked up and the clock on his nightstand read six in the morning. Taija usually left for work around eight.

"I need to fix this," he said to himself. He couldn't let his stubbornness or the fear of giving the last bit of his heart over to a woman he knew he loved deeply keep him from having the kind of relationship he knew he wanted. He wanted Taija, not just in his bed, but in every aspect of his life. He needed her like he needed air and water. She was everything any man could want in a woman. She was his heart and he needed her to know how he truly felt and he needed to do it today. He had enough time to get a shower and stop by her house before she headed into the office.

~ ~

Taija couldn't believe it when her doorbell sounded early in the morning and on the other side of the door would be her ex-boyfriend, Keith. She was not happy when she looked through the peep hole and saw him standing there smiling as if it was the most natural thing in the world to be standing on the other side of her door. She opened the door and made sure she let him know that his presence was not welcomed.

"What are you doing here Keith and at this hour of the morning?" she asked, frustrated as he grinned from ear to ear.

"Are you going to let me in or are we going to stand in your doorway and talk?" he asked.

Taija hesitated, but she let him in. She didn't need her neighbors in her business. After he was inside, she shut the door and turned to him while he took a quick look around at what he could see from his vantage point in her entry way.

"Nice house," he said, casually.

Why was she the only one that thought his reappearance was strange?

"I'll ask again, what are you doing here Keith?"

"I came to town for a friend's wedding on Saturday and I wanted to see you before I headed back to Florida today. I figured you were still an early bird and I thought I would catch you before you started your day. I apologize for the early hour, but I need to get on the road soon and I needed to see you."

"I can't imagine why you need to see me. We have nothing to talk about," she said, trying to remain calm at his intrusion on her territory.

"You have been ignoring my calls and I thought since I was here, maybe if I could see you, we could finally have a conversation. I heard you were back in Atlanta and after all of my futile attempts to reach out to you, I thought this would be the perfect time to have a talk," he said.

"Talk about what? You must have brain damage if you think we have something to talk about. Rather than stand here in my house, you should probably see a specialist for that head injury you must have suffered. We have nothing to discuss," she said fiercely.

"Do you think I could get some coffee? I've been up most of the weekend and I still have a long drive ahead of me."

The nerve of him, Taija thought. She hadn't heard from him in years and here he is at her house like nothing had ever happened. He was right that she'd been ignoring his calls, not sure how he got her home phone number. Not many people had it. Maybe if she got him some coffee, he'd get on his way out of her house and out of her life.

"Sure, but then I need to finish getting ready for work," she said.

Taija headed into her kitchen to get his coffee. When she returned, he'd already made himself comfortable on her sofa.

"Don't get too comfortable, Keith. You won't be here long. Tell me why you're here," she said handing him the coffee cup.

"I still love you and I want to give our relationship another try."

That was blunt and to the point and useless, she thought. What was he talking about? Love? Relationship again? *Never.*

"You are crazy and out of your mind. Now, I know you need a head doctor. I know you did not come up in here talking about love and relationship like it's an easy conversation to have with me after what happened. I'm shocked you can say it with a straight face."

"Taija just hear me out," Keith pleaded.

"Hear what out? All I hear coming from your lips is

gibberish. We broke up a long time ago and you know why. There is no going back and we have nothing to talk about."

"I'm not trying to go back, I'm trying to move forward, hopefully with you. We didn't really break up, you left me. I had no decision in it," he said.

"I left you for a very good reason and you had a lot of decision in it. Your part of the decision was when you slipped, fell and your penis ended up inside yet another sports groupie or have you forgotten that part?" she asked.

Taija didn't think ignoring his phone calls and emails would result in him wanting to talk to her in person. A few days after her move back to Atlanta, she'd started getting phone calls from him. She had a feeling either her mother, who wanted them to get back together or some of the friends they had when they were a couple, who now lived in Atlanta, informed him of her recent move. She did wonder how he knew exactly where she lived. The culprit started to look more and more like her mother, though the internet could have given him her information.

She'd never told any of her friends why the relationship with Keith ended and they were always hoping that the two of them would reconcile. There may have been a time where she would have reconsidered and given him another chance, but that was her pre-Boston days and definitely pre-Duron. Duron was all she needed. He was her dream man. He was strong, but handled her with gentleness. She knew he loved her, but was reluctant to let love guide him. Even though they had a disagreement over the weekend, she was more than willing to give him the time he needed to see that she would never hurt him. She hoped by now he would see how much she truly loved him. She needed him to know that those were not just words to her.

The fact that Keith showed up out of the blue did nothing to lessen her feelings for Duron. Looking at Keith, she felt nothing, but anger that he sauntered to her house without a care in the world. Duron was the love of her life and Keith needed to be gone and stay gone. Seeing him sit in front of her and ask for another chance after the hell he'd put her through sleeping with woman after woman made her appreciate the man Duron was even more. Keith was the reminder she needed that she needed to be patient with Duron and let him get to where he needed to be in their relationship at his own pace.

Sometimes women looked at a man and saw strength and power and they never think to consider how betrayal could crush them. She'd gone through her own betrayal and she knew what it took for her to get over it. It is a known fact that women were the emotional ones and were known to have fragile feelings, but men were just as fragile when it came to matters of the heart. Their hearts bleed and their eyes shed tears when they are crushed by betrayal just as much as women. It didn't make them weak, it verified their humanity.

She loved Duron and nothing Keith could say or do would make her go back to a messy situation and give up on Duron. They may have some things to work out, but she had no doubt, that's what they would do.

If she had known Keith would take drastic measures when she didn't respond to his calls, she would have answered him when he first contacted her to let him know that getting back together would never be a possibility.

"Keith, I'm sorry you drove all the way here, but any conversation is fruitless. We are not getting back together. I'm not giving you another chance and let me state this one major fact so that we are clear, I have moved on. You may not believe that, but it's true. I'm involved with someone, a wonderful man named Duron and I'm very happy. The relationship we had was volatile and not healthy for either one of us. You were in the same relationship I was in and it was a bad one. Why now?" she asked.

Keith leaned back on her sofa like he was planning to stay a while.

"Taija, baby, listen. I have learned a lot while we were apart. I've had time to think about what I want in my life and it's you, baby. It's always been you."

Taija was floored by his admission.

"Wait, did you come to this realization before or after the groupies? Before or after the countless number of women screwed in the name of the signage '*they meant nothing to you*', you declared every time you were caught?"

"Taija, I have changed. I swear to you I have. I know you've kept up with the sports game since I know how big of a basketball fan you are. You have not heard or seen me in the gossip rags with anyone. No stories of late night or all-night parties, no wild parties at all, no long list of beauties always hanging on to me. I've changed and I've missed you. I miss the great times we had. You leaving me was the wake-up call I needed to get my act together. I've done that and now I'm ready to be the man you've always wanted me to be. I can understand that you may be seeing someone, but we were in love. I've learned that good women like you are hard to find. You know what my life was like as a rookie player. I admit there were times when I should have said no and realized what I had at home was enough, but I got caught up in the limelight. All I'm asking is that you take some time and think about the possibility of us. I know you are seeing someone, but I'm willing to wait and fight for us. You mean that much to me. *We* mean that much to me."

"We had some great times when we were involved Keith, yes, but there were so many bad times that they outweighed the good. I'm not that same person I was when I was involved with you. I put up with things and looked the other way many times because I was in love with you and I didn't want to give up on what we had. You took it for granted that I would be there no matter what and you never considered my feelings when you did the things you did. When enough was enough, I walked away and never looked back," she said.

"We were good together and I think we can be good together again," Keith said, not giving up.

"I hold no ill will toward you after all of this time, Keith. If I had not met someone that I love very deeply, who knows where a conversation like this would have taken us. I do believe you have changed and congratulations on finally knowing what it means to appreciate a good woman. I'm not the woman for you, though. Our time has come and gone. My life and my love belong to Duron now and I can't go back."

"I hear you Taija. I believe if you took the time to think on the great times, you would see that they could be great again without all the drama."

"Listen, I've said my peace, Keith. I'm not going to think on it. I am very happy now and I hope you find the same type of happiness. It's not going to be with me. I have to get ready for work before I'm late. I'm sorry you came all this way with hope of a sweet reunion, but please move on. Life is too short to look back," she said.

Keith knew he wasn't ready to give up yet. He needed to buy himself a little more time to convince her.

"Do you mind if I finish my coffee while you get ready for work. I can leave out when you leave, if you don't mind. I want to finish this before I get on the road and not try and drive and drink hot coffee," he said.

"Go ahead and finish your coffee. You'll need it for your long drive back home. I'll be back down in a moment to walk you out as I leave for work."

Taija turned around to head back upstairs to get showered and dressed.

Keith watched the woman he loved walked away from him again as if he were reliving that day from the past when she'd walked out on him before. He sat down, reached for his coffee and decided he was not going to give up on them. He had come too far to make changes in his life to become who he knew she wanted him to be.

He was thankful for her mother who believed he deserved a second chance with Taija. If her mother had not contacted him to let him know she was back in Atlanta, he would not be here practically begging. Seeing her today, even more beautiful than the day she walked out on him, he knew he had to get her back. He had never stopped loving her and given time, she would love him again. Besides, he was Keith Mathers. Women didn't say no to him. Dealing with these women who only saw dollar signs when they saw him and were willing to do any and everything to get him, he needed someone he knew loved him for who he was before all the money and the fame. Taija was that woman and he had always known that. He was not giving up. He would think of something before she came back down. He was not leaving Atlanta until she agreed to at least think about the possibility of giving them another try. It didn't matter that she claims to be involved with someone else. He was Keith Mathers and every woman wanted him. Somehow opportunity would come knocking and he'd have his edge.

18

Duron ran the conversation he wanted to have with Taija through his mind the entire twenty-five minutes it was taking him to drive to her house. He hoped that his macho attitude and his lack of giving her one hundred percent of him, didn't make her lose patience with him. *"I love you Taija."* Duron said it out loud to himself for the first time and it felt good. Those words flowed easily because he was all in with his mind, his body, his soul and especially with his heart. It belonged to her and only her. He couldn't wait to let her know. He wanted her to have all of him, unconditionally.

Finally pulling up to Taija's house, he was about to pull into the driveway when he noticed a Black Porsche Carrera GT sitting in the driveway behind her car. His first thought was, who would be at Taija's house this early in the morning. As he stepped out of his truck and walked around to the curb, he saw the Florida license plate tag. A ton of bricks fell to the pit of his stomach when he saw the personalized tag *MAVRICK*. He knew that name. It was the nickname of Florida NBA star, Keith Mathers, who he knew was Taija's ex-boyfriend. What the hell was he doing here?

Inside the house, Keith sipped his coffee and heard a car pull up out front. He knew Taija was in the shower and wondered who else would be showing up at her house this early in the morning. When he got up to see who had arrived, he saw a white Navigator park at the curb. He watched as a guy got out and came around to the curb, checking out his car. He recognized him immediately from the photo Taija had sitting on her fireplace mantle of her and the same guy he assumed she was currently seeing.

Keith watched as the guy checked out the car in the driveway that he didn't recognize. As the guy looked toward the house, Keith became jealous. This was the guy who was blocking his way to getting back into Taija's heart and life. Taija belonged to him and not this guy walking up to her house. He had to fight for her and find a way to force Taija to think about what they could become if she gave him another chance. He had to think quickly.

The devil sitting on his shoulder whispered a conniving plan to him and before he gave it a second thought, he went with it. He was nothing if he wasn't resourceful. He listened first and could hear Taija's shower still running, so he went into action.

He saw his plan playing out and knew how men thought. He had to make this Duron character disappear and what better way than to add a little doubt in his mind. No man could stand the thought of his woman cheating on him.

Keith knew how angry Taija would be with what he was planning to do. Desperate times, however, led to desperate measures and he was fighting for the woman he loved. No woman had ever left him other than Taija and now that he's seen her again, he wanted her back. In time, she would see that they were meant to be together and forgive him. She always had in the past. She just needed a little help seeing things his way. He knew she would never give it any thought as long as this guy was around. He saw how she lit up when she mentioned his name and he didn't like it.

Acting quickly, he removed his shirt, his shoes and his socks. To add a little more affect, he unbuckled his belt to let it hang out to give the impression he was getting dressed or perhaps undressed. Either way, it was time for her early morning visitor to make his exit. Hearing the doorbell, Keith waited a few seconds, making sure Taija didn't hear it. When he heard nothing from upstairs, he opened the door.

"Where's Taija?" Duron asked without offering any kind of greeting. He was fuming and that was all that he could say when the door opened, though what he really wanted to do was knock this fool out. Standing before him in a pair of jeans was Taija's ex, looking like he had just gotten out of bed.

Keith didn't respond, but gave Duron a look like he was in her house where he was supposed to be. It was time to play dirty.

"She's taking a shower at the moment, getting ready for work. We overslept and she's running a little late. I was just about to finish dressing myself. I didn't realize she was expecting someone this early in the morning. Would you like to come in and wait?" Keith asked.

Keith knew he wouldn't. This guy was busy trying to read what he was seeing. For added measure, he reached down to fix his belt, knowing he was sealing the fate of the relationship Taija was having with this guy and being Keith Mathers, he didn't feel bad at all. He was Keith Mathers and no one got his woman except himself. Taija was his. This scheme was a man thing and he was on a mission.

Duron wanted to kill Keith standing in Taija's house like he owned the place. Rather than cause a scene, which he knew he was about to do, he knew this was not the situation for him where he could lose control and end up in jail, so he chose to leave. Fighting was for kids.

"Just tell her Duron stopped by, but no need for her to call me," he said. Duron turned around, strolled back to his truck, got in and without looking back, he sped away. His last thought before he turned off of her street was that he'd gotten played again.

~ ~

Duron drove not thinking of his destination. He needed to calm down. All he could think of was Taija's betrayal. He thought they were having a great relationship and now he knew why he hadn't heard from her since Saturday and why she had ignored his messages. She failed to tell him Keith was back in her life. She knew how he felt about trust and honesty and how they were most important to him. Two nights ago, she had declared her love for him. He'd actually felt bad about not telling her then what was in his heart and declaring his love for her.

Driving faster than he should be, he needed to pull over and walk off this anger before he had an accident. Seeing a mall parking lot ahead, he pulled in, parked and sat in disbelief at what happened. He had been on his way over to her house finally ready to tell her how much he loved her and wanted to be her all. He was ready to receive all she was ready to give him.

He thought back to the conversation from Saturday. It was a bump in the road, but not an ending. It was after midnight when he'd dropped her home and after checking the inside of her house to be sure it was safe, he left without saying much. There seemed to be a lot of tension between them and he needed some time to think as Taija suggested. He knew that she was still upset with him over his being on guard that she was going to hurt him like his ex-girlfriend had done. Taija had assured him that she was nothing like her and he had believed her. He was finally having the kind of relationship he thought he'd never have again. He had finally found the woman who could fulfill all of his hopes, dreams and desires. Had he been blind to yet another woman's deceit?

Anger beyond anything he had experienced before surfaced and the rage he felt was uncontrollable. He wanted to break something. Had Taija been that upset by his lack of love declaration to her that she would sleep with her ex so soon? Had something been going on between Taija and Keith all along? When did he get in town? He lived in Florida. This was no coincidence. Maybe she was seeing him all along and just stringing Duron along. Apparently, she was no better than the last woman he had been in love with. He was right all along, that women were about nothing. His mother was wrong when she said not all women were like Allison. Taija just proved to him that they were.

Women were playing games men owned the playbook to for centuries. They were just as good at scheming as men were. It sickened him to think of all the times they'd spent together and how it all must have been a lie. He'd been investing a lot into his relationship with Taija. Thinking of her one way and finding out she was a liar and a manipulator crushed any hope he had that when a woman found what she wanted in a relationship, it would be enough to sustain her. He knew they had some small hurdles to cross, but nothing that would lead her to do this to him.

When he woke up this morning, he'd hoped that with her, he'd found the kind of love his parents had been experiencing for the past forty years.

He was furious and he was done. No more giving relationships a try if this is where he was always going to end up. Here he was a brother who was committed, faithful, honest, trustworthy, hardworking and respectful, yet it wasn't enough. *What do these women really want?*

Calming his frazzled nerves, he started his truck back up and headed to the office. Rather than work for the day, he was going to work off the stress in the gym two floors below his office to beat out his frustration on the equipment. Working out always helped him focus and right now, he needed to focus on forgetting about the latest woman who crushed his heart.

~~

Taija came down, fully dressed and ready to head to work. Keith was up, standing near the door, ready to leave, too.

"You look beautiful, Taija. I don't want to continue to pressure you like I did earlier, but I do want you to think about us. Really think about what we could have. I'm a changed man and I still love you with all my heart," Keith said.

Keith wiped from his mind the events of earlier with Taija's soon to be ex-boyfriend and turned his thoughts to getting her back, finally getting what he wanted. He was Keith Mathers. He always got what he wanted.

Grabbing her keys, Taija opened the door, making room for Keith to exit ahead of her.

"Keith, I am in love with Duron. He makes me happy

and I need you to be happy for me. I need you to understand that what we had is in the past and we need to leave it there. We have a lot of mutual friends and I don't want things to be awkward, so can we be friends, declare that the past is the past move on to live our lives? I want you to find the kind of love I have found. Someday you will see that this, you and I, really isn't meant to be. Be safe heading back to Florida and good luck next season," she said.

Keith didn't want to drag this out. He knew when her world soon crumbled around her, she would be vulnerable enough for him to make his move then. He would wait for the relationship with Duron to end, which he was quite sure was already over. He kissed Taija on the cheek then headed to his car, but not before he had the last word.

"Just know that I love you, Taija. I always have and I always will. I would do anything and I mean anything to get you back. I'm not looking to replace my love for you with loving another woman. There is no one for me but you. I will respect your space. If you change your mind and want to give us another chance or to even talk about what we could have, call me anytime."

Keith got in his car, backed out of the driveway and headed back to Florida to wait.

19

Taija tried calling Duron all day. She didn't understand why he wasn't returning any of her calls. She'd found out from his secretary that he'd taken the day off and was unreachable through the office until Tuesday morning.

She'd also tried his cell and his home phones and had not received a return call as of yet. She'd received a few voice mail messages from him on Sunday, but she needed that day to work things out in her mind. This was unlike him to just ignore her. He couldn't still be upset about the other night, could he? She decided to put it out of her mind and try to catch up with him after work. Maybe she would cook a nice meal and invite him over to talk tonight. Surely, they could get beyond this small glitch in the relationship.

She wanted and needed more from him if they were going to take a step forward in a serious relationship. She would love to be under the same roof as him day in and day out, but she didn't want to play house without knowing that the end result would be a happy one for them both. Nothing was guaranteed, but she couldn't allow him to continue to play safe. If he wanted something, it was time for him to put all of his cards on the table and let go of what's keeping him from giving his all to her.

~~

Duron spent the day not wanting to deal with the messages

and texts from Taija. She was talking as if everything was normal, as if he did not walk in on her and her ex after they'd spent the night together. This just goes to show how deceitful women can be. After what he witnessed, he was sure she could win the Oscar for best actress. What kind of woman sleeps with her ex and in the next breath calls her boyfriend as if nothing had changed. Apparently, Keith didn't tell her he stopped by. That meant, she didn't know that he knew what she had done. How long would she play this game with him? He was not a game player, like the ex she claimed devastated her with his infidelity. Maybe their dictionaries didn't define cheating the same way. He needed some breathing space.

He needed to work away from the office. He couldn't think of a better place to do that than at his family's cabin on Lake Allatoona in Northern Georgia. Placing a call to the office, he left a message for his secretary to forward all of his calls to his cell for the rest of the week and that he would be working from a remote location for a few days.

Calling Tyrone, he told him about Taija's betrayal and was shocked when Tyrone told him that Taija must have an explanation for what he saw. He could not believe that the Taija he had come to know, who he knew without a doubt was all about Duron and their relationship, could do something like that.

"D, what did she say when you asked her what that was about? You know, that mess with Keith," Tyrone asked.

"I haven't talked to her."

"Why not? You have to give her a chance to explain, man," Tyrone said.

"Explain what? Explain why he was in her house looking as if answering the door got him out of bed? Or how she was in the shower while her almost naked ex was answering her door. Tell me how many explanations can you think of that would make everything alright from this point forward?" Duron said.

"Man, all I'm saying is I never thought I would see you as happy as you have been since you met her. That can't be all fake on her end. Take the time and talk to her to find out what happened. Even if this situation can't be fixed, you will never get beyond it if you don't know the whole story."

Tyrone was right, but he was too angry to talk to her right now. He couldn't think of facing or talking to Taija until he'd gotten his anger under control.

"I'll think about it. For now, I'll be at the cabin for the rest of the week working on some final plan changes. I need to focus right now so that we stay on schedule. We have a lot more to do since all of the new requested changes have come in. I should be able to have this knocked out by Friday. Let's plan to get everyone back around the table sometime late next week," Duron said.

"Not a problem. We'll hold things down here, but think about what I said. It may not have been what you thought you walked in on. Talking has not always been your strong suit, but do it, D. Don't give up on this too soon. Even though you haven't said it, I know you're in love with her. I was already picking out my tux for your wedding," Tyrone quipped.

Duron didn't respond. Now wasn't the time, he thought.

"Make sure everyone knows how to reach me," Duron said.

"I'll give you a call if anything comes up that needs your immediate attention here at the office," Tyrone said.

"Thanks, Ty. I'll be in touch."

Duron hung up and knew Tyrone that was right, but his pride wouldn't allow him to pick up the phone and deal with this head on. All he could go by right now is what it looked like to him. That was enough for him to deduce that another woman had proven to him that women could not be trusted. Maybe after a week at the cabin, his thinking would be clearer.

Before heading home to pack for some time away, Duron drove to his parent's house to let them know he would be at the cabin for the week working in case they needed him for anything. As he reached the door, he could smell the aroma of his mother baking, her favorite thing to do. The smell of freshly baked cookies met him at the door. Jake's kids must be over for a visit. Whenever his mother baked during the week, it was because his niece and nephew were in the house.

"Anyone home?" he called out.

"In the kitchen, Duron," his mother hollered back.

After announcing his arrival, Duron heard the sound of two pair of little feet making a beeline for him. Bounding around the corner with the speed of light were his niece Lyric and his nephew Milo, with Milo leading the way. Duron knew he had only a split second to brace himself before they threw themselves into his arms. He hunched down to scoop them up as they giggled and wrapped their arms around his neck, almost choking him.

"Hi, Unca D," Lyric said first. He hugged them tightly, giving them each a kiss on the cheek. His niece returned the cheek kiss, blowing raspberries on him as she often did.

"Hey, baby girl. How are you two doing?"

Duron looked back and forth between the two of them.

"We are being good," they replied together.

They were the light of his world. He hoped to one day have children of his own if he could ever get a clue on this relationship stuff.

"Being good huh?" he asked.

They shook their heads vigorously, with his niece shaking her head so hard, her two thick, long black pony tails with pink ribbons on them bounced up and down with her head.

"Well that's good to know. I'm sure grandma is happy to see you and even happier when you're being very good."

"Grandma said if we were very good, we could have cookies. We helped bake them," Lyric said.

"They must be very good then," Duron said, smiling. Even when he was having the worst of days, his Lyric and Milo could make him smile.

"Cookies are ready," his mother stated as she came around the corner from the kitchen. Both kids scrambled to get out of his arms and head for the kitchen.

"Wash your hands first," she told the two fireballs flying by her to get to the cookies.

"Hey, mom," Duron said. He tried his best to keep his somber mood from her.

"How is my favorite son?"

"Oh, today I'm your favorite?" he joked.

When she laughed, Duron smiled because he loved to hear her laugh.

"Sure you are. My favorite is whomever I'm talking to at the time and right now, that's you," she replied.

"Let's head into the kitchen to see how many cookies are already missing while you tell me why you're visiting on a Monday, not that I'm complaining. You never leave the office before nine or ten o'clock at night and yet it's early afternoon and here you are."

Duron took a seat at the island and looked over at Lyric and Milo who were seated at their kiddie table, both with a cookie in each hand. He grabbed a cookie from the plate in the center of the island and wondered how much to share with his mother about what happened with Taija.

"Where's pop, still at the hospital?" he asked, buying himself some time.

"Yes, he called a few minutes ago and said he was heading home. He had a meeting that was running late. When I told him Jake had brought the children by because he had a last-minute surgery and Kim was showing a house later than usual today, he said he was leaving now so that he could spend some time with the kids before they went home," Barbara said.

Duron admired his brother's life. He and his wife had the kind of life Duron looked forward to having one day. Now that the kids were getting older, Duron was thinking of making plans to have them spend a weekend with him. He had done overnighters before, giving Jake and Kim a much-needed night out, but they would drop them off around bed time and picked them up first thing the next morning. He knew they loved animals and wanted to take them to the zoo, a big tourist attraction in Atlanta.

"That's good," he said.

"Back to my question. A visit on a Monday during the day? You didn't work today?"

"No, I took the day off. I have a lot on my mind that I needed to sort out. In fact, I'm going to the cabin today to work for the rest of the week. I have a lot to catch up on and that's always a good place to get it done," he said.

When his mother didn't comment, Duron looked up from eating his third cookie to see her looking at him with concern covering her face.

"What's wrong Duron? You only go to the cabin alone when something is really wrong. The last time was your split with Allison. Is everything going okay with Taija? I really enjoyed having her over this past weekend. She's a lovely young lady," she said.

Duron looked over at his niece and nephew to see if they were focused on watching the old episode of Barney, to see if he should get into this with his mother right now.

Looking back at her and seeing the worry in her eyes, he knew he had to say something.

"I don't think things are going to work out with Taija, mom."

He saw the look of surprise on her face.

"What happened? You were just here on Saturday and you could not have been happier. Taija was simply glowing. Loren told me every time she sees you two together, you seem like the perfect couple."

"I thought so, too, but apparently she had other ideas. I won't go into details, but let's just say that women today are not like you, mom. I would love to find a woman who is as devoted to me and to love and relationships as you are to dad. It's hard to grow up in a home with all this love, trust and understanding and not want to find the same thing for myself. I will be the first to admit, I have had my share of dating lots of women, but they always knew the deal. Those were not serious situations. They always knew forever was not an option and that was a mutual understanding. Having a serious relationship is hard enough for me, but when trust is broken, it's hard to not want to be that selfish, self-serving person that I have been since my last relationship. Taija broke that trust and I'm sure it's not fixable. We never defined what we had as a relationship, but I know for a fact she knew that trust and honor were important to me," he said.

"Most things are fixable son, if you communicate. Have you talked this out with Taija? Are you both in agreement that there is no way things can work out?" she asked.

His mother was saying the same thing Tyrone had said.

"I haven't spoken to her about it," Duron admitted.

Barbara sat down across from him and settled in to soothe what she saw as her baby boy in pain. Duron was the son who always carried his heart on his sleeve. Once he was hurt in a previous relationship, he started staying away from serious, loving relationships and started having one-night stand relationships with women. She had heard all about her playboy son. She didn't want to see him go back to that. She wanted him to find true love. She wanted it for him because she knew it's what he wanted deep down for himself.

"Duron, how could you decide that this situation can't be fixed if you don't sit down and talk to Taija about whatever it was that brought you to this place in your relationship? Going to the cabin to be in solitude for a week is not going to help you. You will spend a week wallowing in self-pity and that doesn't lead to anything good."

Duron was taking in all that his mother was saying. He knew she meant well, but knowing the kind of lifetime love she shared with his father, she couldn't understand.

"She cheated on me, mom," he finally said.

Duron looked at her with pain in his eyes. A type of pain he would only let his mother see.

"Oh, son, I'm sorry. Are you sure?"

"After all she and I shared, she cheats on me. I stopped by her house this morning before work. We'd had a small argument the night of the cookout. This morning I wanted to clear the air. I was going to tell her how much I really loved her. I'd become so guarded over the years and I didn't want to lose her because I couldn't give her all of me when I knew that's exactly what I wanted to do. I got there and her ex answers the door. Let's just say, I have learned my lesson when it comes to unannounced visits," he said.

"I'm sorry, son. I'm really sorry, but you still need to talk to her. I know what it looked like, but things are not always what they seem. I can't believe what you are telling me without there being something else to this. This does not sound like the Taija I met the other night or the one that Loren speaks so highly of. I can't believe she would do anything to dishonor your relationship. Unless you know the entire story, you won't know if it's something that can be fixed. This may simply be a misunderstanding."

Though he knew deep down his mother was correct, he could not get the image out of his head of Keith Mathers standing in her doorway in his pants, opened as if he'd hurriedly put them on. That's the image he couldn't get off of his mind or the image of another man touching, caressing or kissing Taija. He was burning inside with rage at the idea.

"I hear you, mom, but I can't right now. I have that work project I told you all about that I need to complete on time. There is still a lot of work to do and I need to focus, so I'll be at the cabin. I can't deal with talking to her right now. She's been leaving me messages and texts all day as if nothing is out of the ordinary. What kind of woman does that?" he asked.

Duron exhaled when his mother reached out and held his hands in hers as she spoke.

"Son, you'll figure this out, but only after you talk to Taija. Do that and if things don't work out, you move on, but what you don't do is think that all women are scheming and conniving. You were meant to love and meant to be loved. Don't give up hope, okay?" she asked.

Duron smiled. "I won't – I promise," he replied.

"Good. Now, are you excited about your father's hospital benefit dinner next month?"

As the hospital administrator, the benefit his father chaired each year was huge for the city of Atlanta. This event would allow the hospital to continue to operate its free clinic for those who couldn't afford to pay the high cost of health care. He looked forward to helping his father in whatever way he needed. His thoughts jumped to Taija who he had invited to come as his date, prior to the events of the morning. Now, it looks like he'll be flying solo.

"Yes, I am excited and I wouldn't miss it. Dad does excellent work at the hospital for this clinic and my company is prepared to make another big donation this year like we did last year."

"Have I told you recently how proud I am of you? I always knew all of my children would be successful. Any mother would be proud of a son like you."

"Thanks, Mom. Your love and support mean everything to me. Tell Pop I said hey and I'll give you guys a call sometime tomorrow."

Turning to Lyric and Milo who were engrossed in cartoons, he smiled. "See you two munchkins later. Unca D has to head out. Keep on being good okay?" he said.

Lyric spoke up first, as usual. "We will Unca D." Milo was more of the silent type and waved as Duron expected.

"I guess cartoons have more of an appeal than I do. Love you, mom."

Duron left knowing his mother meant well, but as far as he was concerned, things were over between them.

~~

Eight o'clock in the evening and Taija was concerned when she hadn't heard back from Duron. The disagreement they had could not have been this bad. They'd both had time alone for cooling off and she hoped everything was okay. Maybe Loren could shed some light on where Duron was. She grabbed her cell phone to call her.

"Hey Taija. What's up girl? How's my brother treating you?" Loren asked her as soon as she answered.

Taija assumed nothing was wrong with Duron because Loren was her same, cheerful self.

"Everything is good and your brother is incredible. He's a gentleman's gentleman. I've been trying to reach him all day long. He didn't go into the office today and I've been leaving him messages and he hasn't called me back. I thought I would check with you to be sure he's okay. Have you heard from him?" Taija asked.

"I did speak with him earlier today. He sounded a little preoccupied, but he didn't say anything was wrong. I know he's in the middle of something big at work and I figured the preoccupation I heard was because he has a lot going on. I'm sure everything is good. While I have you on the phone, did you want to go together to pick out dresses for the hospital benefit dinner that's taking place next month? Duron told me last week that he asked you to go with him. This dinner at three hundred dollars a plate plus the huge donations given are a big accomplishment for my dad and the hospital. I'm looking forward to it," Loren said.

If Loren said everything seemed okay with Duron, then what, Taija thought, would make him not take a few moments to return her phone calls. The nagging feeling that something was wrong would not go away.

"Sure, I can do that. Let me know what day you want to go and I'll free up my schedule. I could use a day of shopping with my busy life. Listen Loren, I'm going to try reaching your brother again, so I'll talk to you later. Either call or email me with the day and time and where you want me to meet you for shopping," Taija said.

"Will do. Talk to you later," Loren said before hanging up.

As Taija disconnected the call, she sent another text to Duron's phone hoping that if work really was keeping him busy, he would at least call her before the end of the night. She settled in and waited.

20

"Duron, what's going on, bro?" Mike asked when he was finally able to reach Duron by phone.

"Nothing, just finishing up on some work plans and getting in a little fishing. Anything I need to know about as far as work at the office?" Duron asked.

"Don't ask me about work when you're hiding away at the cabin avoiding Taija. Tyrone brought me up to date with your predicament and I agree with him, talk to her. She's an incredible woman. You know I was the first to make fun of you meeting a woman at the bachelor auction, but I've come to know her and I know that she makes you happy. Like Ty said, there has got to be an explanation for what you saw and you won't be able to get to the bottom of it if you don't talk to her," Mike said.

"I can't deal with her right now, Mike. I know what I saw and there can be no justification for her ex being in her house at six in the morning half dressed. What would you think?" he asked.

"I hear what you're saying and I can only image what you saw, but to not give her the chance to explain is wrong. You're going on the premise of what you saw is exactly what it was and maybe it wasn't. You'll never know if you don't ask her. I go out of town for a few days and come back to the best relationship you've ever had being over and done with."

"For now, I'm focusing on work and I'll focus on Taija after I get back. It's Wednesday and I've only been here two days. I'll be back later this week with the work complete and maybe my anger will have tampered down by then and I can confront her. I don't want to do it on the phone and I can't face her right now."

"Alright, bro. I hear you and I'll let it go. I'll check with you when you get back and if anything else comes up before then, I'll give you a call."

"Sounds like a plan," Duron said before disconnecting the line.

He wasn't understanding why everyone in his circle started off defending Taija even after he told them what occurred. She wasn't who they thought she was, especially now that he knew she wasn't who he thought she was either.

He decided to put work on the side for the moment and get in a little extra fishing. The cabin was his place to get away from everything. It was right on the lake where he loved to go out on the pier and fish or sit and think. The lake was a quiet place where neighbors respected each other's desires to be left alone.

There were times as a child that his family came up to the cabin to regroup and focus on each other. It was times like those that caused he and his siblings to be as close as they are. When they came to the cabin there weren't friends to take them away from each other; all they had was each other. They played board games, swam, fished and one of his mother's favorite things, they cooked as a family. The cabin meant a lot to him and if there was one place where he could go to think, this was it. Now, all he had to do was figure out how to deal with Taija. He cared about her, he loved her and he was once again about to make a big revelation to another woman only to be let down yet again. This couldn't be how life was to play out for him. Allison was one thing, but Taija was a different kind of woman. He was older and had learned from past mistakes and thought he'd reached a different plateau with Taija. What did he miss?

Grabbing his fishing pole and his tackle box, he walked to the pier to spend the rest of his day catching fish that he could cook and enjoy eating by the fireplace while reflecting on how he'll react when he and Taija finally do have the talk.

~~

By Wednesday afternoon, Taija was losing patience with waiting. What was wrong with Duron? Her heart was breaking knowing that whatever was going on with him, he wouldn't call and talk to her about it. Did he assume because she chose to go home Saturday night and not stay at his place or talk anymore about their relationship, that the relationship was over? Was he doing to her what she'd done to him when she didn't return his calls on Sunday? She assumed they would both take that day to figure out what was next for them. What she didn't expect was total silence from him for the next four days.

Her phone rang, invading her thoughts. She hoped it was Duron, but it wasn't him; it was her mother.

"Hey, Ma," she said smiling. They hadn't talked in a few days.

"Taija. I haven't heard from you in a couple of days. I thought I would check on you. How are things going in Atlanta?"

"Things are going great. Work has me on overdrive most days, but I'm hanging in there. "How are things with you, Ma?" she asked.

"I'm good and I miss you. I was thinking of coming to Atlanta for a visit soon to check out your new digs."

Did her mom just say digs?

She was excited at the thought of her mother coming to visit and having her to herself for a few days.

"That would be wonderful. When are you thinking about coming so that I can take a few days off and show you around? I don't think you've been here since my college graduation."

"No, I haven't, so it's time I paid you a visit since you are closer now than you were when you lived in Boston. How is that new man you're seeing? Is everything still blissful with Duron?"

She didn't want to tell her mother that she had not heard from him in a few days, not sure of what was going on. Instead, she decided to keep it positive.

"He's fine and yes, everything is all blissful," she said.

"I won't keep you long. I just wanted to check in on you and see if you were up for a visit. I will check my work schedule tomorrow and call you this weekend to let you know my plans. 'll talk to you probably Saturday sometime. Love you."

"Love you too, mom."

She wanted to ask her mother about Keith, but decided it was best to not bring up his little visit. After she got to the office after he left her house, she knew that the only person who could have told him about her returning to Atlanta and where she lived was her mother. She didn't know why her mother would do such a thing, but she wasn't in the mood for a fight with her mother about it.

When she split with Keith after his constant infidelity, her mother was still on the Keith train begging her to give him another chance. Her mother had that mentality that boys will be boys, but that she was the woman he loved. Cheating wasn't love and there weren't enough dollar signs in the world to make her forgive a man who mistreats her. She wasn't a doormat nor would she ever be one. Keith showing up out of the blue still bothered her. She would get to the bottom of how he knew she was back in Atlanta. She hoped he had gotten the point and wouldn't contact her again.

Her mind was still focused on Duron and if what they had was now over because she pushed him too far. She hoped not, but she couldn't make a man move in a direction he wasn't ready for. She had high hopes that he was as ready for her as she was for him. Only time will tell if she's ever able to reach him.

~ ~

Duron had been at the cabin for four days and didn't feel any better than he did when he arrived. Getting a lot of work done, he was able to complete the redesigns in record time helping him stay ahead of schedule. Finishing work early, he'd spent the afternoon on the lake. After catching plenty of fish, he was set to head back to the cabin when he turned and noticed a car pulling up. He stopped moving when he recognized who the car belonged to.

As he made his way up the pier, standing on the bottom step that led up to the cabin was Taija. He wondered which member of his family told her where he was. He guessed it didn't really matter at this point because she was here and he had no choice but to deal.

Approaching her with reservation, it didn't escape him how beautiful Taija was even though he was fiercely angry and disappointed in her. She never ceased to take his breath away. He could see why any man would want her. She must have come up to the cabin straight from work because she was in her work clothes. She looked sexy and his traitorous body hardened, reacting to her presence, reminding him how much he missed her. Before he got too caught up in his body's reaction, he remembered why he was furious at her.

As he reached her neither of them said a word. They simply stared at each other until Taija broke the silence.

"Hi, Duron," she said. She waited for a hi back, but none came. What she did get was a scowl on Duron's face that startled her. He wasn't happy to see her making the entire situation between them more of a mystery.

"What are you doing here Taija?" Duron said glumly.

He was trying to act preoccupied with his fishing pole so that he didn't have to make eye contact.

"What's wrong with you?" Taija asked after getting a miserable greeting.

"How did you find out I was here?" he asked. Duron kept an easy monotone to his voice. He wouldn't be swayed by her beauty.

"I came to talk to you. Your sister told me where you were. Is this the greeting I get after you have ignored me for days? I've called, texted, left voice messages and you haven't responded to any of those. What's going on here? One minute we are all over each other and the next, we have a small disagreement and you take off. Something that small pushed you away from me?" she asked.

Taija tried hard to capture Duron's face to make eye

contact and she became frustrated when he looked in every direction except at her.

Still reeling from her betrayal, Duron was becoming angrier the more she spoke. How dare she push the blame over on him after what she had done? He then looked at her and all he could see was Keith touching her and his skin felt like it was on fire.

"Pushed you away? I pushed you away?" he asked. He raised his voice, something he hardly ever did. This was a trying circumstance.

"What else am I supposed to think when you won't talk to me!" Taija exclaimed.

"All I can think right now is that you are not the woman I thought you were. I thought things were almost perfect between us. Since nothing is perfect I figured that was good enough for now. I guess that wasn't good enough for you, huh?" he asked.

Duron moved to go around her and up the stairs into the cabin.

Taija, stumped by his response had no idea what he was talking about.

"Wait a minute. That's it? I'm confused here. If there is something that I'm missing, maybe you can clue me in so that we are both on the same page. You seem to have one up on me. We had a small disagreement Saturday evening. You didn't seem this upset when I decided to go home that night. You seemed to understand that we needed a little space. Are you this angry because I didn't call you Sunday or is something else bothering you? It would be nice if we both knew what that was? I drove all the way out here to talk to you and you're more distant than ever."

She didn't know what to do or say. Duron's fierce anger

was coming from left field. His mood was more than the small discussion they had on Saturday. Something else was going on. The more they talked, the angrier he appeared to be. She had never seen him upset with her. He had a blank, non-caring look on his face, something he never displayed to her. She needed to get to the bottom of what was on his mind. For some odd reason, he was pissed and she had no idea why.

Duron wondered how long she was going to continue with this star actress role she was playing. Since she was here, at the cabin, maybe it was time to clear the air and then send her on her way back home after finding out he knew all about her and whatever was going on with Keith. He hated even thinking the guy's name.

"Why didn't you tell me you were back to seeing your ex, Taija?" he asked. He waited when no response came from her. There was nothing, but silence.

"What?" Taija was more confused than ever now. His anger wasn't about the argument on Saturday? She looked at him questionably. He needed to give her more than that.

"Why didn't you just tell me you were involved with Keith Mathers again? Can you imagine what I felt like when I realized you've been playing me?" Duron asked, more furious than ever.

The stunned look on Taija's face wouldn't deter him. She almost looked like she had no clue what he was talking about or was it the look of a woman who'd been caught?

"What are you talking about? I am not involved with Keith. Why would you think that?"

Now denial? He was done playing.

"Go home, Taija. It'll be dark soon and I don't want you finding your way out of these mountains after dark. If you're going to play dumb and insult my intelligence, we have nothing to talk about. I don't want to play games with you," he said calmly.

"What does Keith have to do with anything? I don't understand, Duron," she pleaded.

He looked right into her eyes and said again, "Go home."

Taija was shocked. What could make him think that she was involved with Keith. Nothing was further from the truth than that.

"Duron, I will say it again. I am not involved with Keith. Where did you get this come from because I don't understand? This doesn't have anything to do with our discussion Saturday night? This is about Keith?" she asked.

Feeling himself getting angrier, Duron came closer to her until he was only inches away from her.

"Since you're obviously going to make me spell it out for you, well here it goes. I saw him shirtless in your house, Taija. Do you deny that Keith was at your house Monday morning?" he asked.

Realization finally hit her. Monday morning's surprise visit from Keith. When had Duron encountered him?

"Wait a minute. Yes, Keith was at my house Monday morning, but he was not shirtless. He..."

Duron didn't let her finish as he put his hand up to stop the conversation. Rehashing seeing Keith in her home in the state of undress in which he saw him isn't something he wanted to do.

"I'm going to say this and then I'm done. I could not sleep after I got back home Saturday evening. I thought about our relationship for the rest of the weekend. I woke early Monday morning and realized it was time I stop having this guard up around my heart because I didn't want to lose you. I didn't want to continue to make you suffer for the pain another relationship had caused me by not being willing to commit to giving us a real shot at a loving relationship. You meant too much to me."

Taija heard the word 'meant', meaning past tense and her heart ached.

"Meant to you?" she asked.

"I came by your house hoping to catch you before work to lay it all out on the line. Imagine my shock when I pulled up to your house and saw his car. Then to see him answer the door in no shoes, no socks or shirt, pants unbuttoned looking like he just rolled out of bed to answer the door at that hour of the morning, I felt betrayed. He gloated like he knew who I was when he told me you were in the shower. How long has that been going on Taija? How long have you been seeing Keith behind my back? I wasn't enough for you or were you just passing the time with me until playboy Keith got his act together? I know we hadn't defined what we had as monogamous, but I assumed that's what it was."

Duron's words were coming out of his mouth as if he were spitting out nails and she felt every dagger.

She couldn't speak. No words would come in response to his accusation. She realized what this was all about. Duron had come to her house the other morning and had somehow run into Keith. Why would he say Keith was without a shirt or shoes and looking like he'd just woken up? That never happened. Duron was furious and he was wrong.

"Wait. There is a huge misunderstanding going on here. You've got this all wrong. I haven't been seeing Keith and he was not undressed in my house," she said.

Before she could finish, he cut her off.

"So, this is a misunderstanding? On whose end because from where I stood, everything was crystal clear. That fool told me you were in the shower and that you both had gotten up late which was why he was standing in your door undressed and fastening up his pants. I really hope it was good and worth the ending of what we had together," Duron said through clinched teeth.

Realizing now what was going through his mind, she needed to explain because none of this was making any sense.

"Duron, for starters, calm down. It's not what you think at all. I can't explain to you what Keith did or did not have on. When I went to take my shower, he was completely dressed."

She saw his anger boil over when she mentioned him being in her house while she was in the shower. She saw him about to fire off more accusations.

"This isn't helping!" he said loudly.

"Wait before you continue," she said. "You are mistaken about this entire situation. Let me start from the beginning so that I can show you that whatever you are thinking happened, didn't happen at all," she pleaded.

"Oh, you're thinking for both of us now? I know what I saw and you just admitted he was there," he said angrily.

If there was ever a time to diffuse a situation, this was it if they were going to talk this out.

"Look, Keith was there, yes, but nothing happened. I don't know what you think you saw, but he was not in my house undressed."

Duron cringed when he heard her say the word yes, acknowledging that Keith was in her house. He didn't need to hear anything else.

"This conversation is over. Go home, Taija," he said.

"You're not going to let me explain and clear this up?" she asked.

Her heart was breaking. In his eyes, Taija could see that Duron was thinking that she had been intimate with Keith sometime after she had returned home from his place, but he was wrong. She would never, ever betray him like that. She didn't know what else to say because he cut her off every time she tried to explain. She looked at him hoping he could see that she loved him and would never do anything to hurt him. She wished he would let her tell him what actually happened and not what he thought he saw.

"You are not the woman I thought you were and that's all I have to say. You fooled me and I hope the night spent with him was worth it. Go home, Taija. There is nothing going on here with us anymore. I never want to see you again because I'm done."

On that last word, Taija watched as Duron ascended the stairs to the cabin, opened the door, went in and slammed it so hard, she could feel the step she was standing on vibrate. Defeated and not wanting to upset him anymore than he already was, she turned and headed for her car.

Duron watched out of the window as Taija walked back to her car, got in, but didn't drive off. He figured she was sitting there thinking through what had transpired. He could only imagine her thoughts were that she had been caught.

Watching her, he was seething. Even after he told her what he'd seen, she continued to deny anything happened. He was a man, he knew what he saw. In his mind she could offer him no excuse that could justify an ex who had hurt her being in her house that early in the morning half-dressed. All she could do for him was to leave him alone.

Taija sat in her car and wondered what just happened. She came out to the cabin thinking either Duron was having a work issue or that the disagreement had disturbed him more than she thought. She had no idea he thought she was cheating on him. What was he talking about? Keith, shirtless, looking like he'd just rolled out of bed? *Shirtless?* A thought occurred to her. Keith had done something. That snake had done this. Somehow, when she was in the shower and didn't hear the door when Duron stopped by, Keith must have cooked up a scheme to ward off Duron. That type of behavior was exactly who Keith was. The way he professed his love for her, he would do anything to keep another man away from her, she was sure of that. She had endured many years of his scheming and would put nothing past him. She never should have let him in that morning. He had developed such a huge ego, he thought he could do whatever he wanted in order to get his way.

Thinking back to that day, she remembered the scene and thought that Keith was a little too happy when she finally came downstairs. He would have known what Duron looked like from a picture she had on the mantle of her fireplace that they'd taken together at a party. She saw Keith admiring it while they were talking. Duron's good looks would be easy to recognize, especially if he came by that same morning that Keith had been there. Keith must have put two and two together.

Enlighted, maybe she should go back to the cabin and demand that Duron hear her out. This was a misunderstanding and not something she'd had a hand in.

She was wrong for letting Keith in her house, but nothing happened. More important than him taking her back, was him knowing that she would never hurt him like that or do anything behind his back. She wasn't that kind of woman.

Looking up at the cabin, a second thought came to mind. Duron was too angry to listen to her. All she could think about was the man she loved more than anything in this world never wanted to see her again. Until he's calmed down, no explanation could fix this.

Her hurt turned to rage at what it seems Keith had done. That snake had not changed, she thought.

The sun was beginning to set and she needed to get back to the city and figure out how things could have gone so wrong for her. She loved Duron and she didn't want to give up on them. She'd let him have the space he needed, but as far as she was concerned, the discussion was far from over. She turned the car on and without looking back, drove back to town. He'd only been on the road a few seconds when the tears flowed. Her life was shattered.

21

"You're up early on a Saturday morning," Earl Knight said to his wife as she planted flowers in her garden in the back of their Atlanta home.

"Gardening helps me relax, much like baking does. I didn't want to wake you with my tossing and turning. You don't get many Saturday's off."

Barbara smiled when he walked over and handed her the next bunch of flowers to add to her garden now that she'd dug the holes.

"I'm more concerned about what's got you worked up and unable to relax. If it's Duron, he'll be okay. He has to work this out for himself," Earl said.

"I know. He's my baby and I worry about his and that heart of his. He plays that role like he doesn't care, but he's the most sensitive out of the bunch and whatever happened between him and Taija has really got him down. You remember the last time he went to our cabin alone," she said.

"I do and that woman was trouble from the start. She made demands on our son that had nothing to do with love. I believe what he has with Taija is different. Until he learns how to talk things out instead of running away, he will always end up where he is now. He'll be fine. I don't want you worrying yourself crazy over his love life and he's not baby," Earl laughed.

"Well, he's my baby and I worry about all of my children. He happens to need my worrying the most right now. I think he's coming back today and I hope he stops by to let me set eyes on him. I don't like when he closes himself off. I'm glad he has work to keep him focused on something other than the state of his relationship. Do you want me to make you a big breakfast this morning?" she asked, standing and looking around her garden at her morning's work.

"This morning, my love, I'm going to make you a big breakfast. When you're finished out here, get cleaned up and let me pamper you for a change," Earl said, giving her a quick kiss on the lips.

"One of a million reasons by I love you, Earl Knight!" Barbara declared.

"You, my love, are one in a million and you were created just for me," Earl said before heading back in the house.

Cleaning up the empty pots, Barbara did think about Duron and what he was going through. She was expecting him back in town from the cabin and from the few conversations she'd had with him while he was there, things weren't looking any better with his relationship with Taija. She'd hoped he had come to the realization that what happened between them was a big misunderstanding somehow; it had to be. She really liked Taija and she seemed perfect for Duron. According to Loren, Taija had gone up to the cabin a few days ago to talk to Duron and it didn't go well. No doubt, it was because Duron and his stubbornness was too angry to have a civil discussion.

Even though he was a grown man, she still tried everything in her power to keep her children from hurting and to help them heal when it was unavoidable. She would give him some space today if he decides to not stop by. She was scheduled to go with Loren to find a dress for the hospital benefit gala later in the day.

"I'm going to whisper a silent prayer for your situation Duron," she said aloud. "I know there's a way to overcome this hurt and I pray the healing of your heart is a speedy one."

~ ~

Taija woke Saturday morning missing Duron terribly. It was still sinking in that the relationship was over. She'd sat up most of the night disgusted with herself for being caught up again in yet another dramatic situation involving Keith. Even though they were no longer involved, he still brought misery into her life.

After her trip to visit Duron at the cabin, she returned home and checked her caller-ID for Keith's number. She hoped she hadn't deleted it like she'd deleted all of his voicemails. Seeing a Florida number, knowing it wasn't a number for her mother, she assumed it was his. She called him about what Duron said about him and his state of undress. Without missing a beat, he didn't even try to deny what he had done.

Keith admitted it and tried to convince her that his excuse was that he was desperate. He saw Duron as the one person standing in the way of the two of them getting back together and it was a spur of the moment idea. It wasn't until after he'd returned home that the impact of what he had done set in. By then, he was too embarrassed to call her and tell her what he had done.

Taija was livid and she let him know how sickened she was by his calculated move to get her back. Did he think she wouldn't find out exactly what he had done? After that, was he feeble minded enough to think that she would take him back? Wishful thinking of a man who was accustomed to getting whatever he wanted.

She'd had enough of hearing his voice and no matter how much he pleaded with her, she despised what he did to get her back. She felt a little better by telling him to go crawl back under the rock that he slithered out from under and to never contact her again for any reason. Once her call with him was over, she felt better knowing that even though Duron didn't believe her, she understood his anger and what he must have thought about her and Keith.

Duron had ended things with her thinking she was a liar and a cheater. Though she understood his anger, she couldn't believe that after all the time they'd spent together, where she had no time or energy to be involved with anyone else, he wouldn't take a moment to think logically. Did he really believe she would make love to him the way she had that Saturday night and then turn around and have sex with Keith the same weekend? The kind of workout Duron gave her body, she would never have enough energy to share her body with anyone else, not that she wanted to because she didn't. They shared a passion in lovemaking that could only happen between two people experiencing true love.

After talking to Keith, she thought about calling Duron to explain everything, but his anger wouldn't let him listen and she wasn't sure he would believe her. The idea that he thought so little of her as to think that she could hop in bed with anyone that wasn't him, was disappointing and hurt her to her core.

Duron had dismissed her as if she were some lying,

scheming trick. She would let him stew, but they would talk and she would explain and if he still didn't believe her, then she would walk away. At least she would leave knowing she'd done nothing wrong and that it was on him if he was willing to walk away from what they have over a misunderstanding created by a lunatic like Keith. The last thing she wanted to do was to bring hurt into his life.

She had been so caught up in her worry over her relationship, she forgot that this was the day she was going with Loren to find a dress for the hospital benefit gala. She should have told Loren that she no longer had plans to go since she and Duron were not on speaking terms. She needed to call and cancel the outing. If she and Duron weren't together anymore, something he made clear, she wouldn't be attending the gala.

"Hey, Loren," she said when Loren answered.

"Hey, Taija. I was just thinking about you."

"I'm going to take a rain check on shopping today. I won't be attending the gala so I don't need a dress."

"What do you mean you're not going. What's going on Tai?" Loren asked.

"Everything is still where it was with your brother. Nothing has changed. Like I told you after I came back from the cabin, he broke up with me, so I'm going to pass on the gala."

"Oh, I'm sorry to hear that. Is it that bad that you guys won't work it out?"

"Yes, it looks like it's that bad."

The weight of the breakup was finally hitting Taija and her voice started to crack.

"Taija, I can hear you're pretty upset and I'm sure you don't need to sit around on a Saturday wallowing in self-pity. I think you should still come shopping with me. You sound like you could still use a day to take your mind off of things. I'm picking up my mother to go with us. I know she would love to see you, too," Loren said.

Taija was hesitant. "If your mom knows anything about what's going on with Duron and me, she won't be happy to see me. If he's told her what he saw at my house and his accusations that I've been lying to him or that I cheated on him, she won't have good thoughts about me and I'm sure she won't want to see me. I know how your mom is about all of you and she will side with him and it doesn't matter that it's all false," she said sadly.

"That's just nonsense. My mother isn't like that. She loves us all, but she also knows how pig-headed my brother can be. Please come on and go. I was going to surprise you and my mom with manicures and pedicures and have a real ladies day out. Please? I know you could use the girl company today. You can go back to dealing with this mess with Duron on tomorrow. Today, let's get our minds on all things good. Plus, I want to tell you about someone I've been seeing and I need your opinion on it. It's a little touch and I could use some insight from a friend. Deal?" Loren asked.

Taija did need to get out and stop sulking for a little while or she knew she would be in the house all weekend. Plus, it appeared Loren needed an ear and she had been an ear or more than one occasion and it was time she returned the favor.

"Okay, I'll go. Where should I meet you and your mom?" she asked.

"Don't worry about that. I'll stop by and pick you up on the way to my mom's house. I'll be there in an hour. Cheer up. My brother loves you, no matter what he's saying right now. He's angry and needs time to think things through. I believe he'll come around. Then you two can talk it out and work through it. I have never seen him as happy as he is when he is with you. You told me what happened and I never sided with Duron. I love him, but I know you and you and him are meant to be together. That kind of love can conquer anything. Give him some time to work it out. I'll see you in an hour."

After Taija hung up, Loren sat in her office at her interior design business totally disgusted with her brother. She loved him, but he was the most stubborn of all of them. It was like him to not listen to Taija's reasoning. She would let it go for the moment, but if he continued with his mess, she may have to step in and say something about it. He may not want to hear what Taija has to say, but now that Taija has told her the whole truth, she would make him listen to her whether he liked it or not.

22

Duron exited his condo to spend a few hours in the office even though it was Saturday. Most of the staff had the day off and he was expecting to get a lot done. He was walking to the elevator when the door to Mike's condo opened.

"Look who's back!" Mike said.

"What's up, Mike."

"I wasn't expecting to see you here. I saw your car in the garage last night when I got in. You had to pass your house to come here."

Duron thought about staying at his house, but wanted an early start in the office.

"Yeah, I had a lot to get done today. I'll be around all day. You coming in today?" he asked.

"Definitely. This new deal is one of our biggest and I'm doing my due diligence in being prepared. It will be different having you in the office on a Saturday morning. After you met Taija, you spent less and less time in the office on Saturdays. Still no Taija, huh?" Mike asked. He had hoped the few days away would clear things up and they would have worked out their issues by now.

"That's not a good conversation or me."

"I'll take that as a no, then," Mike said. "Pity because that woman is your queen."

"Mike, I told you what happened in great detail and you still think she's my queen?" Duron asked as he leaned against the wall looking forward to hearing Mike's take on things. The one thing he valued was the opinions of his two best friends.

"I know what you told me, but until you let her explain without you interrupting or ignoring her, then I'm going to believe that she's still your queen. You want me to believe this incredible woman you raved about up, down, even sideways turned into some side-stepping woman who was stringing you along? She's not Allison. That woman none of us liked because her trickery was crystal clear. Loren talks about Taija all the time and from what I hear, she's as incredible as you said," Mike said.

Duron as about to respond when something caught his attention.

"Wait, you talk to Loren all the time? What are you talking to her about all the time or at least enough that you're talking about how incredible Taija is?" he asked. When did they become good buddies?

Mike's tongue felt heavy when he realized he said too much without thinking. He needed to think fast to avoid an uncomfortable discussion he wasn't ready for.

"Don't try changing the subject. You need to talk to Taija and either hear her out and still walk away or hear her out and believe what she tells you."

Duron shook his head to try and clear.

"Why is everyone jumping on the Taija bandwagon. Tyrone said the exact same thing. What are you doing, rehearsing what you're going to say to me? What does it matter if I'm seeing Taija or some other woman? There will be another and you'll forget there was a Taija," he said.

Duron knew he'd said too much when he watched Mike shake his head back and forth as if to say he wasn't buying any of it.

"Bro, you're the one who set us straight when Tyrone and I made fun of you meeting a woman at the bachelor auction. Weeks of dating and you sold us on all the great things you told us about her. That one night you had us all over to your house for a little get together and I got the chance to really get to know her and see you two together, I was sold. I don't want to discount what you saw that morning at her house, but if I ask you if you had heard the entire story, what would your answer be? Before you answer, let me answer for you. You don't know because you don't listen. Your anger gets the best of you and you shut down. I'm not going to tell you what to do, but if you haven't listened without interrupting her, you will never know the full truth."

Duron wasn't going to answer the question because he didn't have an answer. He hadn't let Taija fully explain because he didn't want to hear the ending, especially if it was something that would rip his heart out of his chest. His pride was hurt enough.

"I hear you, Mike and I appreciate you and your opinion as I always do. Today, I want to focus on work and make sure I'm as ready with my end as you are."

"I'm always here for you, that is until I'm in California, then we'll have to have these chats by phone," Mike said laughing.

Duron used his key to open the elevator door.

"I'll see you when you come down," he said as the elevator doors closed.

Leaning back against the wall, he thought a lot about what Mike said. He could be short-sighted when it came to letting others explain. He was beyond mad and couldn't shake it enough to hear anything about the details of the rest of Taija's weekend that included her ex.

He would deal with thoughts on the situation later. On his way to his condo the night before, he'd dropped off the plans and files that he needed to go over today and was anxious to get down to business. If these new designs were acceptable with his client, the results would increase their standing in the world of architecture. This would make his firm not only the top one in the Atlanta area, but possibly across the country. They'd already had plans to expand to the west coast with Mike taking over the building and expansion in California. He was going to miss having Mike around the office every day, but they all knew that if they were going to grown they needed to expand to make it easier for other clients to reach them.

Mike had no problems making the change to the west coast since he had a lot of family on that coast already. First, they had to pull this deal off. They were definitely going to be busier than ever once things are finalized. That's just what Duron needed to take his mind off of his troubles with Taija. As with Allision, it was going to take him a long time to get over Taija. She was on his mind night and day. When his thoughts turned to what may have occurred in her bedroom between her and Keith, it made him sick. The thought of any other man touching her in an intimate way had him boiling. He had to stop torturing himself. Why women were being bred these days to not know what it meant to be faithful, he didn't understand. Perhaps it was because other men had messed over them. No one wins in a relationship not based on trust. He wished he could find a book to read that would explain it all to him.

When the elevator opened to the office level of his building, he walked through the halls greeting the few staff members who were in the office. One Saturday a month, they gave the staff the day off with pay, allowing them to spend a long weekend with family and friends. Building their company was a priority, but family was the biggest priority. When employees are valued enough and know that the company they work for finds importance in their home life as they do in their work life, morale is high and productivity skyrockets. It was important to him that work and home life have the perfect balance.

After he and Taija started getting to know each other, he had begun spending more Saturday's away from the office and more time with her. They lived busy work lives during the week and when the weekend came, they loved sleeping in late on Saturdays, making love until their bodies screamed for sustenance. He missed those Saturdays when he woke to her being in his arms. When his body woke longing for her, he was thrilled that her body had the same need. Making love to her was his heaven on earth. Everything about her pleased him, which is why he didn't understand what happened to them.

As he walked into his office, he noticed a large stack of messages his assistant had left for him. A few of them were from Taija earlier in the week. They were taken before she showed up at his cabin to talk. Even in his office, when he looked around, all he could think about was her.

He looked to the leather sectional in his office where they had made love one late night when he'd been working so hard, he forgot to eat dinner. Taija had shown up when Chinese food and some very good loving, exactly what he needed. There was also that one time, like at her office, she'd joined him in the shower in the adjoining bathroom for one of his longest quickies. Thankfully, everyone had left the office to play in a baseball game for charity leaving him to join them later. Taija had agreed to accompany him and act as one of the cheerleaders and when she showed up in an actual cheerleader outfit, he couldn't resist taking it off of her and within minutes, they were naked and in his shower, screaming each other's names as the hot water poured down on them. Of course, they never made it to the game.

Every place he went, there were memories of Taija. Would that ever end?

Duron walked over to the conference table in his office and laid the plans for the new business center out so that he could give them one last glance. Signing the final contracts for the complex was going to be one of the biggest days of his life and he wished he had Taija to share that day with.

23

Taija was nervous as Loren drove them to pick up her mother. She had a lot of respect for Ms. Barbara being the kind and loving woman she knew she would be. When she and Loren were in college together, Loren talked about her mother all the time. She loved their close relationship. She and her own mother had a good relationship, but her mother didn't visit her on the Spellman campus as much as Loren's mother visited her. Loren could have lived at home and gone to school, but she mentioned it was her mother who suggested she stay in the dorms to get the entire college experience of being more independent.

She seemed the perfect mother when they'd met at the cookout. She knew there was nothing she would not do for her children and Taija admired that. She wasn't sure what Ms. Barbara would think of her when she got all of the details of her break-up with Duron, from his perspective. If the time came when his mother did find out, she would make sure she explained herself, letting her know that she would never intentionally hurt Duron. She never wanted her to think that she was untrustworthy or that she had set out to deceive and hurt her son.

"Taija you look like you're about to go in front of a firing squad. Will you chill out girl?" Loren said smiling.

Taija shifted in her seat, not feeling comfortable.

"I'm sorry, Loren. I think I should have stayed home

today. Your mom doesn't want to see me."

"I will admit, Duron did talk to my mom, but she didn't believe anything he said. It's not that she thought Duron was lying, but she thought that there has to be an explanation for what he saw or thought he saw and she knows how stubborn he can be. I told you my mom doesn't place blame and she lets us figure out our own love lives. She loves Duron, but she would never go along with anything he said, especially what he believes was going on with you and Keith. We're hanging out today to have fun so cheer up before I push you out of this moving car," she joked.

Taija laughed knowing she needed to lighten up.

"I miss your brother, so much," she said.

"I know you do and if I know him, he misses you just as much."

"I wouldn't be too sure of that. He said some nasty things to me and I've never seen him behave like that. He was cold and heartless. He wasn't the loving guy who can't keep his hands off of me whenever he sees me."

Loren faked gagging.

"Okay Tai, way too much information. I don't want to think of my brother with any parts of him all over you."

They laughed together.

"Sorry about that. I hate the fact that those hazel eyes that I love to look into were looking back at me with nothing but hate and disgust. It hurt me to my heart to see him hurting like that and I couldn't say anything to make things better."

While they were stopped at a light, Loren turned to her.

"Taija, don't worry, something tells me that soon, everything will come to light and he'll be knocking down your door to apologize and beg you to take him back. Make sure you make him sweat a little bit. Don't make it easy on him. He has to know how to communicate better and not just by talking, but by listening too," Loren said.

"Girl, I won't even begin to tell you my reaction to him when he begs for something. Whew!!" Taija fanned herself thinking of the many times he'd pleaded with her to let up on him when she pleasured him to the point of no return.

"Like I said, too much information about my brother, so don't go there. Keep the faith that everything will work out. It's only been a week."

Taija sat up straight looking shook.

"Is that all? I swear it seems like it's been a lot longer than that. I've never felt like this about any guy before and it hurts."

"That's why I said keep the faith, girl. Can you imagine life without my crazy brother? I think not, so cheer up and get ready to have a fun day and no more dismal talk about Duron and his bad mood. Imagine spending your life with that mood," Loren said before she pulled back into traffic when the light changed.

~~

Duron spent most of the day catching up on a week's worth of work and messages that his assistant had left for him. He was heading out when his phone rang. Since no one else was in today he grabbed it before it stopped ringing and the answering service picked up.

It was his father.

"Hey, son."

"Hey Pop. How did you know I would be here?" Duron asked.

Duron heard his father chuckle.

"Chip off the old block. You like to go to work when everyone else is off so that you can get more done. I'm the same way."

His father knew him well, he thought.

"What can I do for you Pop?"

"I didn't get a chance to see you earlier in the week when you stopped by or talk to you when you called your mother from the cabin the other day. I wanted to check in to see how the plans for the new office park are coming along. It's the talk of the town. People are excited for the new business and all the new jobs this project will bring in. We could use a great boost in the economy in this area."

"Things are moving full steam ahead, Pop. We're having our final meeting next week and construction will begin soon after that. We're still on schedule which is great."

"That's good news, son. Is everything else alright? Your mother seemed to think you were troubled about something else. She's been worried about you all week. Anything I can help you with?"

Duron smiled. He knew a lot of men didn't take the time to inquire with their grown sons about their personal problems, but his father had always been hands on. He and his brothers could talk to him about anything and he always listened patiently, giving them advice. They were all strong, black men because of his father. Nothing and no one could do much about his current situation. He was going to have to figure it out.

"I'm good, Pop. Nothing I can't handle and get myself through. How are plans for the benefit gala coming along?"

"Excellent. The hospital has already sold every single ticket. We're also expecting huge donations this year thanks to support from companies like yours. The free clinic will operate in the black with all the additional funding. You know I'm thankful for your support. Are you planning to come for your mother's Sunday dinner tomorrow?" Earl asked.

Duron loved that his mother planned a dinner once a month for he and his siblings. It was a must that everyone attend. She never accepted any excuses for not making it to dinner.

"Yeah, I'll be there. I already put my bid in for her to make her famous pot roast and potatoes. I'm not eating tomorrow until dinner, so that I can get my fill," he quipped.

He heard his father laugh and it made him smile as well. He had not smiled all week.

"Alright, son. I don't want to hold you. I'll see you at dinner tomorrow."

"Thanks for checking up on me," Duron said.

"Son, you know I'm always here for all of you if you need me. Whatever it is that your mother says has you down, think it through and figure out a way to fix it. You know what I always tell all of you - you have the power in your own hands to make all things right in your own life. You just need to think it through and open up your mind to the possibilities when you let yourself live your best life."

"Thanks, Pop. Your advice always helps. I'll see you tomorrow for dinner."

He hoped no one brought up Taija at the dinner. He never liked discussing his personal life with everyone around the table. This was one situation he didn't need anyone's help with. He had been wronged and from his perspective, only time would heal the mood he was in.

~~

Shopping with Loren and her mother turned out to be what Taija needed to lighten up her mood. She was having a lot of fun and it temporarily took her mind off of her troubles with Duron. Ms. Barbara was her usual cordial self and didn't show any signs that she was upset over what was occurring between she and Duron. She had no doubt that Ms. Barbara knew everything. She hadn't asked Taija anything about him or even mentioned him all afternoon. She found that odd.

They were now at a nice, quaint boutique in downtown Atlanta looking at the most exquisite dresses and gowns. Loren had picked out three that she wanted to try on and headed for the dressing room.

When Taija found a chair to sit in to wait to see how Loren looked in her selections, Ms. Barbara turned to her.

"Taija, aren't you going to pick out a few dresses to try on for the gala?"

Nervously, he responded. "No ma'am."

"May I ask why, unless I'm prying?" Ms. Barbara said. "Loren told me last week that you were going to get something new for the gala, too."

That was before her split with Duron, she said to herself.

"I've decided I'm not going to the gala. I appreciate your family inviting me, but I won't be attending," she said.

Silence from her made Taija realize she indeed did have a clue into what was going on with the state of her relationship with Duron.

"Taija, I know that you and my son are having some problems. I hope that whatever has caused this riff between you can be fixed. Just in case you can't, I don't want that to keep you from coming to this gala and having a wonderful time. I know the invitation to attend came from Duron originally, but you are also invited to attend as a guest of the family. It'll be a great event and it's for a great cause. I hope you'll reconsider and attend. I would love to see you there."

Taija was happy to hear Duron's mother not take sides in the situation. She appreciated that his mother still wanted her to attend, but Taija had already decided it would not be a good idea. She was still upset when she thought of the look in his eyes that day at the cabin. Those hazel eyes that drew her in like a moth to a flame only showed disdain for her. She couldn't bear to see that again and she didn't want the night to be awkward. She also didn't want to ruin that night for Duron either by being a constant reminder of another failed relationship. She knew he would not want her there.

"Thank you for that. I will think about it, but I don't think I'll be able to make it. If I change my mind, I'm sure I have something I can wear. I don't want to get something new and not really need it. Thank you for understanding."

Ms. Barbara didn't respond. She patted Taija on her shoulder in a loving, motherly way to let her know that she sympathized with her. Feeling like she could confide in her, Taija, wanted to come clean about her feelings for Duron.

"Ms. Barbara?"

"Yes dear?"

"I'm in love with Duron. He means more to me than I could ever have dreamed. Years ago, I was able to get a quick glimpse of him on campus when Loren and I were at Spellman and I thought he was the most handsome guy I had ever seen. When I came across him again at the bachelor auction months ago, I saw that as fate. I was excited to connect with him on a more personal level, get to know him and eventually fall in love with him."

"I could see the love between the two of you last Saturday. How you feel about each other was evident to everyone in the family. See the two of you made me happy."

"Did Duron tell you the circumstances surrounding our recent breakup?" Taija asked.

"Yes, he told me all about what he thought was an uncompromising situation at your house one morning."

Taija was afraid of that.

"I know what he thinks, but that's not what it was at all. I wish he would give me the chance to really explain now that I know what happened. At the time, I had no idea what had occurred. It's true my ex was at my home that morning. He stopped by to talk to me about getting back together. He was heading back out of town that morning and stopped by unexpectedly, according to him. What I didn't know was how desperate he was to get me back. When I went to get ready for work and Duron decided to also stop by, Keith, my ex, did something unthinkable. He tried to make it look as if we had been sharing a bed together to ward off Duron. As you know, it worked. I had no idea he had done that. After Duron told me what he saw, I contacted Keith and he admitted to what he had done out of desperation."

Taija took a breather from her explanation when she felt herself about to cry.

She watched as Ms. Barbara came over to comfort her and then she really wanted to cry.

"No tears, dear. I know you're hurting and it's alright."

"I don't know what to do now. He won't talk to me. He

told me he never wanted to see me again. I tried to explain that nothing happened, but he wouldn't listen. I don't even know how to try and tell him what really happened now that I know. I don't want to see the look on his face like the day I saw him at the cabin. It broke my heart even more to see how hurt he was," Taija said, sniffling. Like a typical mother, she smiled when Ms. Barbara handed her a tissue from her purse.

Taija's voice begun to crack at the thought of never seeing or being with Duron again. She loved him and didn't want to lose him forever.

Seeing how upset Taija was, Ms. Barbara leaned closer to comfort her by embracing her like only a mother can.

"My son can be as stubborn as a mule and when he sets his mind on something, he stays with it. It has worked out for him for his good and it's also been his biggest downfall. He gets that from his father. Don't give up on him yet. He needs a cooling period and when he does, you'll have a chance to talk to him and work things out. I have faith knowing that the two of you were meant to be together."

Taija began to sniffle harder and louder, no longer able to hold back the tears that have been threatening to fall since her last conversation with Duron. She had cried when she was alone, but this was the first time she'd done it in front of any one. Hearing Duron's mother's words of encouragement gave her a little hope.

"I know, but I really miss him Ms. Barbara. I know he's hurting and that's my fault. I know how much trust means to him in a relationship. For him to think such things about me is heartbreaking."

"I know, dear. Give him some time. Now, even if you don't want to pick out a gown today, why don't you grab a few to try on. Nothing makes a woman feel better than when she gets to play dress-up."

Taija looked into her smiling face and everything felt good in her world again. She felt better after their conversation and she didn't want to continue to bring down their fun day. She thanked Ms. Barbara and ran to grab a few gowns to try on. Maybe she was right, she thought as she looked through the row of gorgeous gowns. It's possible in the end that everything will work out. Only time would tell.

24

Loren was getting tired of Duron once again moping around. She decided to pay him a visit and shake some sense into him. Taija was hurting as much as he was and she thought that if he found out the true circumstances around Keith's unannounced visit, maybe he would suck it up and get his woman back. It had been two weeks now and they both were miserable apart and having them back together again was the one and only answer.

Her anger at his stubbornness surfaced higher the closer she got to his house. After she parked and walked up to the house, she buzzed hoping he was home even though the house looked dark. It didn't occur to her to call him before she drove all the way out to Buckhead from her place. She was angry at him and wasn't thinking clearly. She waited for him to answer.

Duron had finished checking out his attire for the gala. His tuxedo had arrived earlier in the week. After spending weeks going back and forth to his tailor to get his suit the way he wanted, he was happy when the messenger showed up at his office with everything he'd need from the suit, to accessories to shoes.

He was now alone after his cleaning lady had left. His big house seemed empty. He'd built it as a place to get away, but it had turned into a place where he kept everyone else away. He didn't know when his feelings about the house he'd designed and had built to his specifications had changed. He was once proud of what it stood for and now that he was in it alone day in and day out, he didn't enjoy it as much as he had for weeks when Taija's beautiful presence brought new life to it. He missed that and he missed her.

When he looked at his tuxedo, he was reminded that he was going to be dateless for the gala. It wasn't that he couldn't get another date, he didn't want one. With his relationship with Taija being over, they were no longer going as a couple. It was the evening before the big hospital gala where all of the elite of Atlanta and across the country would be in attendance and all he could think about was how much he missed her presence in his life.

He enjoyed this gala each year, but this year his mood wasn't one of enjoyment. It had been two weeks since he last heard from, seen or talked to Taija. There were times when he reached for her warmth in the middle of the night, only to find himself alone. He missed the late-night phone calls. He missed making love to her. He missed being around her. He missed everything about her.

He was about to settle in for the evening to take his mind off of his troubles by going over some paperwork when his door buzzer sounded. Looking into the security camera view from his theater room, he saw that it was his sister.

He spoke to her through the two-way pad on the wall.

"Use your key, Lo. The alarm isn't set yet. I'm in the theater room," he said.

After he saw her reach in to her bag to retrieve her key, he took his usual seat in the last row, center seat. A few minutes later, after raiding his refrigerator and showing up in the theater room with a soda and sandwich, Loren plopped down in the seat next to him without saying a word. He waited for her usual rambling and when she didn't say anything, he looked over at her.

"What's up? Happen to be in the neighborhood?" he asked with amusement.

He was surprised when she continued looking at the movie screen, eating her sandwich and ignoring him with an expressionless face. He tried again, this time waving his hand in front of her face.

"Hello, you are in my house. Did you show up to sit next to me and not talk or are we going to converse at all?" he asked.

Again, no response from her. This time, he turned off the movie screen and waited for her objection. None came.

"Okay, enough of the silent treatment. What have I done now that has you upset with me?" he asked.

This time she turned her attention to him.

"Not so pleasant being ignored is it D?" she said.

Not knowing what she was talking about he decided to play along. She was definitely upset about something.

"Okay, how about you bring me up to speed on this conversation."

Duron watched as she took a deep breath. This must be good, he thought.

"You're being a real jackass, D," Loren said aggressively.

Whoa, he thought. Anger to the tenth degree.

"Okay, what jackass thing have I done now? I do so many I can't keep up. How about you narrow it down for me. How have I ignored you lately, even though I don't think I have," he said.

"Not me. I'm talking about Taija."

At the mentioning of her name, all of the life went out of any attempt at a conversation they were going to have.

"I know she's your friend Lo, but stay out of it. It has nothing to do with you. You know how I don't like anyone getting in the middle of my relationships, so find your way out of this and exit stage left," Duron said.

Knowing the substance of her anger, he turned the movie back on and increased the volume signaling an end to any further discussion about Taija.

Loren, who didn't like being dismissed so easily, reached for the remote, turned the movie off and turned to face her brother once again.

"D, listen. I know your relationships are none of my business. You've told me on more than one occasion to mind my own business, but this time you really are being a jackass," she said.

Loren hoped he would listen to her voice of reason. They were always able to talk about everything and this shouldn't be an exception because he was feeling hurt.

Duron loved his sister, but he refused to have this conversation with her. It was a touchy subject and he never liked arguing with her. He could see this one turning into an argument.

"Yet, here you are, once again butting in," he said harshly.

He was getting very tired of his sister and all of her drama. He hoped his tone would be a deterrent, but it was having no effect on her.

"How could you not let Taija explain? You don't know what happened. What kind of closed minded person does that?" she asked.

Duron calmed his nerves before he spoke in order to not

upset his sister even more.

"You have no idea about the territory you are venturing into. I'm a big boy and Taija is a big girl. We don't need you to fix this for us."

Loren began huffing and puffing at him and folding her arms across her chest letting him know that she was not going to let up.

"Apparently you do need me to fix this. It's been weeks and you haven't even attempted to make things right."

Shaking her head at the thought of how pigheaded Duron was being, she could not resist going all in with her opinion.

"Stay out of this, Lo, I'm serious. You have no idea what you're dealing with and we're not talking about it. I love you, but we're not having this conversation and I don't have anything that I need to make right, so let it go. What you should be doing is checking your friend, not me," he said dolefully.

Loren whipped her head at him.

"Wow. You are so much like dad. I love him just like I love you, but that stubborn streak is working at a disadvantage for you. You let a woman who loves you more than anything get away because you thought what you saw was more of what had occurred in your past, with that woman whose name I will not mention. You didn't take the time to even talk about it with her to hear what she had to say. Not all situations are what they appear to be," he said.

Duron didn't want to respond anymore because the more he did, the more volatile the situation between them seemed to be getting. He never liked fighting or arguing with her and like him, she too had a stubborn streak and he knew she would never let up as long as he fed into the conversation. He looked down as if he was reading over his paperwork in hopes she would end the argument and let him be.

When Loren noticed Duron had taken to ignoring her, she got up, placed the remote in her now vacant seat and headed for the steps to go back home. Before doing so, she needed to get a few more things off of her chest.

"D, I understand what you went through in your last relationship. You know I know. Of the four of us siblings, you and I have always been the closest. I never mince my words when I talk to you and I'm not going to do it now. I'm going to say this and then I'm going to leave."

Duron crossed his legs and turned his attention to her.

"Say what you need to say," he said.

Here goes nothing, she thought.

"Nothing happened with Taija and Keith. She didn't even realize he'd tried to make it look like more than it was. After you told her what you saw, she called him to find out what you were talking about, since you dismissed her like you have a habit of doing to people without letting them explain. He admitted to her that he set it up to look that way to you when he saw you coming to the door. He recognized you from a picture Taija had of the two of you. She'd told him she was in love with you and it apparently ticked him off. He showed up that morning unannounced while in town for something else for the weekend. He had not spent the night with her. He wanted to talk to her about the two of them and she kindly let him know that there was no them. She let him know that she was in love with you and very happily so. She went to prepare for work, he saw you coming and thought up a scheme to buy himself some time to get through to Taija. She never knew about it,

D. She was just as stunned as you were by his actions. Her big mistake was getting him coffee for his long ride back to Florida and while he drank it, she went to get ready for work. You never gave her the chance to explain these details to you. You ignore her phone calls and texts, acting like a spoiled rotten child and you are being totally unfair. I know you Duron and I know you love her. I can see it every time you mention her name. Unlike all the times where I've said that Allison was never good enough for you, I won't say that this time. As much as I love you, I'm starting to think that maybe, just maybe, you aren't good enough for Taija. She doesn't deserve this treatment from you when she's done nothing wrong. It's time to get over yourself and stop living in the past," Loren said in anger.

Loren was so frustrated that her heart had sped up and she began pacing in place. She took one last look at him and started heading toward the steps, but was stopped by the sound of him calling her back.

He looked up at her as she returned to him. *Could she be telling the truth?*

"Taija told you all of this?" he asked calmly.

"Yes, she did. She would have told you, but you told her you never wanted to see her again. She also told me how much she loves you and that she would never, ever do anything to hurt you. She knows it looked bad, but she didn't know. You have been treating her horribly. Even though you're acting like this, she still loves you and I don't know why. You are a great guy, so I guess I can understand that, but you are wrong here. I love you unconditionally, even when you piss me off like now. Talk to her and stop being this way. You are miserable without her and you don't need to be. You were on your way to true happiness.

The playboy had given up all other women. Oh, yes big brother, you are in love. Don't let your past continue to haunt your present and your future. Let it go," she pleaded.

Duron thought, if what she was saying was true, he was being a jackass. He didn't give Taija a chance to explain anything and he cringed at the thought of telling her he never wanted to see her again. He spoke out of fury and never should have said that. He assumed the worse about her and walked away when what he should have done was talk it out. Loren was right that they could talk about everything and they always had. He was once again being stubborn by purposely dismissing her, something he didn't like doing. He loved his little sister. With her, he could always be honest, like he was about to be.

"I love her, Lo. I love her and I let my pride get in the way of working this out with her. I knew deep down she wouldn't do anything like that to me. I think I was always on guard waiting for something to happen and when it did, I closed myself off. She is nothing like Allison, but I let what Allison did to me touch my relationship with Taija.

Duron was getting angry with himself.

"Taija is nothing like her," Loren said.

"After the way I've treated her, I don't know how to fix this. If I went to her, I don't think she would listen to anything I had to say. I said some nasty things to her, things I can never take back," he said.

Loren felt sorry for him.

"You're right. She may or may not want to hear what you have to say, but you have to try if you really love her and want her back. You have to fight for her. Her mother is in town tonight, so I know this is not a good time to head over there. I will, however, let you in on a little secret. You can do with it whatever you want," she said.

"What's that?" Duron asked.

"Taija is still going to the gala tomorrow night. Mom talked her into coming even with the situation with you. At first, she wasn't going to go. She called me the other night to get the name of the place where I bought my gown because she wanted to get something new for the gala."

Duron felt hopeful for the first time in few weeks. He would try and talk to her at the gala tomorrow evening. He needed to apologize and let her say what she needed to say. Maybe they could work this out.

"Thanks, Lo. Thanks for always having my back and kicking me just when I need it," he said.

She came closer, leaned down and gave him a kiss on the cheek then turned to leave.

"I love you, big brother."

"Wait, are you still leaving? You still mad at me? You don't want to stay and watch a movie since you're already here?" he asked.

"No, I have a date. I wanted to kick you around a little bit and eat a sandwich."

Duron heard nothing after she said the word date.

"Wait, you have a date? With who? I didn't know you were seeing someone. Who is this guy so I can check him out?"

Loren stopped him before he could get all in her business. She wasn't ready for him to know about it yet. Duron knowing could turn her world upside down.

"Don't do it D. It's still early and nothing to tell about it yet. It's a simple date. When it's more, you'll be the first I'll tell about it. For now, you need to worry about your own relationship. Wear your knee pads to the gala, in case some begging and groveling are involved. In fact, why don't you beg and grovel for good measure."

Loren laughed and waved at him as she left.

Duron laughed, but didn't comment because he knew his sister was right, he may need to do some begging and Taija was worth it. t felt good to laugh and smile again. He felt hopeful for the first time in a long while. If he handled things right, he'd have his woman back soon.

25

Taija was enjoying having her mother in town visiting especially while she was preparing for her night at the gala later that evening. They had spent the day getting pampered and her mother spent a few hours with her at the hair salon as she got all dolled up for the evening's events. Now, back at her house, her mother was helping her select the right accessories to accompany the gorgeous gown she'd purchased.

When her mother called a few days earlier to say she was finally coming for a visit, she broke down and explained the situation with Duron. Before that, her mother didn't know they had broken up and with her coming to town, there was no reason to continue keeping it from her. It would be awkward when her mother showed up and discovered she and Duron were no longer an item.

It was during that conversation that her mother explained that she was the one who gave Keith her contact information. She apologized for doing it knowing she was responsible for the end of her relationship with Duron. Her mother admitted she should have left things alone.

Taija had been angry with her mother for what she'd done, but what Keith had done wasn't on anyone but him.

During the conversation, she was angry with her mother because the only thing she could think about was that her mother had a hand in bringing Keith back into her life.

That fact and the idea of losing Duron behind it made her boil over with anger. She abruptly disconnected the call, needing to calm down. In only a short few hours, she had calmed down enough to call her mother back and talk things out. She wouldn't do like Duron had done her. Her mother deserved a chance to explain herself and then they could move on past it. They had only talked about it briefly over the past few days. Most of their time was focused on happier things. This was her mother's last night in town and she wanted to focus on good things like getting dressed up for the gala.

"What do you think about the gold necklace I selected earlier?" her mother said.

Taija looked around for the necklace she remembered her mother taking out of her jewelry chest. When she found it, she smiled knowing it was the perfect piece that would go perfect with the gown she decided to wear.

"I think that's a perfect piece Mom."

"You are going to look gorgeous in that gown with these accessories," her mother said, holding up each piece for inspection.

"I'm actually looking forward to it. I didn't think I was going to go, but now I can't imagine not going," she said.

"Well, no one is happier than me that you're going. I would hate to think that it was due to my butting in that you couldn't go to this event. I know you've been excited about this for a while. You still haven't heard from Duron?"

Taija was sad that she hadn't.

"No, I haven't."

"Do you think it would help if I contacted him and explained my role in this? He may listen to me and perhaps it would be the lead-in to you patching things up. I was looking forward to meeting him."

"I don't think that will work, but thanks for offering. I'm sure I'll run into him tonight and I don't want things to be more awkward than they will be."

"Are you nervous about tonight?"

Nervous was an understatement, but the last thing she wanted was for her mother to worry.

"No, I'm fine. He won't be the only person there and I'm looking forward to the event. You know how much I love any opportunity to dress up."

"You know how sorry I am about your relationship with him. I had no idea Keith would do that. He said he only wanted to speak to you and then when he said he was coming to Atlanta for a visit, he asked for your address to stop by and say hello. I didn't know he had planned to scheme to get you back."

Taija turned to her mother who had been apologizing all week long.

"Mom, stop apologizing. You may have given him my contact information, but you had no hand in what he did. I love you, you know that. If Duron and I were meant to be, we'll figure this out. I still have not completely given up on him. I love him too much to do that. What I will do is enjoy the gala. They have some of the top stars and musical artists around the country performing tonight. I can't keep focusing on Duron. Tonight, it's about looking and being sexy and I think I've nailed that," she exclaimed.

"That sounds like a good idea and yes you do."

"Are you sure you don't want me to take you to the airport before I leave. I still have hours before the event," Taija said. She was sad to see her mother go, but they made plans for her to return again soon.

"I'll be fine. I want to be here when you get dressed. My flight isn't until nine this evening. I can get to the airport with no problem. I do need to get something to eat."

"I have some salmon we can pop in the oven and the makings for a salad if that will work," she said.

"That sounds delicious."

Walking arm in arm, Taija and her mother headed toward the kitchen with nothing but good thoughts.

~~

"Hey, Taija."

Taija smiled when she picked up the phone and Loren was on the other end.

"Hey, Loren."

"I'm checking to see if you need ride to the gala tonight. I didn't realize my dad was sending a limousine for me until today. There is plenty of room if you want me to swing by to get you."

"No, I'm going to drive and besides, three's a crowd. Aren't you going with your mystery date?"

Loren had confided something she promised to keep a secret about the man she was seeing. Though she knew they weren't going to the gala together, she knew she would see them both at the event. She joked about them riding together knowing it would get a rise out of her.

"Absolutely not. No one except you knows that we've been seeing each other and don't forget, I swore you to secrecy. I'm not ready to discuss it with anyone yet. I don't think I'd get the support I'd like to get, especially from my brother. If we showed up together, that would raise too many eyebrows and for now, I want to keep things under wrap. He's coming tonight, but we aren't coming together."

"Oh, this will be an interesting evening. I promise to not

let it slip that I know," Taija said.

"How was the visit with your mother this week?" Loren asked.

"Great! She's still here. She wanted to wait until after I got dressed for tonight before she left. This grown is a crazy knock out. I'm glad it was still there when I went back to the boutique. I saw it the same day you purchased your gown, but I wasn't planning to go back then. I'm glad I changed my mind."

"You're okay that you'll see Duron?"

"Yes, I am. I may space out if I see him with another date on his arm. I'm not ready for that, but it is what it is. Your brother is fine and any woman would be happy to be his date for the evening. I'm going to try and hold onto my composure when I see him, even if he's with someone."

"He's coming to the gala alone. I talked with him yesterday and he's coming alone. He may have said he was through with you, but trust me, he's not over you. Who knows, you may see each other and run into each other's arms like a movie scene," Loren joked.

"Real funny," Taija laughed.

"Don't give up on my bull-headed brother yet. There is hope for him yet and I believe there is hope for the two of you. If the dress you picked out for tonight is anything like that red dress you had on the night you met Duron, he's a goner for sure."

"This white gown puts that red gown to shame. I never liked myself if all white, but this gown is like a second skin, flattering in all the right places. My mom and I selected the perfect accessories and I'm all set. I was about to do a little touching up on my hair and then I'm on my way."

"Yeah! I can't wait to see you. Text me when you arrive

and I'll keep an eye out for you. Remember, no sudden moves when you see my mystery man. I don't want anyone in my family to get any ideas until I'm ready for them to know," Loren pleaded.

"I got your back and I'll see you in a few. Thanks for staying on me about attending the gala."

"Well, I knew you would have a good time, Duron or no Duron," Loren said.

"Bye Loren."

Taija turned in all directions in her four-way mirror and was excited that she was able to find the perfect gown for the event.

"You look incredible!" her mother said entering the room.

"Thanks, Mom. This gown is amazing and I feel amazing in it."

"Let me get that necklace we talked about."

Taija continued her perusal while her mother went into her walk-in closet to pull out the necklace they'd selected earlier. It was the one piece of jewelry she hadn't put on yet.

Tonight, was going to be an exciting night. She excited that she was actually going to see Duron again, not that he would talk to her, but she knew in this dress, he certainly wouldn't be able to take his eyes off of her. She smiled at the one bit of advice her mother had given her earlier in the day. She encouraged Taija to get back on the horse and get her man back. Taija knew she wasn't going to plan or scheme, but she definitely wanted him to know what he was missing out on. It was her beauty that drew him to her once and it would do it again. Though she didn't want that to be the only reason Duron would come to her, she wanted him to do so because he missed her and had calmed down since they'd last spoken. Tonight, she was going to give her all to having a good time and if Duron still wanted to act like she was the worse person in the world, she wouldn't allow it to stop her from enjoying all that the evening had to provide. There would be great food and even greater entertainment and she was ready for both.

Eat your heart out Mr. Knight, she said to herself as she caught a glimpse of herself in her full-length mirror. She had to admit, the full-length white gown highlighted all of her assets, leaving lots to the imagination. Maybe, just maybe, Duron would melt the cold as ice shield that's around his heart a little when he saw her. At least enough so that they could talk. Keeping hope alive, she dipped so that her mother could get the necklace around her neck.

"Tonight, the only thing I want you to focus on is being beautiful, which you already are. Don't make Duron the focus of tonight. If he's ready to talk, then talk. If not, knock everyone in that place dead because you, my daughter are a drop-dead bombshell!"

26

Duron arrived at the gala and looked around for Taija. Not spotting her, he turned and ran into Mike.

"Hey, man," Duron said.

"Hey, D."

"I didn't realize you would be coming tonight. I know you were thinking about it, but the last we talked, you said you were going to send in your personal check and chill for the night. I assumed that meant you had a woman paying you a visit to the condo tonight and she was more appealing than this gala," Duron said.

Even though their company gave a large donation to the gala, he, Tyrone and Mike were giving their own large personal donations for the cause, too.

"Yeah. I changed my mind at the last minute. I didn't come last year and I thought I'd check it out this year. I hear the entertainment is like going to an awards show – the best of the best. Your sister was able to wrangle me up a ticket at the last moment."

"Cool. Who did you bring as a date?"

Duron knew Mike was forever the player, always dating several women at a time and wondered who he chose to bring tonight. He thought it strange when Mike had to hesitate before responding and the fact that he didn't see a woman with him.

"Uh, yeah a date. I didn't bring one. I decided to come at

the last minute, so I didn't bother with it."

"What? Are you ill?" Duron joked.

Mike ignored his quip and changed the subject.

"You dateless tonight, D?" Mike asked.

"Only temporarily. I'm planning on getting my woman back," Duron said straightening his suit and looking like a man on a mission.

Mike patted him on the back.

"It's about damn time man. I thought I was going to have to make my move on her if you didn't soon get your act together."

Duron faked trying to attack Mike. He knew he was only goading him and didn't have a plan to go after Taija.

"You were never thinking that. I know that because you aren't ready to die!" Duron exclaimed.

They laughed heartily and Mike held his hands up in surrender. "You know I'm kidding man."

"Yeah, I know. I'm looking forward to a great night. Everyone who is anyone is here tonight. As for me, I have my eyes on the search for one person."

When Mike didn't answer, Duron noticed he seemed a little distracted, looking around as if he were looking for someone in particular.

"Looking for someone, Mike? I thought you said you came alone?"

Mike tried to hide his obvious search of the room.

"No, just checking things out."

"Cool. Well, I just arrived and I'm heading over to say hello to my family. You coming?" Duron asked.

Mike perked up and Duron laughed at his out of the way behavior.

"Of course. Let's do that," Mike said and started walking

without Duron.

"What is going on with you and this strange behavior?" Duron said catching up to him.

"I'm going to head over with you to say hello to your family and I thought you meant right now," he replied.

When Mike started walking again, he followed.

After greeting his family who were all dressed in their finest, Duron needed to find Taija. He was aching to see her. He'd been at the gala for about thirty minutes and hadn't run into her yet. He assumed she'd be sitting at their table.

Checking for Taija's whereabouts with his sister was a good place to start. He turned to ask her and noticed a crazy look on her face, like she had been flustered. He followed her line of sight and noticed her watching Mike and Mike watching her. He thought there must be a full moon out because the two of them were acting like they didn't even know each other. He didn't have time to ponder their obvious crazy behavior. He needed to find Taija.

"Hey, Loren, do you know if Taija is here yet?" he asked.

"I saw her a few minutes ago. She had just arrived and she may still be over near the entrance. She was talking to some of our sorority sisters who are here," she said.

"Thanks."

Duron headed off to locate her. He looked around as he walked knowing she could be anywhere in the large crowd of attendees after he didn't see her near the door.

He had walked the entire room and didn't see her and was losing patience with himself. His desire to see her, touch her, kiss her and apologize to her was consuming him. Because of him, they had wasted weeks apart from each other and if he could fix that tonight, he was planning on doing so.

He decided to stay in one spot and wait until he could see her possibly pass by him. He started to sway when one of his favorite songs was being played by the band. It must have been a favorite of a lot of people because the dance floor had gotten crowded with couples swaying to the sound of Anthony Hamilton's song, *Can't Let Go*. The lyrics to the song made him think of Taija.

"No matter what the people say, I'm gonna love you anyway, you are my life I can't let go. Even if we fuss or fight, try 'til we get it right, you are my life I can't let go."

Duron was singing along with the words to the song when he spotted Taija out on the dance floor dancing with an older guy. His palms began to sweat, the hair all over his body began to tingle and his heart leaped with love for her. She was beautiful, just like the first night he'd spotted her at the bachelor auction. His reaction now was no different than it had been that first night, only now, his heart was filled with love.

He watched as they swayed to the music and he could tell by the distance between them that they didn't appear to be at the gala as an intimate couple. They were keeping a safe distance between them. He watched as Taija flung her head back and laughed at something the man must have said to her and immediately, he was jealous. He didn't like that someone else could make her smile and laugh like he could. He didn't have a right to be jealous since it was his fault that she wasn't on his arm tonight.

He looked at her glowing in a long white gown that he could only describe as remarkable. He tampered down his jealousy so that he was open minded when they finally had a chance to talk. When the song ended, he watched as she spoke briefly to the man she had danced with then walked away. He watched her to see where she was headed and noticed her heading toward the restrooms.

Making his way through the crowd to try and catch her when she returned from the ladies room, his heart was beating so hard and fast, he felt like he could actually hear it. He felt like a stalker following her, but there was no way he was letting her out of his sight again. She looked magnificent in her evening gown, once again accentuating all of those curves he loved so much. He missed her and he loved her and he had no plans of leaving tonight without telling her exactly how he felt.

Taija knew the moment Duron spotted her. She could feel his eyes on her as she danced and when she made her way through the crowd toward the ladies room, his gaze felt like a heated beam on her body. She was glad that though they were going through something, he still found her attractive.

She'd caught him looking around and hoped his perusal of the room meant he was looking for her. She had decided to wait for him to approach, just in case he was only watching her, but not ready to talk to her. She knew he was there when she arrived, but had not laid eyes on him until she was heading to the dance floor. She looked in his direction when the song came on that she knew was one of his favorites. He hadn't spotted her yet, but she was sure he would. She had a feeling he was as tuned in to her presence as she was to his.

When she entered the gala ball room earlier, she'd heard several women in a group talking about him. They were betting on who would be going home with him at the end of the night. She knew that prior to their relationship,

Duron had a reputation as a ladies man. No woman ever seemed to speak ill of him even though he was the type of man to not commit, but sought out women for physical satisfaction. From what she'd heard about him, women relished the opportunity to be bedded by the handsome bachelor. The story was that he always delivered on a night to remember. Taija was not foreign to that herself. She felt like she was in a class by herself since he provided her with more than just one night of memories, but many, many nights, mornings, noondays and early evenings, too. She blushed at the memories.

She needed to go collect herself and throw a little water on her face, which was why she was heading to the ladies room. She needed to get herself together because it was her plan to finally talk with Duron and get him to listen to her side of what happened.

While in the bathroom stall, several ladies had entered the ladies room. Just as Taija exited the stall to wash her hands and check her make-up, one woman made a comment that she knew was about Duron. She moved about slowly to stick around to see what direction the conversation would go in.

"Girl, I had to save up for months to afford a ticket to this years' gala. Last year, I was close to snagging myself a night with that fine Duron Knight. I think this is my year. Every year I hear about all the fine men who attend and this year didn't disappoint, though I have my eyes on one man and one man only. Did you see how sexy he looked in that tux and when he walks, those bowed legs are every woman's dream. I bet he can do wonders with those legs."

Another woman chimed in.

"I hear you. He is fine and I hear he's still unattached.

Since this is a hospital fundraiser, you know there are some fine doctors up in here, too."

Yet still, a third woman joined the conversation.

"I know. I've noticed a few I'd like to meet in a dark corner. I had to borrow a little extra from my mom who gladly gave it to me if it meant I would end my evening with a handsome bachelor on my arm. You are so right about that fine Duron Knight."

The first woman gave the third woman a look of hatred.

"Don't even think about going after him. That's my Knight tonight."

They all laughed.

The last to chime in had more to say.

"There are enough men here to go around. I bow out gracefully from going after Duron. All bets are off if he's not interested in you."

Taija, pretending to check her make-up, was getting pissed off as she continued to listen in once she exited the stall and stood at the mirror where she could get a look at the women. She wanted to say something, but didn't want to butt into their chat.

"Did you read that article about him and his business partners in one of the issues of Black Enterprise magazine? He looked scrumptious and so did the other two. I think I saw one of his partners here tonight, too. He's also rich which is always a plus. His father is chief of staff or administrator or something at the hospital. That Duron is finer than fine. There is nothing better than a sexy man who I single and rich!"

They all agreed and high-fived. Taija knew what they meant. Duron was certainly all that and then some and no matter the state of their relationship at the moment, as far as she was concerned, he was still hers. Girlfriend in the two sizes, too small dress had better keep her hands off.

Having heard enough, Taija headed for the door, but not before tossing a remark back over her shoulder to all three women.

"Good luck with that," she said, leaving them with bewildered looks on their faces.

She opened the door and headed back toward the gala ballroom. Her time in the ladies room had given her the courage to go and confront Duron. She hoped he was ready for her.

While walking back toward the main ballroom, she was smoothing her dress to be sure everything was in place and she wasn't looking where she was going when she walked directly into someone. Almost losing her balance, her heart skipped several beats when she realized it was Duron. He grabbed her arm to keep her from losing her balance. When she looked up into his gorgeous face, all thought left her mind and all speech remained just out of reach. He seemed just as surprised at running into her. He released her, but continued to stare at her as if he could see into her very soul. Gone was the harsh, coldness of the last time they'd see each other. She could see the look was now replaced by softness and that twinkle in his eyes she had grown to love had returned.

"I'm sorry, I didn't mean to startle you. I was waiting for you to come out of the ladies room. I was turning to be sure I wouldn't miss you when we bumped into each other," Duron said.

"Wow," she said on a whisper. She was surprised to see him when she had been thinking about him. She assumed she'd see him again in the ballroom, not in the hallway.

"Taija, are you alright?" he asked.

Shaking off being stunned by his sudden appearance, she finally found her voice.

"Yes, I'm fine Duron. How are you?"

Then his statement rang in her head.

"I'm better now," he said.

"Wait, you were waiting for me? Why?"

Taija didn't want to get too excited by getting her hopes up.

"First let me say that you look exquisite tonight in this white gown. I'm sure every eye in this place is on you tonight. I know I can't look away," he said.

He did a slow pass up her body with his eyes. Taija knew that look and her body's response to his look was instantaneous. Duron was standing before her, better-looking than she'd even remembered.

"Thank you. You look mighty fine yourself tonight."

Not knowing what else to say, they stood staring at each other. Realizing someone needed to say something, Duron pulled her further to the side, out of the main path of traffic in and out of the ladies room.

"I was wondering if we could go someplace and talk, that is if you can stand being in my presence after the way I've treated you lately."

Taija knew the best idea she'd ever had in a long time was to come to this gala tonight. She wanted to talk to Duron as much as he wanted to talk to her.

"Sure. Where do you want to go?" she asked.

Taking her by the elbow, he led her toward the terrace doors.

"Let's go out here. It's a lot quieter than inside."

It was a beautiful night. Duron came to a stop at the

railing that overlooked the immaculately kept gardens and the beautiful, starry night made it a perfect setting to talk about love. He turned so that he and Taija were facing each other.

"What a beautiful night," Taija said.

"Everything about tonight is beautiful, especially you. Again, I need to say you are absolutely stunning tonight. You are doing wonders for this gown."

She blushed as he once again perused her body. He had a way of always making her feel like the sexiest woman alive.

"Thank you," she said.

"I wanted to talk to you tonight to apologize for the way I've been acting. I have been acting like a fool or as my sister so kindly put it, a jackass and I'm sorry. I never gave you an opportunity to explain to me what was going on. I jumped to a conclusion that was apparently the wrong one and for that I am deeply sorry. I know I can't take back the things I said to you, but I want you to know I didn't mean them. I spoke them in anger. That's not an excuse. It's just a fact. My words and my behavior are inexcusable, but I hope they are forgivable," he said. He looked deep in her eyes before continuing. "Taija, baby, I miss you."

Looking at her and hoping she could see his sincerity, he moved a little closer.

"You do?" she asked, surprised at his admission. She was all set to plead her case with him tonight, but he took the lead in doing that.

"Yes, and I love you. I love you so much I've been in agony without you. I never thought I would say that again. I think I fell in love with you the night of our dinner, following the auction. Before you, it had been a long time since I'd connected with any woman the way I felt with you. I know we have some small issues due to my lack of being able to commit to you the way you needed. I was being selfish and I had no right to take you for granted. The morning that I came to your house and saw Keith, I was going to tell you how much I loved you and wanted to commit to what we had. I arrived with hope for us, but when he opened the door, I was shocked to see him and I was hurt. I was finally ready to open up myself to someone and my first thought was that it was being snatched away from me. I want you to know right now that I love you, Taija Charles and if you'll still have me, I want to be with you. I'm open to begging, groveling and anything else it would take for you to forgive me."

Duron reached up to caress her cheek. He couldn't resist touching her, having felt like he had been in jail, unable to touch her for so long.

Taija felt dizzy. She didn't have to pour out her heart and demand that he listen to her. Duron was standing in front of her declaring his love for her. He wasn't only apologizing, but he was confessing and telling her everything was his fault because he jumped to a conclusion.

"I don't know what to say," he said and she was being honest. His words were unexpected.

"Tell me you're open to giving us another chance," Duron said.

He saw tears forming in her eyes and didn't know if they were tears of joy or tears of sorrow for what he'd put her through by walking away. When she didn't respond, but continued to look at him with tears that slowly leaked from her eyes, he didn't know how to react. He stood still, waiting for her to say something. He could see that she needed a moment to get herself together in order to speak. He let her have her moment.

When Taija was ready to speak, she first looked down, away from Duron's gaze and whispered a silent thank you to God for answering her prayers. When she looked back up at the love of her life, she knew that they were meant to be together.

Reaching up and capturing his face in her hands, she was overwhelmed by how deeply her love was for him.

"I love you, too. I love you so much, baby. These weeks away from you have been some of the hardest in my life. I had given up on this working out for us, not knowing how to get through to you. I felt hopeful once I spoke with your mother and she told me to be patient. She told me that true love always wins out over everything. I believe that and I believe you," she said.

She leaned up closer to him and placed a sweet kiss on his lips. The instant tingle she felt was what she had been missing. He returned her sweet kiss and all was turning out right in her world.

"I'm sorry for the weeks we've been apart. If you'll forgive me, that will never happen again. I'm learning to express myself better when things go wrong. I never want to lose you again," he said, feeling hopeful.

"Of course, I forgive you. I probably would have had the same reaction had the shoe been on the other foot. It's hard to understand a situation without having the whole story. If you want me to lay it all out for you I will. I want you to know that there is no other man for me and there has not been since we met. You were it for me the night we had dinner after the auction. I had enough love for us both, so I knew it would sustain us while you fought to rid your mind of past demons and past hurts. I saw it and you needed to find your way to see it, too. I'm happy knowing that's what you were coming to tell me that morning. I'm glad you finally shared it with me today. Baby, I love you and I want nothing more than to be with you."

Duron needed to seal their love with the kind of kiss he had been thinking about giving her all evening. He pulled Taija close to him and leaned in for the kiss he was about to pour every ounce of love he had for her into. He wanted her to feel his love for her every time his lips came in contact with hers. He wanted this kiss to signal that there was no doubt about his love for her. As he deepened the kiss and Taija opened her mouth to invite him home, he sighed his very own thank you that things had worked out. She was his everything and he would never let her go again.

This night was turning out to be more than Taija could ask for. She was in Duron's arms and he was kissing away the hurt and replacing it with his love for her. She had the man she loved back in her arms and he loved her. That was enough for her. She knew what it took for him to get to this point and knew he didn't utter the words lightly.

Ending the kiss, with his eyes still closed, Duron touched his forehead to hers and they stood that way for several seconds. The moment was perfect for reflecting on the time they'd missed and happy that the distance between them was in the past.

Duron opened his eyes and knew he didn't want to spend another day or night apart from her. Doing what his heart was telling him to do, he whispered words of love and devotion to her. They were words he missed saying to her over the weeks they had been apart. He looked into her eyes again and saw unconditional love looking back at him and he knew the time was right. There was no need for any hesitation.

"Marry me, baby," he said.

To say his words shocked her was an understatement. The look on her face made him smile. He knew he had caught her off guard and he wanted this moment to mean more than them getting back together. There was and never will be another woman for her. She was all he thought about and the only woman he wanted. He had to let her know how he truly felt about her. He loved her and he wanted to spend the rest of his life with her.

Taija wasn't sure her hearing was working. Somewhere in the back of her mind, she could have sworn Duron had just said something about marriage.

"Um, what did you say?" Taija said placing her hand over her chest, holding her breath.

"Breathe, baby," Duron said. "You're not hearing things. You heard me correctly."

Did she speak her thought out loud? She couldn't find any words.

"Did you....?" she asked, unable to finish her thought. Perhaps, she was in shock because additional words wouldn't come out.

"Say you'll marry me and make me the happiest man alive. Now that I have you back in my life, I don't want to be without you. I want to marry you, make love to you every day and night, wake up to you every morning and go to bed with you every night. I can't wait to see your belly swell with our babies and I want to grow old with you, making our love last for an eternity. I love you that much. I want you to know how deeply I feel about you. I have no doubt about my love for you and where it's leading. I hope we're on the same page," he said.

Taija was trying to speak, but she was overwhelmed. She was afraid to speak, scared that she had not heard him correctly.

"Duron did you just ask me to marry you or am I just wishing that's what your lips are saying?"

Duron leaned down to kiss her again to let her know they were not in the midst of a mutual delirium.

"You heard me correctly. Marry me, baby. Say you'll be my wife," he said against her lips as he kissed her lightly on them over and over again.

"Yes, Duron. I will marry you. I love you and I can't wait to be your wife," she said, finding her voice.

Duron was so excited, he picked her up and spun her around. He wanted to get away from this place so that he could be alone with his wife to be.

"How committed are you to being at this function tonight?" he asked.

Taija replied without any hesitation.

"Not at all. Once I turn in the donation check from my company, my commitment is done," she said.

He smiled brightly as he grabbed her hand and led her back to the terrace doors. Taija had to walk quickly to keep up with his long strides. She giggled at how anxious he was to get her alone and she could hardly wait. His take control attitude was a major turn-on. She almost ran into the back of him when he stopped suddenly and turned to her. Leaning down again, he grasped her lips in an intense kiss that stole her breath away.

"I needed to do that again. I wanted to be sure this was real and my hand was holding yours again," he said. "Let's get out of here. I need to be alone with you baby. I've missed you and I want to show you just how much."

Holding her face in both of his hands, he kissed her again, deepening the kiss to the point that Taija felt lightheaded with need for him. She wanted him to stop talking and get them someplace where they were alone.

When he lifted and looked into her eyes, she only cared about being in his arms again.

"I'm ready to go whenever you are," she said.

"Good. Let's say our goodbyes to my family. I also need to thank Loren for coming by and giving me a smack in the head for being a jackass. She told me how Keith schemed to make me jealous and how I was crazy for letting you get away. It'll never happen again."

Taija nodded. She needed to thank Loren, too.

"Do you want to tell my family our big news tonight, before we leave?" Duron asked.

"No, not tonight. I want to keep this between you and I for tonight. Let's tell them tomorrow," she said happily.

Walking toward his family who were seated and about to eat dinner, Duron kissed his mom and told her he was heading out. She didn't seem surprised by his sudden need to depart, especially when she noticed he had brought Taija to the table with him and their hands were locked together.

"Thank you for telling Taija to be patient with me," Duron said to his mother.

Taija said hello and goodbye to Duron's family and when she gave Loren a hug, she held on a little longer, thankful for her friend who intervened on her behalf.

When Taija went around to give Duron's mother a hug, she stood up to give Taija a tight, motherly embrace.

"Take care of my son's heart. It belongs to you now and

only you. I had a feeling I wouldn't see the two of you the entire night. I'm glad I was right. Come by the house soon."

"I will," she replied.

Taija spotted Duron giving his father one last hug and was about to venture in his direction when she saw the women from the ladies room heading toward Duron. She guessed they finally got up the nerve to approach him. Little did they know that their efforts were for naught. She walked around the table to where he stood and reached him at the exact moment the first woman who spoke about him in the ladies room started throwing herself at him with both feet, arms and a few other body parts as well. Something about her looked different than when she saw her in the ladies room. She could now see more skin around the cleavage area. That must have been the area she adjusted when they were in the restroom, she thought.

Duron looked a little uncomfortable when the women circled him like he was prey. She saw him look over their shoulders searching for her. Her mind took her back to the night of the bachelor auction where she had to rescue him from another group of women. She was more than happy to oblige again.

Interrupting little missy as she made her play for her man, Taija cleared her throat, interrupting the woman mid-sentence.

"I'm sorry. I know you had your heart set on this bachelor tonight. I think I even wished you luck on that in the ladies room, but I didn't really mean it. You never had any luck with this one," she said pointing at Duron to make her point.

"Excuse me?" one of the women said with more sass than Taija appreciated.

She stepped a little closer. "Let me be a little clearer. You'll have to go in search of another bachelor. Duron's bachelor days are over and his reserved card is now permanently turned down, indicating his out of service status. It now says, permanently reserved for Ms. Taija Charles, so go away. There's nothing for you here," Taija said, feeling empowered by the love that flowed from Duron to her.

Leaving the woman clearly stunned and feeling exposed, Taija took a very happy Duron by the hand and headed towards the door, leaving miss bold and not so beautiful standing, wondering what just happened. She turned and saw the faces of his family who were shocked and not sure what they'd just witnessed. When the women walked away and Loren broke out laughing, everyone else at the table did, too. She saw Loren and Kim, Jakes wife, give her the thumbs up and she smiled.

"Why do I have to keep rescuing you from crazy women who want to claim you as theirs? Do I need to make a permanent sign that says *bachelor not for sale* for you to wear around your neck?" Taija said laughing.

He hit her with his famous one-hundred-watt smile and she knew her answer.

"Well, the sooner you marry me, I think the ring that I'll be sporting on my left hand will do the trick and if it doesn't, I know you'll be in the corner with your boxing gloves on making sure no woman thinks she has a chance. I know I'm scared of you, so I know any woman who sets her sights on me would be scared, too," he said.

Smiling in agreement, Taija leaned up as Duron leaned down and prepared for the explosive kiss she knew was about to happen. When it did, she saw stars. She couldn't wait to have this experience for the rest of her life. When they separated, they had several pairs of eyes on them that said, get a room. She wanted that more than anything.

Since he'd arrived in the limousine with his family, they waited for the valet to return with Taija's car. When he handed Duron the keys, he whispered to her, "Your place or mine?"

This time she made the decision right away.

"Yours which will soon be mine because as soon as we can make it happen and as long as you still want me to, I'll be moving in. I don't know what my hang up was about that and since we'll be getting married, I don't want to prolong being away from you. I want my forever with you to begin tonight," she said.

"I will always want you and whenever you are ready, my place is your place, making it our place. Do you need to let your mom know you're not coming home tonight? Loren told me she was in town."

"No, she left right after I left to come to the gala. She's in the air as we are talking. I'd like for you to meet her and I'm sure the moment I tell her we're getting married, she'll turn around and come back to Atlanta to meet you. We'll save that for another day because tonight, I have other plans for you that do not involve mothers," Taija said, adding a sexy tone.

After getting her into the car, Duron got into the driver's seat and sped through traffic to get to her house.

"Can you not kill us before we get there," Taija laughed.

"What? Do you know how long it's been since I've been inside of you? Too long!" Duron declared. "You're lucky I haven't pulled this car over and hiked that dress up. I'm seriously considering it. I think my zipper is about to pop open there's so much force behind it," Duron said.

Taija doubled over laughing. Duron's amorous appetite is what kept the fire burning hot in their sex life. She missed that as much as she missed him. She hoped he didn't have plans for the rest of the weekend, because she wasn't planning to let him up for air. To tamper down her own overzealous body, she turned on the radio and enjoyed the music in hopes that it would distract her until they reached his house.

"Do you need clothes or anything from your house?" Duron asked.

Taija looked over at him. "If I need clothes, we're not on the same page," she joked.

"Oh, it's like that?"

"Yeah, baby, it's like that," she smiled.

Finally pulling up to his house, Duron parked Taija's car alongside one of his garage doors.

When they exited the car, he stopped before heading in the house and stole another scorching kiss from her. Barely getting the door shut and locked, Taija went to work on the buttons of Duron's shirt as he reached for the zipper on her right side to lower her gown. This was all happening as they continued to kiss and make their way up to the bedroom. No words were said because none were needed. Their hearts, minds and bodies were in harmony.

By the time they reached the bedroom, they were both naked. Not forgetting to protect them, Duron reached into his nightstand and withdrew condoms, tossing a handful on the top. When Taija saw the number of condoms he produced, she got excited about what was in store for her for the rest of the night.

Duron caught her smiling and knew why.

"I have a lot of time to make up for and I intend to start tonight. I have plans to work my way through every last one of those condoms unless I have an objection from you, my love," he said as he moved her to the center of the bed.

Taija didn't speak as she looked up through the skylight over the bed into the dark, starry night. She looked forward to going to bed to that view every night. It gave the effect that they were making love outdoors.

Pulling Duron down on the bed until his body covered hers, she opened her mouth to receive his kiss and at the same time, she opened her legs to receive his deep thrust. Taking the full impact of him, the delight of the feel of being with him once again caused her to climax right away. She had been holding that one in for weeks and her body was excited to feel him again. She was right where she wanted to be, making love with the man who'd made her believe in love again.

The last thought she had before Duron started thrusting into her deeper and deeper in order to take her over the edge again was that he would get no objection from her about using every one of the condoms he'd produced. She planned to make up for lost time all weekend long, starting with tonight.

Epilogue

Six months after the hospital gala, the wedding of Duron Knight and Taija Charles was the talk of the town. The wedding guests were a who's who of Atlanta.

"This day is perfect, Mrs. Knight," Duron said to Taija as they enjoyed their first dance as husband and wife.

"I agree and everyone is having a wonderful time," Taija said.

"You look beautiful in your gown. Vera Wang is definitely a designer you should get use to because this was made for you," Duron said, admiring his lovely wife.

"I needed to get something that would amaze you and I'm glad it worked," she said.

As they danced, the wedding coordinator told everyone else to join the happy couple on the dance floor. When others joined them, Taija noticed Loren and Mike dancing together and it wasn't because she was the maid of honor and he was the best man. She smiled to herself knowing that she was the only one Loren had confided in that she and Mike were secretly seeing each other. She wondered how Duron would feel about it because he was overly protective of Loren and he knew Mike's penchant for being a playboy. They lived in condos side by side and she knew Duron had seen many women come and go on various occasions.

No one was going to be prepared to hear the truth, especially Duron. She didn't think he would like anyone who was interested in his sister, let alone one of his friends and definitely not Mike. His reputation was as bad as Duron's when it came to the revolving door of women in his life. That's not the kind of guy he'd want for his sister.

Duron was happier than any other day of his life. He was holding in his arm, not just the woman he loved, but his wife. They were swaying to his favorite song by Anthony Hamilton and he wanted her to know that he meant every word of his vows and every word of the song he was singing into her ear. He wasn't the best singer around, but seeing Taija's distraction with something just over his shoulder had him wondering what could take her focus away from even his awful singing.

Turning and following her line of sight he saw Loren and Mike dancing together. He looked at them saw the way Mike was holding Loren. Something seemed a little too cozy to him. The hold was more than just a friendly hold or the best man dancing with the maid of honor. He wondered what it was that he was seeing. The way Taija was looking at them smiling, he figured she might know what was going on.

Duron had an uncomfortable feeling about what he was seeing and he didn't like it. Perhaps he was reading too much into it, something he was prone to do. Reading too much into a situation is what caused him to almost lose Taija. He promised he would stop making assumptions. He would hate to come unbenefited with Mike for making a play at his sister.

He turned his attention back to Taija after several looks back and forth at Loren and Mike.

"Baby, would you tell me if you knew something was going on between Loren and Mike? I know how close you and Loren are."

Taija looked at Mike and Loren again and knew that anyone looking at the two of them would be able to see more than just friendship was happening. She didn't want one of those people to be during. She turned his face back to her when he turned to look at them again.

"Your focus should be on me, not Loren or Mike. They are dancing like everyone else. They should dance together because they are the best man and maid of honor. Look, everyone else is dancing who were matched together as groomsmen and bridesmaids. Even my best friend, Victoria, the other maid of honor is dancing with Tyrone. You didn't make a comment about how close they're dancing," she said.

"Victoria isn't my sister and things look a little too cozy," he said and tried to turn to look at them again.

Taija stopped his turning head.

"Focus on your bride and leave your sister alone. Don't start getting in her business," Taija said.

"Wait, Loren has business that involves Mike?" he asked.

"Duron, stop it. They are dancing and Loren is a big girl. Now, if me in this gown isn't enough of a distraction for you, something's wrong."

"Baby, you are more than enough for me and I love it My focus is all over you tonight and I can't wait to get this gown off of you sooner rather than later," Duron said leaning down for another sweet kiss. They smiled when everyone on the floor clapped for them.

"Good, now leave Loren alone," she said.

"All I'm saying is I'm looking at them dance and it looks like more than just a dance. Look at how he's looking at her and how close he's holding her. Now that I think about it, I don't think I've seen him talk to anyone, especially women, other than Loren. There are more than a few single women in attendance here tonight. He better not be trying to run his player game on my sister. I don't care how close we are. Loren is off limits to him and Tyrone and they know it. I know too much about each of them to ever let them around my sister," he said.

Taija could tell by Duron's body language that what he was seeing was not sitting well with him and she promised Loren she wouldn't tell anyone, especially him. He was becoming distracted from what the day was to be about and she needed to fix that.

Reaching up and turning his face back to look at her once again, she wanted to draw him back into the moment where only the two of them existed.

"I'm sure they're just dancing and its nothing. Let's not worry about what someone else is doing today. Your focus should be on me and only me."

The tension that Taija had noticed briefly in Duron's body started to dissipate as her words about their day started to sink in.

"You know how much you hate for your family to get involved in your personal business, so don't you dare start worrying about what Loren is or is not doing or Mike either. It looks like a simple dance to me and it's a slow song. How else is he supposed to hold her?"

Moving close so that her lips were a whisper away from his ear, Taija spoke seductively to the man who was now her husband.

"I have enough business for you to get into that you won't have enough time to be in anyone else's."

That brought Duron back to where he should be, in this space and time with his wife. He liked how her mind worked. Smiling down at his new bride, he couldn't wait until they could be alone.

"I love you, Mrs. Knight."

Taija looked sweetly up at her husband.

"I love you, Mr. Knight."

She saw that all-too familiar look in Duron's hazel eyes that told her exactly what was on his mind even before he shared his thoughts with her.

"As much as I love seeing you in this wedding gown, all I'm imagining is all of those luscious curves underneath of it that I love exploring. I want to hear, in private, about all this business you have that I need to get into," he said adding a little more to his grind while dancing with her and hoping no one else saw his seductive move.

Taija gave a little squeal that only he could hear and he knew that she could feel how anxious he was to get her alone.

"Oh," she said looking up at him. "Did you bring a large powerful weapon to our wedding or are you just happy to see me?" she said in her Mae West voice.

He leaned down to whisper in her ear, an act he knew drove her wild with want.

"Both. How long do we have to stay anyway? Can we leave now?" he asked.

Duron nipped her ear lobe, something else that drove her crazy in a way that made tremors pass through her entire body, which he could feel.

Shivering from his affection, Taija could not resist

looking up into the face of the man of her dreams and moving closer for a kiss that would tell the story of what their first night as husband and wife would be like.

When she needed to breathe, she broke off from his passionate kiss and responded with her own sexy whisper.

"We have the rest of our lives baby. Let's give our families a little more of our time and then I'm all yours. All of me."

Taija winked and Duron knew what that meant. She was just as hot for him as he was for her.

"I love you, baby," he said.

Taija would never tire of hearing those words come from Duron's lips.

"I love you, too. Thank you for being a bachelor for sale only for me."

"For sale for you and only you," Duron replied.

As the music stopped and they headed back toward their table for the next part of the evening, Duron couldn't help, but let his eyes wander to his sister and Mike. They were too cozy for him and he didn't like it. He didn't like it one bit.

Will Loren and Mike be able to keep their affair a secret from Duron and the rest of the Knight family much longer? Read Mike and Loren's story in *A DESIGNED AFFAIR*.

To leave a review for Bachelor Not for Sale and to check out other novels by this author, visit
www.amazon.com/author/cherylbarton

Book 2 – *"A Designed Affair"*

In the follow-up to *"Bachelor Not for Sale"*, Loren Knight has been engaging in a secret love affair with her brother Duron's best friend and business partner, Michael Bailey. He is everything she could want and more in a man, but she believes the risk is too great for any type of relationship with him beyond the bedroom door.

Michael Bailey has been fighting his attraction to Loren for years. He has stayed away from her out of respect for his best friend and business partner. Now that he and Loren have finally given into passion that they both have been craving, can Michael convince Loren that what they share is worth the risk?

Book 3 – *"A Perfect Combination"*

In the second follow-up following *"Bachelor Not for Sale"* and *"A Designed Affair"*, Tyrone Davis is the king of one-night-stands; nicknamed, Mr. Love Them and Leave Them. He learned to perfect it from his two best friends, Duron

Knight and Michael Bailey. He never imagined a one-night stand would have such a lasting impact, but that's exactly what happened.

Victoria Alston couldn't forget the incredible night she spent with Tyrone Davis, someone connected to one of her best friends. The next day, she disappeared, returning to reality and the fiancé she'd left in Boston while on business travel. They both soon discovered that it wasn't just a one-night stand, but a perfect combination for love.

Book 4 – "Love at Last"

In the third follow-up to *"Bachelor Not for Sale"*, they had the perfect love...That's what Brian Knight thought of his relationship with Sherry Braxton until he looked up one day and she was gone and never wanted to see him again. Two years later, he discovered that there is the possibility that Sherry may have been pregnant with his child. Hurt and angry at her deceit, he takes a flight to Baltimore to fight for his rights as a father and realizes that the love and passion they once shared had never died. Is it possible he could still have the kind of love he thought would last a lifetime? Can he still have his love at last?

Get the entire "Bachelor Series" at www.cherylbarton.net

OTHER ROMANCE NOVELS BY CHERYL BARTON

Bachelor Series
Bachelor Not for Sale
A Designed Affair
A Perfect Combination
Love at Last
Twelve Bachelors for Sale – Coming 2018

Amorous Occupations Series
The Artist
The Bookkeeper
The Chef
The Dancer
The Electrician

A Lovers' Heart Series
Heartthrob
Heartbeat
Heartbreaker – Coming 2018

Stand Alone Romance Novels
Holly for Christmas
Snowbound
Cupid's Arrow
One Wish
His Halloween Promise
Home for Thanksgiving
Holly for Christmas
A Better Man
Bossy
Un-Break My Heart
Love on Top
Take a Knee
Love at First Sight
My First Love
Black Love

www.cherylbarton.net

About the Author

Cheryl Barton lives in Maryland and in her spare time she loves to read espionage novels, cook, watch Sci-fi movies, spend time with family and friends and enjoy Maryland steamed crabs.

Indulge in more romance and inspirational novels by visiting Cheryl's website at www.cherylbarton.net.

I am because you read and I thank you! - Cheryl

Connect with me

Website at www.CherylBarton.net

Twitter – @Author Cheryl Barton
Instagram – AuthorCherylBarton
Facebook at Author Cheryl Barton
Email – Cheryl@CherylBarton.net
Blog - https://mswriterinmd.wordpress.com/